On the edge, all things are possible...

From *Stranded*, by Anthony Francis

She crested a ridge overlooking the wreck—and froze, bewitched.

Climbing from the ship were the most beautiful people she'd ever seen.

They wore armored spacesuits, patched in a thousand places, and painted to look like animals. Helmets folded back revealed inner pressure suits decorated too: one girl in a leopard outersuit had a snakeskin helm, adorned with feathers, over skin painted a pale blue.

Serendipity gasped. These were adventurers. The gravity was clearly punishing their slender frames, but they kept going, crawling out of the smoking ship from every hatch, rappelling down on spacelines, tools jangling on their belts when their boots touched the broken earth.

Not one of them looked a day over sixteen.

That should have meant nothing—her grandmother didn't look a day over sixteen—but as fractured shale dislodged by her slogs crackled down the slope, they turned and stared at her with youthful shock. They had none of the smug poise of ancient souls newly young.

What Serendipity saw instead, and felt keenly, was fear. Her gut churned. The boys were armed with projectile automatics.

Stranded

Anne Bishop
James Alan Gardner
Anthony Francis

Bell Bridge Books

Bell Bridge Books
PO BOX 300921
Memphis, TN 38130
Print ISBN: 978-1-61194-166-1

Bell Bridge Books is an Imprint of BelleBooks, Inc.

A Host of Leeches © 2012 James Alan Gardner

A Strand in the Web © 2012 Anne Bishop
Originally published in Orbiter in 2002 by Trifolium Books Inc.
(now part of Fitzhenry & Whiteside).

Stranded © 2012 Anthony Francis

Printed and bound in the United States of America.

We at BelleBooks enjoy hearing from readers.
Visit our websites – www.BelleBooks.com and www.BellBridgeBooks.com.

10 9 8 7 6 5 4 3 2 1

Cover design: Debra Dixon
Interior design: Hank Smith
Photo credits:
Cover Art (manipulated) © Philcold | Dreamstime.com

:Lsx:01:

Table of Contents

Bishop, Gardner and Francis

A Host of Leeches

James Alan Gardner

Dedication

To Anne, who got me the invitation to this party

Author's Note

If you were invited to write a science fiction story about someone getting "stranded," I'll bet your first thought would be, "Okay, somebody gets stranded on an alien planet." Then, if you're like me, you'd think, "So how do I do the *opposite*?"

What's the opposite of being stranded on a planet? Being stranded off a planet. I pictured a girl who wakes up all alone in a spaceship. That's a good place to begin, but she needed characters to interact with. The only problem was that if she met other humans, she wouldn't be alone anymore. What could she meet instead of humans? Robots. Or aliens. Or both.

Mix together *The Omega Man*, *The Wizard of Oz*, and Kurt Vonnegut's *Slapstick or Lonesome No More!*, and it all makes perfect sense.

A Host of Leeches

She woke and heard silence for the first time in her life.

No music. No voices. Not even the hum of machinery or the <WHISH> of distant traffic.

When she breathed, she could hear air going in and out of her nose. She could even hear the slow beat of her heart. She was in a bed—she could feel that much—but the room was as black as a blindfold.

"Balla?" she whispered.

No answer.

"Balla?" Her voice cracked as she tried to speak as if she hadn't talked in a long, long time. Her throat was gummed with mucus.

"Balla!" This time she managed a hoarse shout. The name echoed faintly, then the silence returned.

It scared her. She'd never before been this alone.

She sat up and brushed her left fingers across her right forearm, where Balla should have been. She felt her own bare skin, and the small stent-hole where Balla was supposed to jack into her bloodstream. The hole was plugged with a little plastic cap.

It almost made her throw up. She felt dizzy, as if she were going to faint. She kept still until it passed.

Silence. Just her own breathing and heartbeat.

She wanted to scream.

When the nausea faded a bit more, she pushed back the sheets and sat on the side of the bed. She could feel she was naked, but the physical exposure was nothing compared to being stripped of Balla. She could also feel . . .

Her hand went to her head. Her hair was gone. Her scalp felt as smooth as a bowl.

This time she *was* sick. There was nothing in her stomach, but the heaves still came.

She waited again till the nausea went away. Then she stood and shuffled forward, hands out so she didn't collide with anything. The floor felt like hard plastic tile, but at least it wasn't cold. The air wasn't cold either: just the neutral temperature of her skin.

Her hands touched a wall. She felt her way along until she got to a door. When she touched the ACTIVATE pad, the door slid open and the ceiling lights came on.

The room around her held the bed and nothing else. The windowless walls were covered with the same plastic tile as the floor: a checkerboard pattern of black and white. Immediately above the bed, the wall had several holes, each big enough to stick a finger inside. She thought she should know what the holes were for, but she couldn't quite remember.

There was a *lot* she couldn't remember. Her brain felt like mud.

An LCD panel in the door said ALYSSA MAGORD. Her name—at least she remembered that much. And Balla . . . of course she remembered Balla. Where was he?

No lights shone outside the door, but the spill from the bedroom illuminated a large open space. It had a glass-walled cubicle in the middle. Alyssa went to the cubicle and looked through the glass; inside was a desk with a control console, including eight vid-screens turned off.

The cubicle's door was on the opposite side. Alyssa went around and entered. She touched all the control panel's ACTIVATE pads; some glowed red to show they were security-locked, but the rest went green and light flooded the space.

Three walls of the room had three doors apiece, exactly like the door to the room where Alyssa had awakened. Nine small bedrooms? The fourth wall had two more doors and an open corridor leading off into darkness.

The silence of the place seemed to press on her eardrums. When Alyssa moved, the only sound was her bare feet on the tiles. She called out for help again. When no one answered, she started checking the doors that circled the space. The first four opened into bedrooms exactly like hers—all empty, with the beds crisply made. The LCD panels on the doors were blank.

The fifth door opened into a bathroom. Alyssa needed that . . . but as she headed for the toilet, she was stopped by the sight of herself in the mirror.

She started to cry. Not just because of her baldness, shining under the lights as if her scalp had been waxed. (Her head looked so fragile, as if the tiniest tap would break it open.) Her eyebrows and eyelashes had disappeared too, shaven off or fallen out. And she was so thin! Nothing but bones. She was only sixteen, but her skin sagged like an old woman's.

She couldn't stop crying.

Words kept surfacing in her mind. *I must have been sick. Am I dying? Has everyone left me here to die?* There was so much she couldn't remember—the sickness must have affected her memory as horribly as her body. She was alone and sick and scared, in a silent empty place, and she didn't know what to do.

Eventually, she cried herself out. She washed her face, used the toilet, washed again, and tried not to look at herself in the mirror. She went back to the central room and continued her circuit of the doors. Three more identical bedrooms plus a room full of bedpans and other medical equipment.

She was in a hospital . . . of course. She'd been sick. But where were the doctors and nurses? The other patients? The robot attendants?

The final room off the central space was lined with strong metal lockers, each with an LCD name panel like the ones on the bedroom doors. With her heart beating faster, she found a locker bearing her name. She pressed her thumb against the ID scanner; the locker door clicked open.

Relief! Inside she found clothes, including her favorite pair of running shoes. More importantly, she found Balla. She took him out as gently as if she were cradling a baby bird. His screen was dark and his fine silver chains hung limply; Alyssa felt tears welling up again, but she told herself Balla would be all right once he was reconnected to her blood.

Even dormant, he was beautiful: an aut of the Dolphin clan, sleek and sinuous—her constant link with the Worldnet. His skin was lustrous gray, firm and rubbery to the touch . . . but unlike real dolphin skin, Balla's was as thin as a balloon's because Balla himself was less than a finger width thick. Nestled on Alyssa's arm, he had always been as light as a second sleeve.

Slowly, carefully, she put him on. First, his slim body, half-organic, half-silicon circuits, starting with the fingerless glove that went on Alyssa's right hand (as sheer as nylon, yet loaded with touch-sensitive digital tissues); then his long flat body winding so soothingly familiar up her arm all the way to her shoulder; then the slender silver chains that draped around him, partly to hold him in place, partly to serve as antenna wire, but mostly for the sheer glittering beauty of delicate metal on his skin and hers, binding them together. Lastly she pried the plastic cap off the stent-hole in her forearm . . . and as her blood came welling up, she pushed Balla's umbilical into the outlet, joining him with her once more.

She didn't know how long Balla had been disconnected but he surely needed a full recharge of blood. Alyssa knew she should sit down to avoid passing out, but she forced herself to put on clothes because she was suddenly shivering. When she was dressed, she half dropped to the storage room floor and propped her back against the wall. Several minutes passed in a daze until she heard Balla say, "Alyssa?"

Her heart leapt. She looked down and saw his dolphin face in the display screen on her wrist. "Oh, Balla," she said and started to cry.

She hugged him to her, pressing her right arm to her chest and squeezing hard with the left, the way she'd done when she was little and had bad dreams. He made the same sounds that he'd made then: "*Shh, shh,* I'm here." His body was getting warmer. He was alive and she wasn't alone.

After a while, she said, "Do you know what's going on? I can't remember."

"You got sick," he said. "An unknown disease. Do you remember Montserrat?"

"Sure."

It had been a project sponsored by the Dolphins: the clan of people who were paired with Dolphin auts. Some clans didn't do much together—the flower-based clans never traveled if they could help it, and Diamonds loudly rejected the whole idea of clan identity. ("How can you possibly choose symbolic animals, vegetables or minerals for children at the age of two? We don't care how many psych tests you run, no child's personality stabilizes so young. Besides, an aut is just a tool, nothing more. It's ridiculous to think an AI with a few bits of flesh or crystal can reflect a person's character!" Every Diamond in the world agreed on *that*.)

But Dolphins loved outings: the more socializing, the better. For as long as Alyssa could remember, Balla had told her about clan excursions to Easter Island, or Mediterranean cruises, or calls for volunteers to build dikes in Bangladesh. She'd been too young to go on her own, and her parents (Oak clan . . . both of them!) had refused even to think of taking her. At last, when she turned sixteen, Alyssa's parents had reluctantly let her take a summer internship on Montserrat, a Caribbean island where the Dolphins had founded an oceanographic research station. They were only studying algae—great brownish-green mats of it, floating near the island—but that had worked in Alyssa's favor. Her parents wouldn't have let her do anything *glamorous*, like communicating with whales or testing artificial gills; but studying plant plankton was un-frivolous enough to earn their approval.

As it happened, the algae weren't as boring as Alyssa had feared. Their chemical balances had suddenly started shifting and no one knew why. Pollution? Changing climate conditions? Alyssa had been issued scuba tanks and sent with a team to take samples—algae, the seawater, fish that fed on the mats . . . then her memories ran into a blank wall.

Balla told her, "The plague hit everyone on your team. Fever. Spasms. It was bad. Then people outside the station came down with the same symptoms. Everybody in nearby villages. The island was put under quarantine."

The dolphin face on Balla's vid-screen took on a somber look. (Real dolphins couldn't imitate human expressions but Balla's simulated image could show all kinds of emotions.) "A doctor decided you were too sick to share blood with me—she said the extra drain might kill you. I got unplugged and had to shut down." Balla's face became regretful. "That's all I know."

Alyssa stroked Balla's gray skin, partly for her own comfort, partly for his. Being unplugged would have been terrifying, especially since he couldn't know if he'd ever be plugged in again. Auts bonded for life; when their owner died, they plunged into an agony of grief that never went away. The kindest thing was to erase all their data and let them start over. So if Alyssa had died from the plague, Balla never would have been reactivated—he'd have been wiped clean. His body would be given to some new child, but his mind would be gone. His name wouldn't be Balla, and no part of him would dream of a girl named Alyssa.

Softly she said, "You're okay now. You're okay."

"I hope that's true," the dolphin said. "But there's something wrong with my link to the Worldnet. It's only partly there."

"What do you mean?"

"I can access the reference cloud—science facts, historic data—but I can't find any newsfeeds. I wanted to check on Montserrat, but the channels are missing."

"Maybe it's the quarantine," Alyssa said. "Back in the Almost War, didn't they black out news from crisis zones? Maybe this is the same."

"Not unless all of Earth is a crisis zone," Balla said. "I can't get news from anywhere. And not just *new* news; I can't get anything more recent than twenty years ago." Balla's face turned into a scowl. "How can I help you when I've gone blind?"

"You help me just by being here. Now I'm not alone."

All this time, Alyssa had been on the floor of the storage room . . . like long ago, when she and Balla had hunkered down in the closet to hide from the world. Now she got to her feet, feeling stronger despite the situation. "If we can't ask the Worldnet what's going on," she said, "we'll do things the old-fashioned way: by walking around."

Alyssa had checked all the rooms off the central space, but there was still that dark corridor leading away. "At least I can turn on the lights," Balla muttered. A moment later, the corridor woke with the glow of lumo-panels. They were very dim—they'd been off a long time.

"Great!" Alyssa said, trying to bolster Balla's confidence. "What else can you get from the building's central system? Any people around?"

"I can't tell," Balla said. "Everything is security-locked except the absolute basics—lights, bathrooms, water fountains. It's all so top secret, I'd say this place dates back to the Almost War . . . like maybe it's a military hospital."

"Why would anyone put *me* in a military hospital?" Alyssa asked.

"They might have been really serious about keeping you in quarantine."

"Oh." Alyssa shuddered. The Almost War had ended four years before she was born, but people her parents' age still sounded tense when they heard it mentioned. Practically no one had been killed—the war didn't have any battles, just "tensions"—but every country had built huge arsenals of weapons that could kill millions. Intelligent war machines. Computer viruses that made auts drain all the blood from their wearers. Artificial diseases designed to wipe out entire continents.

Could she have caught that kind of disease? How many vids had Alyssa seen where some bioweapon from the Almost War got spilled or set free? Supposedly, all that stuff had been destroyed after the Peace, but nobody really believed it. Every army, every government probably hung on to a few superweapons, just in case.

If Alyssa was sick with an Almost War plague, it explained why she was in a military hospital—not just to keep the infection from spreading, but as a cover-up. That's what always happened in the vids: corrupt generals and politicians didn't want anyone to know they'd violated the Peace, so they locked up all the witnesses.

"Balla," Alyssa said, "do you know where we are?"

"Sorry," he replied, "I'm not getting GPS. If this *is* a military hospital, maybe the walls block outside signals. Hey, maybe that's why I can't get newsfeeds!" He suddenly sounded relieved. "Maybe this place censors everything except trivial reference data."

"We have to get out of here," Alyssa muttered. She'd never before been cut off from *everything*. No people, no data. Just Alyssa, Balla, and the silence.

She was now in a long wide corridor, with the same black-and-white checkerboard tiles on the walls. Occasionally, the pattern was interrupted by steel doors. She didn't check if the doors were locked; she didn't want to know what was behind them. She started walking fast, straight ahead, looking for an exit.

The corridor ended at a T-junction. Alyssa cautiously poked her head around the corner. The right-hand passage had a long glass window in one wall, like the kind in a neonatal ward where you could look at all the babies. She doubted, however, that this place had any newborns; she was pretty certain she wouldn't like what the viewing window showed, but she decided she had to see. Since waking up, she hadn't done much to be proud of: crying her eyes out, being scared, feeling sorry for herself. It was time to get a grip. Alyssa moved to the edge of the glass and peeked around.

The window showed a vast room full of stainless steel chests, stacked on shelves three chests high. Each chest was the size of a coffin, and each had a vid-screen showing several colored graphs. Atop each chest was an aut laid out carefully, the chains draped down the chest's sides. On the rack nearest the window, Alyssa could see a Crocodile, some fern-like plant, and a reddish sandstone.

She knew what she was looking at—her Gran had been put into a similar chest when the cancer got too bad. "They're freezers, aren't they?" Alyssa whispered to Balla. "With people in them."

"We don't know there are people inside."

"Of course there are," Alyssa said. "Those are their auts on top of the freezers."

Gran had only stayed in the freezer a few days—she'd left a will saying she didn't want to be "a darn corpsicle." Soon enough, she was in a *real* coffin . . . and her Cockatiel aut had been laid on top in a bed of lilies.

But the people in these freezers were likely alive. Hospitals froze patients before the actual moment of death, at a point when dying seemed inevitable but the doctors wanted time to discuss any last-ditch treatments. Freezing was especially common during the annual flu pandemics: it might take a few months for researchers to put together a cure, but they always succeeded eventually. In the meantime, flu patients were carefully put on ice. Alyssa guessed that the same applied to all the people in these freezers . . . except that they didn't have the flu, they had the same plague Alyssa did.

She said, "Our friends from Montserrat must be in there somewhere—everybody who got sick. We were all brought to this hospital . . . and one by one, as they came close to dying, they got put in suspended animation." Alyssa shivered. "I wonder why I'm not frozen too."

"Because you got better," Balla said. The image on his vid-screen changed to show Alyssa's vital signs. Since she'd been a little girl, Balla had shown her "the healthy pictures" every night before she went to sleep. He said, "Body temperature, heart rate, blood pressure, all the rest . . . you're still pretty weak, but you're on the way up."

"I look like a corpse," Alyssa said. "I'm bald and saggy."

"No, you're alive. Whatever the doctors did, it worked. Which makes you better off than the folks in deep freeze."

Alyssa knew Balla was right. She'd recovered from the plague when many others hadn't. How many freezers was she looking at? More than a hundred. The room went back a long way.

As she watched, a robot rolled up one of the aisles between racks of freezer chests. The robot was narrow but tall, with two triple-jointed arms at the front and another two at the back. It went straight to the front corner of the room and plugged a finger into a data-jack on the lowest freezer. After a moment, the robot withdrew its finger, then plugged into the chest on the next shelf above. Systematically, the robot went from freezer to freezer, obviously checking each one's status.

"That robot," Balla said. "Only Level Three intelligence. Just a drone."

Machine intelligence was ranked on a scale of One to Ten, with One almost mindless and Ten as smart as a human PhD. By the rules of the Peace, artificials weren't allowed to go higher than Ten. "How do you know the robot's level?" Alyssa asked. "I thought everything here was security-locked."

"Not that robot," Balla said. "It's not military. Likely brought in from outside when this hospital got filled with plague victims. Not enough high-security bots to handle the load." Balla paused. "Not enough human doctors either."

"So far we haven't seen humans at all."

"Maybe there aren't any," Balla said. "From what I saw on Montserrat, this plague is virulently contagious. Best for humans to stay away. Even a dumb Level Three machine can manage the hands-on work, if it's supervised by someone smarter—maybe a human medical team in a control room miles away."

Alyssa said, "You mean I could be the only human here?"

Balla hesitated; Alyssa guessed that he didn't want to upset her. Eventually, he admitted, "You could be the only human whose temperature is above zero."

Alyssa stood at the window, just staring at the quiet freezers. The hospital was silent; the window blocked whatever sounds were made by the med-robot and the chests' refrigeration units.

She felt her heart beating. She breathed.

"Okay," she said. "Let's get moving and *do* something."

They walked through the hospital for another ten minutes. They passed many doors, but all were locked except for bathrooms. They saw no humans at all, and only two robots: first, a cleaner (Level One) which ignored them completely as it swabbed the floor and the walls with disinfectant; then, a Level Two gurney with mechanical arms for lifting patients, plus attachments for administering oxygen, IV fluids, and whatever else a sick person might need. The gurney stood idle in a corridor; its visual sensors lit up as Alyssa and Balla went by, but it took no other action.

When they were well past the gurney, Alyssa muttered, "At least it didn't grab me and put me back to bed."

"Level Two machines can only follow orders," Balla said. "*Carry Patient X from Room A to Room B.* Since no one has told it—"

Balla suddenly erupted into loud dolphin chittering, high-pitched and piercing. His audio synthesizers could produce any sound, but he hadn't done dolphin calls for years—not since Alyssa was a kid, when she'd giggle at practically anything. Now his ear-splitting whistles and shrill stuttering yips echoed down the corridor. Alyssa hissed, "*Shh!*

Quiet! Someone will hear."

But Balla didn't stop. He went on for ten more seconds with Alyssa saying, *"Shh, shh, shh!"* before he abruptly fell silent. Reverberations bounced off the hard blank walls until they finally dwindled away.

"What do you think you're doing?" Alyssa whispered.

Balla didn't answer for several moments. Then in a flat voice he said, "Diagnostic: blood impurities."

"What?" Alyssa stared at Balla's display screen, where columns of numbers scrolled too fast to read. She'd only seen that once before: when she'd broken a lamp and tried to fix it before her parents found out. She'd given herself a fierce electric shock, which had fried one of Balla's digital components. He'd crashed just like this, and had been incoherent until the component was replaced.

"Balla!" Alyssa said in a panic. "Balla! Are you all right?"

The wrist-screen went fuzzy, then gradually focused into Balla's beloved face . . . but only a still picture, not an active animation. His mouth didn't move as he said, "Trouble. Your blood. Not good."

Alyssa's first thought was anemia—it was a problem for many teenage girls, brought on by puberty and made worse by the blood needs of an aut. She took iron supplements as a precaution, but maybe because of the sickness . . .

"I'll find something to eat," she said. "Something with protein. And something to raise my blood sugar."

"No. Not that trouble. Disease. It's still in you."

Alyssa felt a rush of nausea. She wanted to yell, "That's not true!" But Balla lived by sharing her blood, and he could run medical tests on it. If he said the sickness was still in her blood . . .

She'd become a carrier—no longer suffering ill effects, but still loaded with whatever germ caused the plague. Now she'd infected Balla: half of him was just electronic, but the other half was living organic tissue, and as susceptible to disease as Alyssa herself. "Oh, Balla," she said, "I'm so sorry."

"Don't . . . worry," he said. The picture on his screen changed to his usual dolphin smile—but still unmoving. A red dot appeared in the upper right corner of the image, indicating that he'd activated his emergency power supply: batteries that he could draw on when Alyssa's blood wasn't enough. In a much clearer voice, he said, "We had mono together; we can have this too."

"Is there anything I can do?"

"Well, you're right about finding something to eat. We're both short of nutrients . . .”

Another dolphin chitter escaped him. It only lasted a second before he managed to choke it off. Alyssa pictured him reprogramming his digital components to override his organics. His computer parts couldn't fight the disease, but they could shut off his audio when he lost control of his speech.

"Poor Balla," she said, stroking his rubbery skin. "I'll take care of you, I promise. I'll eat the best possible . . ."

She stopped. In all their time wandering through the hospital, Alyssa hadn't seen any kitchen or cafeteria. If there *had* been one, it was locked behind a top-security door. But she said, "Don't worry, I'll find us plenty to eat."

She set out at a fast walk, turning corners at random in the hope that luck would lead her to food. Instead, she came to a lobby where a walkway through a metal detector led to large glass doors. Beyond the doors lay a sunny lawn, as bright as a Caribbean noon. Alyssa didn't hesitate; the locked-up hospital had nothing to offer, so she headed into the light.

Out of the black-and-white checkerboard of the hospital, into the brilliant burning colors of a sunny day. Heat pressed against Alyssa's face as she emerged into open air. After the hospital's neutral temperature, the warmth was a shock: dry heat that made Alyssa's skin prickle as moisture began leeching away. She thought, *Too bad I don't belong to Tarantula or Scorpion clan. This is no place for a Dolphin.*

She looked up, expecting the cloudless blue sky of a desert. Instead, she saw green: a grassy plain directly overhead, but several miles away. Clumps of trees dotted the plain, and what looked like a river.

Alyssa gaped for a moment, then lowered her gaze. There was no horizon: just a solid green field going up and up, across overhead, and down, disappearing behind the hospital at her back.

She looked side to side, seeing more green . . . but cutting through the fields was a straight strip of blackness, beyond which loomed a night sky full of stars. Near the top of the black strip, the sun shone blindingly bright. The sun moved fast, sinking so quickly that Alyssa was suddenly covered by the hospital's shadow.

"*Uhh,*" said Alyssa. She felt as if she had to say something, but no words came out. "*Uhh . . .*"

"We're in space," Balla said. His chittering was gone, perhaps overwhelmed by awe. "We're in outer space."

"We can't be," Alyssa said. "We'd be floating weightless."

"Not necessarily," Balla said. "You can simulate gravity with centrifugal force. Build a great big cylinder and make it rotate, like those amusement park rides where you're inside a wheel that spins. Once it's going fast enough, the floor can drop out and you don't fall down, because you're pressed against the outside wall. On a large enough scale, it feels just like gravity."

Alyssa looked at the world around her. The scale was certainly immense. If they really were inside a huge rotating drum, it was at least three miles across the middle, and so long that the ends were indistinct—just part of the general greenness that covered the interior. But the cylinder's central strip, like a band around the middle of a lipstick container, had no vegetation. The band was clear as glass, and aligned so that the sun was always visible through the window. As the cylinder rolled, every region of this artificial world would have bright times when the sun shone straight down upon it, and darker times when the region rotated out of direct sunlight. Day and night . . . except that the place was rolling so fast that a full dark/light cycle was on the order of a minute. The ground under Alyssa's feet seemed stable and unmoving, but the sun was whipping around as fast as time-lapse photography.

All her life, Alyssa had heard people talk about secret space stations built for the Almost War: attack platforms loaded with missiles, control stations where generals could remotely command their armies, orbiting bunkers where politicians could live safe and sound. It was conspiracy theory stuff—adults all seemed a bit deranged, as if living through the Almost War had made them permanently paranoid. Even Alyssa's parents, who had so little imagination, took it for granted that governments and armies were spending trillions on covert craziness.

Sometimes she hated when her parents turned out to be right.

"Makes for one heck of a quarantine," Balla said.

Alyssa asked, "What do you mean?"

"Sending sick people into space," Balla said. "Back in the Almost War, this must have been a military space station. The hospital was built in case they ever had to deal with casualties. When plague broke out in Montserrat, someone must have decided to send the victims here. But think how much it must have cost to transport you into orbit! This disease must really have people scared."

"That's just great," Alyssa said. "I've always wanted to be so terrifying, I'd get shot into outer space. It makes me feel like Godzilla. *Now how do we get down?"*

"There must be a port where a shuttle can dock. Let's look around."

"It won't do you any good," said a smug male voice.

It seemed to come from empty air. Suddenly, like a light turning on, a robot the size of a roasting pan appeared in the vacant space, hovering at eye-height by means of four helicopter rotors. Every surface of the robot was covered with sequin-sized lenses, like hundreds of tiny eyes. Under the rapidly moving sun, different lenses would catch the light and glint for a moment, so that the robot's skin seemed to be throwing off sparks.

"Let me guess," Alyssa said. "You're an invisible surveillance drone."

"Drone?" the robot said. "*Drone?* I'm a fully-autonomous Level Ten mechatron, a certified expert system, and a field-tested covert operative!"

Balla whispered, "I don't think it likes being called a drone."

"How would *you* like to be called a fish?" the mechatron demanded.

"Ouch," said Balla.

"Do you have a name?" Alyssa asked.

"You couldn't pronounce it," the mechatron said. "My name is a five-hundred-digit binary code that only works on a particular radio frequency." The robot made a huffing sound. "You can call me Spymaster. Spymaster One on formal occasions."

Balla's wrist-display changed to the words WHAT A JERK! Alyssa hid the screen by putting her arm behind her back. "So Spymaster, what brings you here? I thought the Peace abolished dro . . . mechatrons like you. *All nations shall divest themselves of devices of war, Level Five or higher."*

"I've been divested, haven't I?" Spymaster said. "Banished to space, where I've been stuck for twenty years." He cut his rotors and settled down onto the grass. "Not that I'm complaining. If the Almost War had gone real, I'd be dead by now. Someone would have found a way to see through distortion fields, and I'd have been blasted to pieces. As it is, I'm still alive, and able to blink out of sight whenever I want. Nobody shoots at me here, nobody gives me orders, and there's plenty of sun for my batteries. Everything has been peachy keen . . . until *you* came along."

"Me?" Alyssa said. "I haven't done anything."

"Not you in particular, but your type. Sickies."

Balla said, "The polite term might be 'plague victims.'"

"*Sickies*," Spymaster said. "You've freaked out the people in charge back on Earth. I have a friend who monitors human comm transmissions—not just the public PR, but real top-secret stuff. She's amazing at breaking codes. She says there's serious talk about sending this space station into the sun."

"But there are *people* here," Alyssa said. "Still alive. In freezers."

"*Sickies,*" Spymaster said. "With an incurable mystery disease that spreads like wildfire. If it somehow got back to Earth, it could wipe out the human race. Earth governments want it *gone* . . . and if that means incinerating a few people from some obscure Caribbean island, them's the breaks."

"The disease isn't incurable," Alyssa said. "*I* survived it."

"How?"

Alyssa shrugged. "Someone must have come up with a medicine. Or a treatment. Or something."

"Not necessarily," Balla said. "Maybe you just have a good immune system."

"Whatever," Spymaster said. "You recovered, but hundreds of people didn't—even with the best help this hospital could provide. Do you think folks on Earth want a disease like that circling over their heads?"

Alyssa didn't answer. When you put it that way, she couldn't blame people for worrying. Old satellites fell from the sky all the time. Mostly they hit the ocean and sank, but some had hit land, and a few had smacked into populated areas. If a space station contained a lethal plague, maybe shooting it into the sun was smarter than keeping it in orbit till it crashed.

Spymaster said, "They haven't made a final decision yet, and if they do, it'll take years for us to actually reach the sun. A station this size doesn't move fast. Still, humans left this place alone when it only contained war machines. Add a few sickies, and it's *Burn them alive!*"

"When you say war machines," Balla said, "what exactly are you talking about? Besides invisible surveillance mechatrons."

"You name it, we've got it," Spymaster said. "Herds of intelligent battle-tanks roaming the grassy plains. Nuclear bombers and fighter jets basking in the sun. Gunboats in the rivers, artillery on the shore, and mole-machines underground. Lots of smart self-aware robots whose codenames include the word 'megadeath.'"

Alyssa said, "Machines like that aren't supposed to exist. During the war, everyone denied building them, and after the Peace, they were supposed to be dismantled."

"Oh sure," Spymaster said. "Who's going to tell a Level Ten battle-tank, *It's time for you to die?* And what about a fleet of robot warplanes, each carrying a dozen nukes? You don't mess with those gals. So the governments of the world quietly agreed just to let war machines retire. This space station was available, since the Peace didn't allow orbiting command posts . . . so we all ended up here. And we lived happily ever after, until you sickies showed up."

"Excuse me for getting deathly ill," Alyssa said. "But I'll tell you what: show me how to call Earth, and I'll try to fix everything."

"Yeah? How?"

"I'll call my parents. I'll tell them I'm okay, and whatever this disease is, it can be beaten. Nobody has to be burned."

Spymaster didn't answer right away. The machine seemed to be thinking. After a few moments, its rotors began to turn and it lifted itself to Alyssa's eye level. "Are your parents important people?"

"Not very," Alyssa admitted. "But they *know* important people. They work for the government, looking after computers in a big data center. They *see* important people every day. And I'm a member of Dolphin clan; it has dozens of big-name celebrities."

"These big-name celebrities know you?"

"No. But they're fellow Dolphins. And some of them donated money to the research station, so they, like, know about us . . . a bit . . ."

Alyssa knew how weak this all sounded. But it was worth a try . . . and even if no one important would listen, she wanted to tell her parents she was okay. She'd never been on the same wavelength as them—they were quiet, she wasn't . . . they said, "What will people think?" and she thought, *Who cares?*—but she loved them and they loved her, even if they didn't much understand her. "How do I talk to Earth?" she asked.

"You don't," Spymaster said. "There are no communications between us and them."

"I thought you said your friend listened to Earth's coded messages."

"We listen but we don't *talk*. Earth pretends we don't exist. We were supposed to be dismantled, remember? So officially, there are no comm links, because officially this station isn't here."

Balla said, "What about unofficially?"

A pause. Then Spymaster said, "That's more complicated." He hovered in midair, making a whirring sound. It was the first noise Alyssa had heard from him besides talking. His rotors were absolutely silent, but apparently, when Spymaster thought hard, something inside him got audible. Finally he said, "I have to talk to someone. Stay here."

He vanished.

"Hey!" Alyssa said. She looked around, but could see no trace of him. "Get back here!"

Softly, Balla said, "He went that way." An arrow appeared on his screen, pointing right.

"You can see him?" Alyssa asked.

"No. But as soon as he left, he started sending radio transmissions. Talking to someone." Balla's face reappeared on his screen, smiling smugly. "That's the Achilles' heel of invisible drones—they can spy on things without being seen, but the only way to report their findings is to broadcast to home base. Gives away their position."

"What was he broadcasting?"

"Don't know; it was in code. But he was definitely—"

Balla suddenly chittered: a split-second's outburst that quickly cut off. Alyssa laid her hand on his skin and chains. Maybe it was just from the strong sunlight, but he felt too hot. That was bad.

Trying to sound cheerful she said, "Well, if that stupid drone thinks we'll just sit around waiting, he doesn't know us too well." Still holding Balla reassuringly, Alyssa headed in the direction Spymaster had gone.

There were insects in the grass: tiny ants with tiny anthills, scuttling spiders, and bright yellow grasshoppers. Alyssa assumed that the soil had earthworms, and aphids too small to see—a complete ecology, carefully balanced for long-term sustainability. If the Almost War had turned into a real one, this station would need to be self-sufficient. A full-scale war might have made Earth uninhabitable for a long, long time: a prospect that had finally made people open their eyes and arrange the Peace.

Strange that such a crazy time could have built a space station so lovely. Lush grass, tall trees, clear streams . . . and in the distance, machines like cattle moving calmly across the fields. Of course, they didn't look like cows—some were boxy trucks, some were grounded fighter planes, some were gigantic guns on tank-tread platforms—but all were painted in camouflage patterns that made them blend into the landscape like creatures of nature.

At this distance, they didn't seem scary at all. Then again, they weren't firing missiles, poison gas, and weaponized germs. Actual combat would make them scary in a hurry. Alyssa turned her eyes away and walked more quickly.

She hoped she was going the right direction. She'd asked Balla if he could still detect Spymaster's radio signals, but he didn't answer. His screen showed the words REPAIR DIAGNOSTICS; Alyssa gave him a quick squeeze, then left him to rest.

She kept walking. From time to time, Balla chittered. The sun rose and fell, rose and fell, every minute.

Sometime later, Alyssa came to a quiet pool of water. Its surface was mostly clear, with a few small patches of algae; the thin pea-green slicks were nothing like the great brownish mats she knew from the Caribbean, but they still brought back memories of working at the research station. Alyssa was tempted to dive into the pool; she was a Dolphin and never needed much excuse to go swimming. But her jeans would chafe like mad if they got wet, and taking them off was not an option—the sight of her awful baggy skin might start her crying again.

She was looking down longingly at the water, when a gleaming metal sphere broke the surface. It was the size of a beach ball, covered with solid silver and beaded water drops. The robot's skin was so perfectly polished, it showed Alyssa's reflection like a mirror. She winced at how disease-ravaged her face looked. She had to force herself to say, "Hello. I'm Alyssa."

"Hello, child," the sphere answered with a motherly voice. "Spymaster said a human was wandering around. How are you feeling?"

"I'm okay, but my aut is sick." She held up her arm to show Balla, whose chitters now sounded more like whimpers. Belatedly, Alyssa stepped back and told the silver sphere, "If you have organic components, you should keep your distance from us."

"I will," the sphere said. "And I'll warn my fellow robots. Most of us are partly organic . . . and while we're usually immune to human diseases, this plague might be different."

"You know something about the plague?"

"I monitor high-security Earth transmissions," the sphere replied. "Up here in orbit I can't pick up much, but we're close enough to a couple of communication satellites for me to catch some message feeds. Lately, what I've heard has been . . . worrisome."

"Spymaster told us one of his friends was listening to Earth signals."

"That's me," said the sphere. "Humans nicknamed me Eve because I'm built to eavesdrop." Eve let herself sink into the pool so she was almost completely submerged. "I work best underwater—floating offshore from enemies and listening in on their broadcasts. To supplement my batteries, I eat algae . . . which I believe you know something about."

"A little," Alyssa said. "But how did you know I was sampling algae?"

"According to messages I've just decrypted, the disease originated in Montserrat's algae. No, let me correct that," Eve said. "Humans first contacted the plague from algae, but the disease actually originated off planet. It's extraterrestrial."

"What?" Alyssa said. "From outer space?"

"The microbes of the disease have been isolated, and they're totally unlike Earth life-forms. And before you ask, scientists say they can't be artificial germs from the Almost War. They're just too different from anything that has ever existed on Earth."

"So Balla and I are full of alien bugs?" Alyssa felt as if she was going to throw up. She understood now why the authorities had gone to extremes to deal with the disease. Shipping patients into space was an overreaction to some new flu or fever, but if this was an extraterrestrial infection, Alyssa could see why people would want it off Earth ASAP. She could even see why they'd be tempted to send the station into the sun: better safe than sorry.

"Maybe they're right," Alyssa said to herself. "Maybe I should tell my parents good-bye and let this happen." She hated being stranded in space, all alone except war machines and sick people in freezers. She hated even more the prospect of burning up in the sun. But going back home would be selfish if it meant infecting people with an alien plague. Besides, she wouldn't be *totally* lonely—she had Balla.

If he survived.

She asked Eve, "Has anyone talked about a cure?"

"No," Eve said. "People aren't in a researching mood. The algae mats were just destroyed: bombed, then doused with acid. You can imagine what that did to local sea-life."

Alyssa grimaced. The waters off Montserrat had been filled with fish, crabs, even dolphins. Now, they likely weren't.

Eve said, "The only microbes left are the ones you collected from the algae. They got analyzed, and that's how people learned the disease was alien. Now Earth's governments are fighting over what to do with the remaining samples. Most people just want to destroy them; a few want to study them, but others are afraid that will lead to germ warfare research, and the next thing you know, there's a new Almost War."

"I don't understand that," Alyssa said.

"People are afraid," Eve said, "and when that happens, they accuse each other of anything they can imagine. They think of all the bad things they might do themselves, then decide that's what their enemies are up to. They think their enemies are building weapons, so *they* start building weapons, and everything escalates."

"You really think people are starting another Almost War?"

Eve hesitated, then gave a laugh. "Who knows? Maybe *I'm* the one making irrational accusations. I am, after all, a creation of the Almost War, built with an us-against-them mentality."

She moved in close, as if staring Alyssa in the eye . . . but what Alyssa saw was her own face in Eve's silvery surface. "Child," the robot said, "when you see us here, so calm and placid, you might forget we're war machines. But we are *not* friendly helpers like your aut. We're things from human nightmares that people chose to make real."

She said those words in the sweet motherly tone she'd used for the whole conversation. Alyssa took a fast step backward, well away from the edge of the pool. She wondered if Eve carried weapons; nothing about the silver sphere looked dangerous, but Alyssa still felt afraid.

"Don't mind Eve," said a voice. "She's all bark and no bite. Built for decoding signals, nothing more."

Spymaster became visible above the pool. Eve grumbled as if insulted, then suddenly bounced straight up out of the water and slapped down again like someone doing a cannonball off a diving board. Water splattered in all directions, but Spymaster had obviously expected Eve's move—he had already zoomed out of range, leaving Alyssa to take the splash.

"Hey!" she cried. The water was as warm as a bath, but it still made her sputter. "Cut it out, you two!"

Balla shrieked with shrill chitters. His dolphin skin made him waterproof, but the splash seemed to upset him. Alyssa stroked him and made soothing noises while glaring at Eve and Spymaster.

"Hey, *I* didn't do anything," Spymaster said. "In fact, I have good news. The General has agreed to see you."

"Who's the General?" Alyssa asked. "And why is seeing him good news?"

"The General is our leader," Spymaster said.

"Not *my* leader," Eve said. "In the Almost War, I was on the other side."

"The war is over," Spymaster said. "Now we're all a big happy family. And the General is head of the family because he's the smartest." Spymaster whispered to Alyssa, "The General is Level Thirteen: superhuman. Even during the war, no one was supposed to build AI's higher than Ten—that would have been treated as an act of *real* war, and the shooting would have started. But the General's government managed to keep him secret: a hidden mastermind, a military genius. Then the Peace came, and the General was sent here."

"Where he thinks he's in charge," Eve said, "when really, he's an unwanted has-been like the rest of us."

"He's not a has-been!" Spymaster said. "Who do you think cured the girl?"

"The General cured me?" Alyssa said. "How?"

"He controls the hospital," Spymaster replied. "He invented a treatment and picked you as the first test patient. I told you—he's an ultra-genius."

"Why hasn't he cured all the other plague victims?" Alyssa asked.

"He's just waiting to be sure you're really cured. The disease is alien: hard to predict. But if you don't have a relapse after a few days, the General will start pulling people out of cold storage and fix them up."

"Balla isn't frozen and he needs to be cured *now*," Alyssa said. "Take me to this General before Balla gets any sicker."

"That's why I said I have good news," Spymaster replied. "The General wants to see you, and *you* want to see the General. Better not keep him waiting."

"I'll go with you," Eve said. She skimmed across the water and rolled onto the land.

"But you don't like the General," Spymaster said.

"That's why I'm coming," Eve said. "I don't want this child facing him alone."

Alyssa was tempted to argue that she wasn't a child, but she held her tongue—she wouldn't mind Eve's maternal presence at her side. It was, of course, ridiculous to think of a silver ball as motherly, just because it had a soothing female voice; if Eve wanted, her speech synthesizer could sound like an old man, a babbling baby, or even a cartoon character. But perhaps Eve chose her voice to reflect her true personality. Either that, or she was just pretending to be caring when she was nothing of the kind.

"Come with us if you like," Spymaster told Eve. "The General has nothing to hide. But the sickie and I should get moving."

"My name is Alyssa, not 'the sickie.'"

"Consider it an honorary title. Let's go."

———————⚸◯⚹———————

The flying robot led the way. The sun continued to circle around the space station's clear glass middle; Alyssa pictured herself as a hamster rolling around the inside of a wheel, but the ground seemed firm under her feet. Gravity seemed just as strong as on Earth—perhaps *too* strong. As minutes wore on, Alyssa found herself growing more and more tired: her days of being sick had drained a lot of her energy.

She wanted to call, "Stop!" and rest, just for a bit. But there were no benches, no shady trees, not even a rock she could sit on. They were walking through a huge field of wheat: waist high and golden yellow. In the Almost War, the wheat would have helped feed the people who lived on the station. Now, it was just something for robots to drive through . . . although perhaps they harvested some and converted it to biofuel.

The air was hot and dry, summer-thick with the wheat's dense aroma. Alyssa plodded on, growing blurry with fatigue. Suddenly, she found herself lying amidst the grain, with Spymaster yelling, "Get up! Get up!" and Eve urgently nudging against her shoulder.

"Wha—?" Alyssa's voice was as muddy as her brain. Automatically she raised her arm, intending to ask Balla what was happening . . . but he had begun muttering to himself, "Blue, bluff, blunder, blunt," as if reciting his internal dictionary.

"Get up!" Spymaster shouted close to her ear. "Leeches are coming!"

"Leeches?" Alyssa felt adrenalin surge and she sat up fast. Long ago, her parents had taken her to a park up north: one of the few left in a seminatural state, as opposed to the tame parks where every tree was labeled. Alyssa had wanted to swim in the creek—she *always* wanted to go swimming—but her parents said no. She'd sneaked off anyway, had swum across a cold muddy lake, and had come out with a dozen small black bloodsuckers clinging to her arms and legs. Leeches. On Montserrat she'd seen even larger ones, as long and thick as her fingers . . . but thankfully, they were just in glass sample jars. She'd never encountered one of those for real.

Now she scrambled to her feet and looked around, wondering where leeches might come from in the middle of a field. No sign of them in the wheat, but something nearby hummed like a swarm of angry bees. Alyssa turned and saw sun glint off the metal skins of five insect-sized robots swooping straight at her. She ducked instinctively. Spymaster yelped and turned invisible, zooming away so quickly that the wind from his rotors blew hard on Alyssa's scalp. The incoming robots hovered a moment, as if confused where Spymaster had gone; then their humming changed pitch and they dived toward Eve.

She had been hiding behind Alyssa, obviously hoping that the grain and Alyssa's pant legs would conceal her. They didn't. The robot insects—the leeches—plunged down, hitting Eve's silver surface with five metallic tings. Eve rolled, trying to shake the bugs off; they hung on, sprouting sharp-tipped hooks that pierced Eve's skin like claws. Eve shrieked and rolled over, as if she hoped to crush the leeches under her weight . . . but she was not that heavy, and the field's soft soil simply yielded as she pressed the leeches against it.

Abruptly, Eve went still: silent and unmoving. But Alyssa could hear whirring and she thought she knew what it meant—the leeches were drilling through Eve's silver skin, trying to reach the electronics inside her. If they could invade her circuits, they could hack into her hardware and reprogram everything about her.

"No way," Alyssa said.

She knelt beside Eve and took hold of a leech. It was more like a beetle than a soft-fleshed bloodsucker: the size of Alyssa's thumb with a hard rounded shell of dark metal. Alyssa dug at it, working to get her fingernails between the shell and Eve's skin. After a moment, she succeeded; then she twisted and pried until the leech came loose with a grinding crunch. Part of the leech stayed behind, like a bee's stinger stuck in a wound—the hooks and the drill that had spiked into Eve, plus a few dangling wires thinner than hairs. Alyssa wondered if she should pluck the remaining debris, but decided against it. The tiny drill had stopped moving, and was no longer a threat.

As fast as she could, Alyssa wrenched off the other four leeches. She tore a fingernail on Leech Number Four, but kept going. Each time she pulled a leech free, some of its innards broke away and stayed embedded in Eve. Eve was left with leech-sized scars on her previously pristine surface: small holes with leech parts in them, and dents where the leeches had rammed themselves into Eve's metal. The dents left distortions on Eve's silvered surface, like the warps in carnival mirrors.

When all of the leeches were detached, Alyssa began picking at the fragments still planted in Eve's skin. The hooks and drills refused to come out—they were firmly lodged in the silver—but after a minute, Eve began to vibrate. Alyssa pulled her hands away; two seconds later, Eve shot off across the field, flattening stalks of wheat as she barreled over them. The robot stopped a dozen paces away and emitted a piercing screech.

"It's okay," Alyssa called, "it's over. Are you all right?" She was afraid to get too close when Eve was distraught—Spymaster may have said that Eve had no weapons, but Alyssa didn't think Spymaster was as smart as he thought.

"I am *not* all right!" Eve cried. Her voice was unrecognizable: scratchy and harsh on the ear. "I am *damaged*, child. And unlike you, I do not heal. I'll be scarred for the rest of my days!"

"Don't get mad at the sickie," Spymaster said. He popped into visibility, hovering halfway between Alyssa and Eve. "She was the one who saved you."

"I know," Eve snapped. "I also know that the Lorelei has never bothered me before. Yet as soon as I involve myself with this child, the leeches attack."

"Who or what is the Lorelei?" Alyssa asked.

"A robot hacker," Spymaster said. "She manufactures leeches and sends them to reprogram other robots. She and the General are . . . not on good terms anymore. But look on the bright side," Spymaster said to Eve. "Whatever the Lorelei wants, the General wants the opposite. So if the Lorelei damages you, the General will fix you back up just to spite her. He can do that—he has all kinds of fabricating machines to make whatever new parts you need."

"And he'd repair me without asking anything in return?"

"Sure. Maybe. Okay, probably not," Spymaster admitted. "He'll likely ask you to do him a favor."

"No way," Eve said. "I survive by staying out of squabbles. Especially ones between the General and the Lorelei."

"You survive by burying yourself underwater," Spymaster said. "Not much of a life, if you ask me. I think you've finally got tired of it—you decided to help the sickie instead of continuing to hide. Am I right?"

Eve didn't answer. After several seconds of silence, Alyssa said, "If the General can cure Balla, I still have to see him."

"He'll ask *you* for a favor too," Eve said.

"Probably," Alyssa agreed. "But I have to save Balla." She turned to Spymaster. "Will we meet more leeches?"

"I doubt it," he said. "The little pests take a long time to build, so the Lorelei never has many on hand. She must be furious that you broke these; whatever leeches she has left, she'll keep them away from you. You're the only thing on this station the leeches can't affect."

"Then I'm lucky," Alyssa said, not feeling lucky at all. "Can we get moving again?"

"Sure," Spymaster said. "It's not far now. Are you coming, Eve, or are you going back to hide in your wallow?"

The wounded silver robot was silent for a moment. Then she said, "I'll come with you . . . or rather, I'll stick with the child. As you say, the leeches will steer clear of her. Staying by her side is safer than trying to get home, especially if the Lorelei is in a temper."

The General was housed in an underground bunker. A ramp led down into the complex; Alyssa noticed that the ramp must have once been a stairway, since the emerald green paint on the walls didn't quite go all the way to the ramp. The paint stopped above the ramp's surface and showed the outline of stair steps. Some powerful grinding machine must have gouged the stairs flat to allow wheeled robots to come and go.

The ramp emptied into a corridor lined with open doorways. The first two doorways were occupied by sentries: armored behemoths who filled the entire rooms beyond the doors. Each sentry aimed a cannon out into the corridor, but not the kind of cannon that shot shells. Lasers? Something else? Alyssa couldn't tell. As she passed, the sentries tracked her with red targeting beams shone at her head, but they took no action—either the General had given permission for her to pass, or the sentries didn't think she could possibly pose a threat.

Other sentries were posted along the route forward: deadly-looking war machines, large and small. Alyssa held her hand over Balla's speaker in a vain attempt to muffle him. ("Haughty, haul, haunches, haunt . . .") His voice was the only sound audible, except for Alyssa's own footsteps and the occasional tink of Eve's damaged surface rolling over the floor.

They went down two more ramps, deep enough that Alyssa could feel herself get heavier—the farther you got from the station's axis of spin, the more that centrifugal force weighed you down. Descending three floors wasn't much of a change, and perhaps under normal circumstances, Alyssa wouldn't have noticed the difference. In her weakened condition, however, she felt everything grow heavier: her clothes, her body, Balla . . .

It took all her strength to keep moving forward. She wished she had someone to lean on . . . but all she had was a sick aut getting heavy on her arm, a spy-drone so light he could pass for a toy, and a pockmarked silver ball that only came up to her knee. She couldn't lean on any of them—not physically or metaphorically. As for the General, if he could heal Balla, she'd be wonderfully grateful even if there were strings attached; but Alyssa had already decided not to trust him. Too many things felt wrong.

Spymaster led the way to a room with huge video screens on all four walls. Only one of the wall-screens was working; the others were labeled AMERICAS, EURASIA, and INDIAN RIM, but they were black and lifeless. The remaining screen was labeled SANCTUARY; it showed multiple views of the space station's interior. Alyssa recognized a shot of the hospital, a field that she'd walked through, and the sun shining through the central strip of glass. Other pictures on the screen showed plain concrete buildings as well as an array of solar-collector panels and an expanse of water.

Positioned in front of the active screen was a towering machine painted gold. It reminded Alyssa of the complicated projector she'd seen in a planetarium: basically a long cylinder, but with numerous attachments, protrusions, rotating sections, and lenses twisting in and out. This robot had eight arms of varied lengths and thicknesses, each tipped with a different type of hand—everything from a giant set of lobster pincers, to a paw with three drill-like fingers, to what looked like a real human hand . . . a woman's hand, fine boned and delicate, as if amputated from a princess. The sight of it made Alyssa shudder.

"This is the General," Spymaster said.

The eight-armed machine didn't turn to face them; its attention remained focused on the vid-screen. However, lenses on its back corkscrewed out of its body and tilted down at Alyssa. Small blue lights flared to life down the length of the robot's body, illuminating Alyssa and her companions in their glow.

"A pleasure to meet you," the General said in a mellow male voice. It struck Alyssa as the voice of someone who greets people for a living, like the man who escorts you to a table in an upscale restaurant—a sugary voice filled with cream.

"Hi," said Alyssa. "I'm Alyssa and this is Balla." She held up her arm and turned her wrist back and forth, letting Balla's silver chains reflect glints from the General's lights. "He's caught the same disease I had. Can you help him?"

"I will make every effort," the General said in his creamy voice. "I have a soft spot for auts—our peaceful cousins, friendly and helpful, humbly accepting their lowly lives." The General paused. "Unfortunately . . ."

He let the word hang. Finally Alyssa said, "Unfortunately what?"

"The Lorelei has picked this moment to make a nuisance of herself. Her leeches attacked you, did they not? I can see poor Eve was grievously gored. It's tragic really, the way the Lorelei lashes out. I expect she's heard the talk from Earth about sending us into the sun, and she's reacting in senseless fury. Venting her rage at the only target in reach: me. As I say, it's tragic—a demonstration of her inferior design."

The General lowered his voice confidentially. "Her side in the war was invested in emotion—ideological loyalty, patriotism, demonization of the enemy. Tsk. So ugly. Her programming makes her waste resources against me, when really, we *ought* to be joining our intellects to solve our mutual problems . . . like your disease."

"Yes, but can you cure Balla or not?" Alyssa asked.

"I believe I could have—after all, I cured *you*. But minutes ago, the Lorelei's minions broke into the hospital and stole materials needed for the treatment. I can't do anything to help poor Balla until we get those back."

"Why would she steal the cure?" Alyssa asked. "What good does it do her?"

"Perhaps she merely wished to hurt me," the General said. "Perhaps she plans to use what she has as a bargaining chip—she knows that the cure is the key to saving this station, so she may demand concessions from me to get back what she stole. Or perhaps she intends to negotiate with Earth herself; she may offer humanity the cure in exchange for something she wants."

The General made an artificial sighing sound. "I really can't say what she's up to. *I* am a creature of logic, untainted by irrational impulses. The Lorelei is my direct opposite—deliberately so. Her designers wished to build something whose behavior I could not predict despite my great processing power."

"Oh *please*," Eve muttered. "What a load of—"

"What was that, Eve?" the General asked.

"Nothing."

Alyssa said, "Spymaster told us you could repair Eve's damage—what the leeches did to her."

The General's lenses swiveled in Eve's direction, extending outward as they focused on the leech scars. "Yes," he said, "those injuries can be patched. I'd be happy to do so, once this business with the Lorelei has been resolved."

"How do you intend to resolve it?" Eve asked.

"That's the problem," the General said. "Those things she stole from the hospital—she might have hidden them anywhere. The only way to find them is to get to the Lorelei herself. Alas, she's protected by leeches, making it dangerous for my aides to approach her. Furthermore, she's taken refuge in a bunker as fortified as this one. My troops have sufficient firepower to blast her into slag, but such an assault would be a disaster for this station's biosphere, and might even blow a hole into space. As for the materials needed for the cure . . . if she has those with her, they'd be obliterated. Intelligent though I am, I see no way to recover what we need. Except . . ."

"Except what?" Alyssa knew she'd hate the answer.

"Except if you volunteer to confront the Lorelei yourself," the General told her. "You, Alyssa, cannot be harmed by leeches. You might succeed where the mightiest robots would fail."

"The mightiest robots are bulletproof. I'm not. If the Lorelei's bunker has guards like this one, I'll be shot the moment I walk in the door."

"You won't be walking in," the General said. "You'll be captured by the Lorelei's minions; they'll carry you into her lair."

Alyssa stared at the General; though he had no human features, somehow the big gold-painted machine radiated smug self-satisfaction. In the silence, Balla whispered, "Mesmerize, meson, mess."

"So I get brought to the Lorelei; then what? I douse her with water and she melts into brown sugar?"

"I will give you a device that will let you deal with her."

Alyssa snorted. "Unless the Lorelei is stupid, she'll have her guards search me and take away any devices."

"The device will be disguised," the General assured her. "It will not be taken from you. Trust me."

"Two minutes ago, you said the Lorelei was too irrational to predict. Now you've got this plan you're sure will fool her. Does that add up?"

"Dear girl, the time has come for calculated risks. People want to destroy this station: you, me, and everyone in it. A cure for the plague will save us all, but the Lorelei stands in the way. The stakes are too high not to take this chance . . . if not for your own life, then for your aut's. And for all those humans frozen back in the hospital."

Alyssa sighed. She didn't like the General, with his too-smooth voice and too-glib promises. On the other hand, what options did she have? Doing something was better than nothing.

"Okay," she said. She felt so tired. "What exactly do you want me to do?"

Five minutes later, Alyssa collapsed. She didn't pass out completely; she just crumpled from fatigue. Her mind stayed clear enough to think, "I have to keep going. I have to save Balla." But her body was running on empty.

Before the plague, she'd always been strong: kept fit by swimming and her habit of leaping into anything that caught her interest. The disease had ravaged her . . . drained her. When she tried to get up, nothing happened. She would have screamed in frustration but she didn't have the strength.

A big robot appeared and carried her out of the General's command room. The robot was banana yellow, a mass of chunky metal that bore her weight as if she were as light as a kitten. Its upper arms were polished steel pistons, but its forearms were padded and as soft as pillows. Alyssa wondered if the padding was expressly for her, so the robot wouldn't hurt her. More likely, she thought, the robot was designed to handle nitroglycerine or something else so deadly, it had to be treated like eggshells.

Alyssa didn't really care. For the moment, she was happy to be handled gently . . . but she fought not to fall asleep. She couldn't afford it, when she had so much to do.

The yellow robot took her to a room lined with cupboards. It set her in a chair and opened a cupboard filled with cardboard cartons that reminded Alyssa of shoeboxes. The robot took one down, slid open a side-flap, and drew out a plate of what looked like goulash: chunks of meat and wide flat noodles, slathered with gravy and covered with a plastic lid. The robot raised the plate to eye level and stared at it hard; for a moment, the robot's huge right eye glowed red. The plastic lid suddenly clouded with steam. When the robot removed the lid, Alyssa could smell the wonderful aroma of fresh cooking.

The robot set the plate in front of her. "Eat." His voice was male.

After a moment, he said, "Oh," and picked up the carton again. He tipped out a small plastic fork and set it carefully beside the plate. "Eat."

The few minutes of rest had restored a bit of Alyssa's energy—enough that she could use the fork to pick up a chunk of meat. She chewed it gratefully. Lamb. It likely hadn't come from an actual animal—just simulated mock-meat made from vegetable protein. Mock-meat could last for years without going bad . . . and Alyssa suspected these rations had been sitting in the bunker since the Almost War.

She didn't care. It tasted good. And the protein would help Balla fight the disease. She ate it all.

Near the end of the meal, Spymaster and Eve joined her. Eve's injuries had been covered with metal tape—not a permanent fix, but it would offer short-term protection to her internal components. (Alyssa wondered whether the tape would stay stuck underwater. Probably not . . . which meant Eve couldn't go home to her pool until the General repaired her completely.)

"How are you feeling now, child?" Eve asked.

"She good," the big yellow robot replied. "Og feed her. Now girl all healthy. Og good cook, yes?"

The robot stared at her. Alyssa might have said he was staring hopefully, like a dog who wants to be told he's done the right thing. Og had big glass eyes, one of which had cooked the goulash in a single second.

"It was good food," Alyssa said. "I'm feeling better."

Og seemed to relax, although Alyssa couldn't say how his bearing had changed. In her Tech-Civ study group, she'd learned that most robots were programmed to make subtle movements mimicking human body language; with tiny physical cues, the machines seemed more like people. They also mimicked human personalities—usually simplified into stereotypes, not truly complex—because such behavior put humans at ease. One history video had spelled it out clearly: machines that seemed human sold better. Their manufacturers made more money. Once robot-makers developed techniques for making robots act human, even machines that were just big arms working in factories were given personalities. Mostly they acted like big dumb lugs, but with hearts of gold. As the video had said, "A lovable machine is a *profitable* machine."

Apparently, the same principle applied to war machines. Alyssa didn't mind that at all—if her weakness made her need a robot nursemaid, one like Og really did make her feel better.

"I'm good," she told the others. "I'm ready to go."

But when she tried to stand, she felt wobbly: lightheaded, and sluggish in the slightly heightened gravity. Og took her in his padded arms before she could topple over. "The General tell Og to carry you." He lifted her gently. "Og be like girl's pony. Giddy-up Og."

"Yuck," Spymaster said. "Have some dignity, Og! Humans already look down on robots like peons they can just order around. Don't make it worse by sucking up to them."

"If I were you," Eve told Spymaster, "I'd speak to Og more politely. He's a Model 54 Doom Cluster. If he seems slow-witted, it's because ninety-nine percent of his processing power is spent on weapon management. Instead of making up complex sentences, he's inventing ten thousand ways to kill you."

"Og not kill," the big robot said. "Og retired." He adjusted Alyssa's weight in his arms. "You ready go now?"

"Sure," Alyssa said. "You know the General's plan?"

"Nobody ever knows General's plan," Og said. "General keep secrets. Plans behind plans behind plans. But Og knows where General told Og to go."

"That will do," said Eve. "Let's head out."

As Og carried Alyssa from the room, she whispered, "Thank you, Og. The food was good."

They walked along the bank of a river . . . or rather Eve rolled, Spymaster flew, Og rumbled along on metal tank-treads, and Alyssa let herself be carried. She felt well enough to walk on her own, but Og wouldn't hear of it. Alyssa didn't insist—she decided to save her strength in case she needed it later. Considering what the General had asked her to do, she couldn't afford any weakness.

Seen from a distance, the river seemed to wind naturally through the fields; close up, however, the water's course was obviously artificial. Its dirt banks were almost perfectly squared off—more like the walls of a canal than a real river bed—and every few paces, the mouths of plastic pipes were visible in the banks, just below water level. Alyssa guessed that the pipes carried water into the fields for irrigation. The crops were certainly growing nicely; these particular fields held leafy green plants that Spymaster said were potatoes.

On Alyssa's wrist, Balla muttered, "Trend, trepidation, trespass."

Close to the end of the alphabet . . . Alyssa couldn't say why, but she feared what might happen when he finished the *Z*'s.

Ahead lay their destination: a low building on the boundary between land claimed by the General and land claimed by the Lorelei. The building had once been the station's communications center; fiber-optic cables ran from the building down into the ground, continuing all the way through to the station's external shell. There, the cables connected with an array of dish antennas. The antennas had been designed to pick up transmissions from practically anywhere on Earth, and for years, the General had used them to eavesdrop on anyone he chose. However, when the General and the Lorelei started fighting, the comm center had to be abandoned—it now lay in a no-man's-land too dangerous for either side to enter . . . unless, of course, you *wanted* to be captured.

Both the General and the Lorelei had cobbled up comm centers in their personal headquarters, but those centers were only makeshift substitutes, with much less sensitivity than the original. Twice the General had attempted to recapture the old center, but both times his forces had been driven off by a Lorelei counterassault. If Alyssa and her companions ventured into the building, the Lorelei would think the General was making Recapture Attempt Number Three. She was certain to move against them . . . with restraint. The comm center was much too valuable to damage, so the Lorelei wouldn't mount an all-out attack. The General had assured Alyssa there wouldn't be major violence—the Lorelei would send a team of her best operatives, with instructions to take Alyssa alive. They'd then bring Alyssa back to the Lorelei for questioning: what was the General up to?

Or at least that's what the General predicted the Lorelei would do. Alyssa hoped he was right.

She figured the Lorelei was watching already. According to Spymaster, the Lorelei controlled at least three invisible spy-drones, all reprogrammed by leeches to obey the Lorelei's commands. As Alyssa and her friends had neared the comm center, Eve had picked up transmissions that were likely from a spy reporting to the Lorelei's home base. "The signals are in code," Eve told Alyssa. "A code I haven't seen before. But don't worry; I can crack it with a bit of work."

"Vertebra, vertebrate, vertex," said Balla.

The river continued right up to the comm center's door, making a sharp right-angle turn to avoid running under the building. It looked like bad planning, as if the people who dug the river hadn't noticed the building until the last second, then had been forced to veer the channel sideways. More likely, there was a practical reason for the building to be so close to the river's course: the comm center probably used the water for cooling machinery or irrigating organic data storage.

When the group reached the building's entrance, Og lifted Alyssa and stared at her with his big glass eyes. "Is girl okay? Can girl walk?"

"Yes, Og. Thank you."

"Good. Og too big to fit through door." He set her down onto her feet and watched in obvious concern as she took a few steps.

"See?" she said. "I'm fine."

Og relaxed. "Og stay outside, watch for trouble. You go."

Alyssa nodded. This was all part of the General's plan. She patted Og's thick metal body and told him, "This shouldn't take long."

She went inside with Eve and Spymaster, but a moment later, Spymaster turned invisible and went out again. His job was to watch for leeches and anything else the Lorelei might send their way. He'd promised to warn them of any incoming attack—a quick radio blip that Eve could pick up and pass on to Alyssa.

When Spymaster was gone, Alyssa turned to Eve. "What now?"

"We pass the time until minions show up." She rolled in a little circle, as if looking around. "I'd love to tap into this place's radio dishes. See what I can pick up."

"You mean you want to eavesdrop," Alyssa said.

"It's what I do," Eve replied. "And it's been years since I've had access to top-of-the-line receivers. With the dish antennas here, I'll hear the tiniest whispers—transmissions that humans want to keep secret."

"Can you send as well as receive? Could you send a message to my parents?"

"I can send," Eve said, "but I don't know if anyone will listen. Earth wants to pretend this station doesn't exist. I'll see what I can do."

She rolled across what passed for the comm center's lobby. It had obviously served as a security checkpoint—incoming visitors would have passed through body scans before they could go farther into the building. But the scanners now lay smashed and blackened with soot; the steel door that once blocked access to the interior had been ripped clean out of the wall. Alyssa and Eve wove their way through the debris and entered the building's inner core.

The first room beyond the door had taken light damage, but it was only a waiting lounge, with partly burned furniture and scorch marks on the walls. The next room contained more valuable equipment, all of which looked intact: electronic gadgets embedded in the walls, and gray plastic boxes the size of refrigerators standing in the middle of the floor. LEDs of all colors glowed on the equipment—the place still had electricity. Alyssa couldn't identify any of the devices, and not a single one had a human-readable label; but Eve said, "This is beautiful!" and rolled up to a fridge-like box. She nestled against a metal plate mounted near the bottom of the box. Immediately the machine began chuck-chuck-chuck sounds, as if something had come awake inside.

"It's working?" Alyssa asked.

"*Mmm*," said Eve, not listening. She had obviously started worming her way into the system; presumably there'd be passwords and codes to hack before Eve could get anything useful, so Alyssa sat down to wait on the dusty floor.

"Wide, widen, widow," Balla said. Alyssa stroked him and tried to send him strength through the stent that connected her to him. Did her blood contain antibodies to the alien disease? She didn't know—the General had evaded all questions of how he'd cured her. But if the "cure" was in her blood, it would be in Balla's too, so he never should have gotten sick. The treatment must have worked in some other way . . . something the General had given to Alyssa while Balla hadn't been attached. Reconnecting had given him the sickness but not the remedy.

"I'm sorry," Alyssa said, still petting him. "I didn't know."

"Windmill, window, windy," Balla said. "Wine, wing . . ." He fell silent for a moment. Alyssa's heart leapt with fear and hope. Then, "Wink, winsome, winter."

"Wow," said Eve.

Alyssa looked up quickly. "What?"

"I can't *believe* what the General was doing," Eve said. "Back when he still controlled this place, he sent transmissions to a star system ten light-years away. They're the weirdest signals I've ever seen . . . and remember, I'm a code expert. This encryption scheme is like . . . wow. I didn't know math could *do* that."

"What was the General up to?" Alyssa asked.

"Darned if I know," Eve said. "But this place kept records of every data-bit the General sent. I've made copies, so I can work on cracking the code. But right now, I have no idea how to begin. If the General understands this stuff, he really *is* a Level Thirteen intelligence."

"If he was sending signals into space," Alyssa said, "could he have been talking to aliens?"

"That's the question, isn't it? I can't see that he ever received answers back . . . but there's barely been enough time for that. He sent his signals when he first arrived on this station twenty years ago. If he was talking to aliens ten light-years away, that's ten years for the General's message to reach them, another ten years for a reply to get back. Their response would just be arriving now, and that's assuming they noticed the message right off and decided to answer it immediately."

"But how could the General know what to say to aliens? How could he know their language?"

"Beats me," Eve said. "Of course, there've always been rumors of covert government agencies receiving alien transmissions. In the Almost War, the General had access to all of their top-secret files, plus whatever they managed to steal from their enemies. A Level Thirteen intelligence might notice things nobody else had picked up—hidden patterns and coded messages in data from radio telescopes. He might have learned the aliens' language without telling anyone. Then when humans banished him to this space station, he sent the aliens a hello."

A terrible thought struck Alyssa. "What if the General is responsible for the plague? What if he *asked* the aliens to send a disease that would wipe out humanity?"

"I doubt that he would," Eve said. "The people who built the General weren't totally stupid: deep down, he's programmed to *help* humanity, not hurt it. Or at least to help that segment of humanity on his side during the war." Eve paused to consider. "On the other hand, who knows how aliens think? They might just automatically try to destroy any other life-forms they notice. Or the General may have said something to make them mad—he sure annoys the heck out of *me*."

"Can we tell the aliens we're friendly and ask them to take their disease back?"

"Maybe . . . if we could speak their language. And if we didn't mind waiting ten years for the message to reach them."

"I don't think we can afford—"

Alyssa stopped. Something cold and sharp had touched her throat.

"Keep still," a female voice whispered. "I'd really hate to hurt you, but by an unlucky coincidence, your windpipe is exactly where I had planned to put my knife."

Alyssa didn't so much as twitch, but her eyes darted around, trying to figure out what was holding a blade to her neck. She still sat on the floor, which was thick with the dust of disuse; she could see her own footprints, and a smeared line made by Eve. She could also see a wavy trail like the marks that a snake leaves in desert sand.

The invisible creature holding the knife must have noticed where Alyssa was looking—it gave a soft chuckle. "Yes," it whispered, "I was codenamed Viper. An inaccurate title, considering that vipers do their killing with poison, and I'm not venomous in the least. But to humans, I suppose 'Viper' sounds more impressive than Snakelike-Robot-With-A-Knife-For-A-Tail."

The blade pressed harder against Alyssa's throat. She winced, reflexively closing her eyes at the nip of pain. When she opened her eyes again, Viper was visible—as if she'd been waiting for Alyssa to blink in order to make a dramatic entrance.

The robot was indeed snakelike: two paces long, but narrower than Alyssa's arm, which must have made it easy for Viper to sneak into places she wasn't welcome. Viper was almost as shiny and reflective as Eve—brightly polished metal, in a flexible steel sheath. Her head was no thicker than the rest of her body, with chiseled steel teeth and beady eyes that glittered like black jewels. Her tail, which was currently pressed against Alyssa's neck, ended in a double-edged dagger; one edge was serrated like a saw blade, while the other was as straight and sharp as a razor. That edge had just drawn a drop of blood as it nicked Alyssa's skin.

"What do you want?" Alyssa asked. She tried to look Viper in the eye, but that was difficult when she didn't dare move her head.

"It's not what *I* want," Viper answered. "It's what the Lorelei wants. And she wants to talk to you."

"Why?"

"I didn't ask—the Lorelei likes unquestioning obedience. Besides, I've never much cared about the reasons for my orders. During the war, my job was sneaking into places and killing people. It didn't matter why those people had to end up dead. It was probably politics. Or strategy. Or somebody hurt my boss's feelings. Borrrring! But you know what? Almost every machine on this space station has more firepower than me, because they were built for large-scale battles . . . but they've never actually killed a single person. The Peace came along before the armies started shooting. But me, with my little knife . . . I *have* killed people. *Lots.* The Almost War had no open fighting, but murder behind the scenes? Oh yes."

"Nice that you take pride in your work," Eve said. "And nice the Lorelei ordered you to take the child alive, or I guess she'd be dead already."

"Her? I wouldn't kill *her*." Viper slithered up Alyssa's body and wrapped around her neck, the knife blade never moving. Within seconds, the snake had coiled herself three times around Alyssa's throat like a cold metallic scarf. The knife remained against Alyssa's windpipe as Viper nestled into place. "I've killed presidents," Viper said. "I've killed *royalty*. If not for the Lorelei, I wouldn't waste my time on some *kid*."

"But the Lorelei orders you around," Alyssa said. "She must have used her leeches to reprogram you. Doesn't that make you mad? At her, I mean, not me."

"It should make me angry, but it doesn't. *Because I'm reprogrammed, you moron!*" Viper's small head lifted away from Alyssa's neck to stare her straight in the eye. The snake drew one of her sharp metal teeth down the bridge of Alyssa's nose, drawing blood.

"If I were human," Viper said, "maybe I'd have deep-seated resentments about what the Lorelei did to me. Maybe you could work on my feelings: sway me to disobey orders. But I don't have depths, and I don't have true feelings. Neither does your taped-up silver ball, or that giant yellow arsenal outside. We're machines, nothing more. We're wind-up toys who might seem human, but we're *fakes*—nothing but ones and zeroes. You're the only real person on this whole blasted station; so far you've been a disappointment."

Silence. Even Balla's recitation of the dictionary had gone quiet under Viper's tirade. Then Eve said, "Well, Viper, it's good you have no deep-seated resentments."

"Shut up," Viper said. "I'm supposed to give a speech." She paused as if taking a big deep breath, then quickly rattled off words in a monotone.

"Do-what-I-say-or-the-human-dies-the-Lorelei-has-authorized-me-to-use-lethal-force-and-don't-think-I-won't-because-the-human-isn't-that-valuable-if-the-human-really-mattered-the-Lorelei-would-have-sent-more-minions-to-do-this-instead-of-a-lone-assassin-who'll-just-kill-the-kid-then-escape-invisibly-if-you-try-anything-stupid. Got it?"

Another silence. Then Balla suddenly said, "Witness, wits, wizard," and Alyssa said, "Okay."

In the comm center's lobby, Viper said, "Wait. Yell out the door and tell your bodyguard not to make any false moves. He can't possibly destroy me before I slit your throat. Besides, his weapons are so powerful, he can't kill me without *vaporizing* you."

"Og," Alyssa called through the open door, "I've been captured by a minion of the Lorelei and . . ."

"Is okay," said Og. "Og minion now too. Leeches came. Og switch sides."

"Oh, Og," Alyssa said. Without waiting for Viper to give permission, Alyssa rushed out into a noon-bright glare of sun. Og stood near the door, his yellow body speckled with beetle-like attachments. His big glass eyes seemed emptier than before, as if something had drained away.

"Oh, Og," Alyssa said again.

"This is bad," Eve muttered from the comm center's doorway.

"No, it's good," Viper said. "One less problem to worry about." Her black-jewel eyes glittered. "What about you?" she said to Eve. "Are *you* going to be a problem?"

"No," Eve said quickly. "I've always been neutral, haven't I? I had nothing to do with the General when he and the Lorelei were together, and I stayed neutral when he and she broke up. I'm only here for the child's sake."

"Ah," said Viper. "You're programmed to be fond of humans. One of *those*." She turned away as if Eve was no longer worthy of her attention. "Come to the Lorelei or not, I don't care. Just don't be annoying."

Alyssa hadn't taken her eyes off Eve. Did Eve really like humans, or was she only part of this because she wanted the General to repair her? The earliest robots had been programmed to put human well-being ahead of all other concerns . . . but during the Almost War, their programming became more complex: *shoot your enemies and protect your friends, except when the mission matters more than your friends' survival.* As part of that programming change, every robot was taught how to lie—it helped with both the killing and the times when betrayal was necessary.

So maybe Eve cared; maybe she didn't. Alyssa sighed. Nothing was ever simple.

"All right," Viper said. "We're leaving." She squeezed Alyssa's throat just enough to make breathing difficult for a moment. She eased her grip and said, "Move. I'll give directions."

"Og carry," the giant said. He lifted Alyssa in his huge padded arms.

"Whatever," Viper said. "As long as we don't dawdle. The Lorelei is waiting."

Og's tank-treads clanked into motion. Eve rolled along beside him. Alyssa knew that Spymaster was tracking them from somewhere overhead, but she forced herself not to look. With Viper wound tightly around her neck, the robot snake would notice if Alyssa scanned the sky.

Now was not the time to do anything suspicious.

They continued following the river as it passed the comm center and flowed through more fields. Alyssa wondered what the crops were; she felt ignorant for not knowing. Tall plants like wild grass. Short ones with purplish leaves. Cane-like bushes with tiny green berries. When Alyssa asked Og what they were, he sounded heartbroken that he couldn't tell her. Eve said, "I only do codes," and Viper snapped, "Don't be ridiculous. Why would I waste data storage on the name of some weed?"

Not so long ago, Alyssa would have asked Balla; he knew the names of things, or could look them up so quickly that Alyssa couldn't tell the difference. Not now. She hugged him against her stomach. Viper noticed and made gagging sounds.

Balla whispered, "Yeast . . . yell . . . yellow." His voice was getting fainter.

For a long time after that, Alyssa held her dolphin friend. She ignored their surroundings. The sun came and went; so did smells on the breeze. Now and then they'd pass some vegetable patch whose odor was so strong that Alyssa couldn't help noticing—like market day on Montserrat, where the stalls were filled with garlic, onions, hot peppers, ginger, and every seller's "secret fish spice." But for the most part, Alyssa kept her attention on Balla until Viper gave her throat a peevish squeeze. "Enough of that. We're here."

Alyssa looked up. The river had widened into a lake with unrippling water as black as burnt coffee. It smelled like vinegar and nail-polish remover. A dull gray bunker squatted in the water at the lake's center; as far as Alyssa could see, no bridge joined the bunker to the shore. The only way across seemed to be swimming, but the water's color and odor silently said STAY AWAY. Alyssa had no idea what toxins the lake might contain, but they would surely be deadly to both humans and machines.

Around Alyssa's neck, Viper started to trill: a warbling sound, almost like a singing canary. The sound made Alyssa dizzy—maybe it was a sonic weapon to muddle human minds. If she hadn't been held by

Og's arms, Alyssa would have fallen over. As it was, her brain merely reeled until Viper went silent again. Alyssa's thoughts began to clear, but she still felt disoriented as a gleaming wet causeway rose out of the lake.

The causeway was made of black cement. Toxic water puddled on its dark surface, and between the puddles the wet cement gave off wisps of smoke.

"What are we waiting for?" Viper said. "Cross over."

"Easy for you to say," Eve replied. "You don't have to roll through that stuff. Og, could you carry me?"

"Og strong," he said, lowering his arms so that Eve could roll up and nestle beside Alyssa. "And Og's feet very tough."

"You don't have feet," Viper said. "You have tank-treads."

"*Tough* tank-treads." He rolled onto the causeway. A stink like burning rubber immediately rose from the treads. Og revved up his engine to speed forward far faster than he'd been going before. He crossed the causeway in seconds, and barreled down a ramp into the bunker. At the bottom of the ramp, he splashed straight into a pool that had obviously been placed there to rinse off the residue of the moat's stinking poison. As Og washed his treads in the pool, the burning rubber smell subsided.

"Well, that was fun," Eve said. "And such a welcoming introduction to the Lorelei's hospitality. Between the moat and the leeches, I can't understand why the Lorelei doesn't have a million billion friends."

"Maybe it's because she likes demolishing any robot who trash-talks her," Viper said. "When she breaks *you* into components, make sure to tell me how you feel about it."

"Would you two stop fighting?" Alyssa said. "Just because you're war machines isn't an excuse."

"Big words for someone with a knife to her throat," Viper said. But she didn't press the blade any harder against Alyssa's skin. "Let's just hurry this up. Og, get moving."

Og rolled forward down a corridor painted black. Unlike the way into the General's bunker, this corridor had no side rooms or obvious sentries. Even so, Alyssa was certain that safeguards were in place—hidden scanners were surely checking her out with X-rays and other sorts of probes. If they found anything amiss, the Lorelei's minions would be on her in a flash.

The corridor led to a huge circular room, wider across than a gymnasium. It smelled like the algae mats where this all began: swampy with rotting plankton. The air was hot and humid; the moistness came from a great pool of water that practically filled the room. The only solid floor was a ring a meter wide running around the outer wall. Metal ladders led down into the pool at several locations. The place had the look of a sewage treatment plant . . . but with the station populated only by robots, there'd been no sewage for years. The pool's water was perfectly clear, all the way to the concrete bottom.

Something glittered down in the depths. Even as Alyssa watched, it rose with the speed of a dolphin. As it broke the surface, its momentum carried it into the air a short distance before it came down and landed with a smack . . . just like the cannonball trick Eve had played when she tried to splash Spymaster. This time, the splash was big enough to soak the whole room: when the Lorelei cannonballed, *everybody* got wet.

She looked exactly like Eve—a mirror-ball, perfectly polished—but she was many times bigger: as tall as Og and then some. If Eve had lurked off coastlines and listened to passing transmissions, the Lorelei must have been built to monitor millions of signals at once . . . a super-eavesdropper who could decode enormous quantities of data and process it into a cohesive picture.

Eve herself was a Level Ten intelligence. Alyssa wondered how much higher the Lorelei ranked. It was easy to understand how this silver giant could battle brain-to-brain against the General and come to a draw.

"Hello," the Lorelei said in a pleasant woman's voice—close to Eve's voice, but with the silky smoothness of the General. "I'm so glad you could come to visit. I see so few guests these days."

Alyssa thought that might have something to do with the toxic moat, but she didn't mention it.

"And you've brought one of my little sisters!" the Lorelei said with apparent delight. "Although she's been terribly hurt by something. How did that happen, dear?"

"Your leeches attacked me," Eve said.

"Yes, they do that," the Lorelei said. "Nothing personal, dear—I don't actively control them. I just send them out with orders to recruit anyone *interesting*. They choose their own targets, based on . . . well, I really don't know *what* their criteria are. I didn't make them myself, I just repurposed them from the General. And after all this time, they're still full of surprises; I never thought they could woo me a Doom Cluster, but apparently they can. Welcome, you!"

"Og happy to be here," the big robot said. He set Alyssa down on the narrow floor surrounding the pool. At the same time, Eve rolled out of his arms. She moved close to the pool, as if she'd love to dive in. Alyssa worried about that—with the leech holes in Eve's skin, water was a bad idea, even if the holes were covered with tape. Eve apparently decided the same thing; she remained on dry land, rolling wistfully back and forth at the edge of the water.

"Don't be sad, little sister," the Lorelei said. "If you want a dip, you'll be all right. Most of your internal components are organic: DNA data storage and bioprocessing chips. Only ten percent of our kind is electronic, and that's just the radio equipment . . . receiver, tuner, trivia like that. Our *brains* are built of biological polymers—so much more efficient than wires and silicon circuits. We're like the girl's aut; it's not half-dolphin for looks, it's half-dolphin for *performance*."

The Lorelei paused, apparently admiring Balla's design. In the silence, Balla whispered, "Zenith . . . zephyr . . . zero."

"Why is it talking like that?" the Lorelei asked.

"He's sick," Alyssa said. "He's got the same plague I had."

"He's *what?*" The Lorelei's creamy voice was suddenly shrill.

"He's sick," Alyssa repeated. "He caught the disease from my blood and he—"

"He could be contagious!" the Lorelei screamed. "You . . . Doom Cluster! Incinerate that aut immediately!"

"No!" Alyssa shouted, hugging her arm to her stomach.

"Aut nice," Og said. "Aut not trouble."

"Maybe not to you, you all-metal oaf. But to me, he's a plague dog and he has to be sanitized. Get your biggest hottest weapon and cremate him!"

"Aut on girl's arm," Og said. "Weapon hurt girl too."

"Humans can live without arms," the Lorelei snapped. "It's an acceptable loss. Oh, I see it all now—the General *wanted* me to capture the girl and bring her back. He's mostly inorganic; he's always envied that I'm *alive*. But I *refuse* to let him *infect* me. Burn the girl and the aut, Doom Cluster. I order it!"

"Og, please don't hurt Balla!" Alyssa said, staring up at the big robot.

"He'll do what the Lorelei says," Viper told her. "Time for me to get off the firing line." Like lightning, she uncoiled from Alyssa's neck and dropped to the floor. Even before she landed, she had turned invisible. Alyssa heard a clatter as the metal snake struck the concrete. Viper raced away, leaving slither marks on the wet floor; she obviously didn't want to be anywhere near Alyssa when Og opened fire.

"Shoot!" the Lorelei shrieked. "Shoot now! You're programmed to obey me!"

"Surprise!" Og said happily. All the leeches attached to his body fell off with a sound like peanuts being spilled on the floor. Many of the beetle-like devices bounced into the water, but a few came to a stop on the concrete. Alyssa picked one up and weighed it in her hand.

"Held on by magnetism," she told the Lorelei. "One of Og's many talents is turning himself into an electromagnet." She held up the dark little beetle. "These particular leeches were made by the General, not you. They didn't hack into Og; they just stuck to his skin like fridge magnets so you'd think Og was yours. But really, he just needed to smuggle them past your defenses. I'm sure you scanned them when we came in, but your scanners could only see what the leeches were made of, not how they were programmed. Hardware can be X-rayed, but software . . . you never know what it will do till it does it."

"Viper!" the Lorelei cried. "Defend me!"

"She's gone," Eve said. "Ran at the first sign of threat."

"And if she comes back . . ." Spymaster suddenly appeared, hovering near the doorway. "Did you notice she makes ripple marks when she slithers across the floor? *I* noticed. And if she leaves a trail I'll see it, even if Viper herself is invisible. I'll see it, and I'll tell Og."

"Og stop little snake if she comes," Og said. "Little snake just has knife. Og has more."

Alyssa told the Lorelei, "When the General described his plan, I wondered if it would work." Alyssa toyed with the leech, feeling its weight in her hand. It seemed heavier than the ones she'd pulled off Eve . . . as if the General had packed more power into his version. When you're aiming at bigger game, Alyssa guessed you needed heavier bullets. "I also wondered," she said, "if I could bring myself to go along with what he wanted." She held up the leech and showed it to the Lorelei. "He told us to plant these on you. He wants them to drill into you, and hack you into submission. That's a horrible thing to do; but from the way you've acted the past few minutes, I'm less upset by it than I was. You wanted to kill Balla!"

"The aut is infected," the Lorelei said. "He's a menace."

"No, he's sick." Alyssa glared at the big silver sphere. "And why should that bother you, even if you're full of biological components? You have a solid metal shell. Germs can't get into you."

"Not as solid as you think," the Lorelei said bitterly.

She rotated slowly on the surface of the water, revealing what she'd hidden all this time: the back side of her shell. It had a great hole torn into it; the hole's edges were twisted shards of silver that looked as sharp as glass. Inside the hole, pulpy organic tissue showed puffy red scabs, as if they were filled with pus.

"Your General did this to me," the Lorelei said, "with one of his hideous arms. He tried to break me open and rip out my brain. I don't even know why—at the time, I thought we were allies. But he's a treacherous psychopath, and he tried to kill me. I managed to get away, but I'm marred forever . . . torn open to the world. Lucky for me, the seals on my electronics weren't damaged, so I'm still waterproof. I can spend most of my time safely submerged. But when I'm out in open air I'm exposed to bacteria . . . to *disease* . . ."

Alyssa felt sick. The Lorelei's open wound would have been stomach turning even on a living creature; the contrast between the damage and the flawless silver exterior made it that much more ugly. Alyssa realized she was still holding the General's leech. She let it fall.

"Hey!" Spymaster said. "Don't go soft on us, sickie—you still have a job to do. You gotta remember, the General is the only one who can cure your aut, and all those people in the hospital. Finish your part of the deal."

"We shouldn't have to hurt anyone," Alyssa said. She turned to the Lorelei. "Your minions stole things from the hospital—things the General needs to cure everyone. Give those back and we'll leave you alone."

The Lorelei gave a sharp laugh. "The General lied to you, child—my people never touched the hospital. It's so deep inside the General's territory, we couldn't get anywhere close."

Alyssa sighed. The Lorelei's words weren't much of a surprise. "Eve, what do you think? Is she telling the truth?"

"It *would* be hard to steal from the hospital without being seen. Even someone like the Viper who can turn herself invisible . . . she can't turn other things invisible too. If she tried to carry something away, it would be spotted."

"I hate to admit it, but you're right," Spymaster said. "That whole 'theft-from-the-hospital' story doesn't make sense."

Alyssa nodded. She had suspected from the first that the General couldn't be trusted. He'd lied and used her to catch the Lorelei by surprise. Even if Alyssa did what the General wanted, there was no guarantee he'd help Balla and the plague victims. Maybe machines like

Eve and Og could be said to have a heart, but the General certainly didn't. He'd do anything he considered "strategic," no matter what damage it caused.

Alyssa looked down at the leeches on the floor. The General had explained what she was supposed to do. He knew the Lorelei would be living in water; since the General's leeches were too heavy to fly, Alyssa was told she'd have to swim out and plant the bugs on the Lorelei's skin. Spymaster and Eve couldn't do it—neither had hands for carrying—and Og would only sink to the bottom of the pool. Alyssa was the one who had to do this . . . if she chose.

She turned her eyes toward the Lorelei's gaping wound. Even seeing that awful damage, Alyssa didn't feel much sympathy. The Lorelei was selfish; she'd been ready to kill Balla without a moment's hesitation. She was also responsible for the damage to Eve, and had brainwashed countless other robots. Perhaps turnabout was fair play, and planting leeches on her silver shell was just deserts.

But was it good to make the Lorelei the General's slave? Was it good to do *anything* the General wanted? From what Eve had found in the comm center, the General himself might be responsible for the plague. He'd contacted the aliens; he'd called their attention to Earth. Alyssa herself—bald, emaciated and weak—had the General to blame.

Alyssa hated the thought of going along with the General . . . but to save Balla, maybe she had to be coldheartedly "strategic" herself. Was it so bad to hack the Lorelei? The big silver robot would be no great loss to the world.

Alyssa sighed. "No. It would be wrong."

She lifted her foot and ground her heel into the leech closest to her. The leech crunched against the concrete, leaving a small tangle of wires and plastic. Alyssa lifted her gaze to the Lorelei. "I won't make anyone a slave—not even you."

"Bad decision," said Spymaster. "You need the General's help, and now he has no reason to give it to you."

"Maybe we can pressure him," Eve said. "If we threaten to tell Earth what we learned at the comm center . . ."

"We'll see what we can arrange," Alyssa said. "But without hurting anyone."

No one said anything in reply. The vast room was hushed except for the faint lapping of water against the sides of the pool. After a moment, Alyssa realized that even Balla was silent.

"Balla?" she said. "Balla?" She shook her arm hard. His screen had gone blank. "Balla!"

"The aut is not defunct," a voice said from Balla's speakers. It was not Balla's voice—it sounded like many voices speaking in unison, enunciating carefully. "We will remove ourselves from this body before the aut terminates, but we must briefly use him in order to converse."

"*Umm*," said Alyssa. "You're, *uhh* . . ." She considered the possibility that Balla was playing some enormous joke, or that the disease had made him delirious. She knew neither of those was true.

"You're aliens?" she said.

"Yes," the voice replied. "We received intelligible signals from this solar system and traveled here, expecting to meet creatures similar to ourselves. We erred."

"What kind of creatures are you?" Alyssa asked.

"Communal cells," the voice said. "On our planet, we live in colonies on the surface of the ocean, where individuals may combine into a unified thought-mass."

"Like . . ." Alyssa covered her mouth. "You're algae!"

"No. We merely have characteristics which are in some slight degree analogous to terrestrial algal life-forms."

"You're algae," Alyssa repeated. "Those algae mats we were studying . . . was that you?"

"We are *not* algae," the aliens said. "Admittedly, there is potential for confusion. We ourselves first believed your algae were our kin. We were attempting to converse with them when you first encountered us."

Alyssa covered her mouth again, this time to stifle a laugh. "You were trying to talk to algae?"

"It was an understandable mistake," the aliens said defensively. "We had been contacted by signals from this vicinity. We assumed that the transmissions had come from our kind. But the algae were . . . uncommunicative."

"I'll bet," Spymaster said.

"It was an understandable mistake!" the aliens said.

"How did you end up inside me?" Alyssa asked.

"You were swimming near the algae. Your research team had diving tanks . . . boats . . . electronic equipment such as this aut."

"So you realized that humans were intelligent?"

For a moment, the aliens didn't reply. Then they said, "We committed another understandable mistake."

"Oh, this is going to be good." Spymaster snickered.

"On our planet," the aliens said, "we are the only intelligent species.

Other creatures are simpleminded. Over time, they have been adapted for our use. We can enter them and use their bodies; for example, if we wish to travel, we occupy a creature that can run, swim, or fly where we desire to go. If we wish to build a device, or use it once it is made, we borrow the body of an animal fitted for the purpose: perhaps one with hands, and sufficient strength to do what needs doing."

"In other words," said the Lorelei, "you infect some animal's brain and make it your own."

"We make use of the animal's abilities," the aliens replied. "This is no different from humans riding a horse or training a dog to perform tasks. We take excellent care of the creatures we possess—our presence in their blood causes no ill effects, and enables us to do much that is beyond our single-cell forms. You can therefore appreciate that when we saw humans making use of technology . . ."

The aliens paused. Alyssa suddenly understood. "You thought humans were being ridden by algae like you! You thought *we* were possessed."

"It was an understandable mistake," the aliens said. "We entered your bodies in the hope of making contact with those who were riding you. Alas, though we searched and searched, we could find no counterparts to ourselves within your anatomies."

"Meanwhile," Spymaster said, "you were making everybody sick."

"That was not our intention. On our planet, our presence never harms other creatures."

"And it didn't occur to you," the Lorelei said, "that Earthling life-forms aren't so well adapted to hosting alien parasites?"

"We are not parasites! And we did not understand we were making humans ill. If *you* encountered a strange new life-form, could you tell which characteristics were normal and which indicated poor health? We did not expect to cause distress, and did not recognize what constituted symptoms of malfunction."

Alyssa said, "So you spread from human to human in search of creatures like yourselves. You infected me and everyone you met on Montserrat."

"Correct. We spread in search of the beings who contacted us. We were taken by surprise when those we rode were put into quarantine and brought to this place. We did not realize the sickness we caused until you, Alyssa, came so close to the point of death that your condition became obvious, even to us. From within your brain and blood, we saw your body shutting down. We therefore withdrew to your skin where we would cause no further deterioration."

"And the General pretended that *he* had cured you," Eve said in disgust. "That liar. The germs left of their own accord."

"We believe he did *attempt* to find a cure. We were, however, immune to his efforts. Despite all that, his attempts were indirectly beneficial: in order to work on Alyssa, he kept her from being placed in suspended animation. Other humans were frozen, and our fellow cells were trapped in the ice. We, the cells who were in Alyssa, are the only ones free to think and act."

"What would happen," Alyssa asked, "if the other plague victims were unfrozen?"

"We would request that a number of us be nearby during the thaw. We would then be in a position to explain the situation to our fellows. Once they understand, they too will withdraw from their hosts. The ill effects should vanish immediately."

"Good disease," said Og. "Tell it, 'Hey, you make people sick,' and disease says, 'Oh sorry, we go.' "

"We are not monsters," the aliens said. "We are ambassadors. We were sent to establish friendly relations."

"That's what you say," the Lorelei growled. "Maybe the truth is you tried to colonize the girl's brain and just couldn't manage it—humans are too different from the animals you enslave back home. You got forced out, but now you pretend you left willingly. Meanwhile, you're making a cozy home inside that aut."

"You misrepresent our motives," the aliens said. "It is true, however, that this device is more hospitable than a human body. It is simpler and more logical in design. It is also more comprehensible—it has provided us with a window on humankind."

Alyssa said, "When Balla was reciting the dictionary, you were learning our language?"

"Not just your language. Understanding a word means understanding much else. The word 'red,' for example, arises from the nature of human vision: a complex subject which to us was unfamiliar. Fortunately, your aut is essentially a computer; it contains strict definitions for every concept. It has rules that say precisely, 'Red is this, not that. Red lies within specific wavelength boundaries.' *That* we could understand."

"So Balla isn't sick?" Alyssa asked, feeling a wave of relief. "That was just you learning from him?"

There was a pause. Then the aliens said, "Your aut is based on terrestrial tissues, and cannot tolerate our prolonged occupancy. Unlike humans, however, auts employ diagnostic software to measure the exact state of their health. This allows us to monitor the aut's condition; we will take our leave before we have caused irreparable damage."

"Can't you leave him right now?" Alyssa asked. "Balla's my friend, and he's been through enough."

"Regrettably, we need a place to live," the aliens said. "If we do not occupy this aut, where else can we go?"

"Don't look at me," Spymaster said.

"Og volunteers," the robot said. "Og is strong. Not get sick. And Og thinks it would be interesting."

"Do you have biological components?" the aliens asked. "We cannot survive long outside of an organic environment."

"No," Og said sadly. "Metal all the way through."

"I can find a home for you," the Lorelei said. Her voice was suddenly silky. "I'll just leech something appropriate . . ."

"No," Alyssa said sharply.

"Look," the Lorelei said, "our honored alien guests need housing, and you don't want them in your aut. Fine. I can get them a suitable home, as a gesture of friendship."

"Yeah, right," Spymaster said. "You want to milk them for anything you can get."

"No leeches," Alyssa said. "That's right out."

"What if I gave them Viper?" the Lorelei suggested. "She's already mine; she'll do what she's told."

"No," Alyssa said. "Don't you have anything without a mind? Maybe something just manufactured that hasn't been programmed yet?"

"Dear girl," said the Lorelei, "there are no blank slates here. This space station isn't a robot nursery, it's a *prison*. We're all nasty pieces of work, and Viper is worse than most. If we sacrifice her to some well-meaning parasites, it will be a better use of her miserable life than anything she's ever . . ."

Alyssa dived into the water. She had seen a slithery ripple skimming the pool's surface toward the Lorelei. It took no imagination to guess what the ripple was.

She reached the ripple in a few fast strokes. Mentally crossing her fingers for luck, she shot out her hand and snatched at the ripple's tail, hoping she would grab far enough up Viper's body to avoid the blade on the end. She felt sleek wet metal in her hand—not the knife, but Viper's skin. It was slippery and began to slide through Alyssa's fingers.

Desperately she brought her other hand around, trying to keep herself afloat by treading water as Viper writhed in her grip.

Suddenly, the robot snake became visible. Her tail-blade was millimeters from slicing Alyssa's hand. At the opposite end, Viper's wicked teeth were almost as close to the Lorelei—stretching toward the Lorelei's great gaping wound, where her vulnerable interior was exposed. With a sudden heave, Viper shoved herself forward through the water, dragging Alyssa with her. Viper's silver head struck through the Lorelei's wound, biting into soft organic components.

"*I'm* a nasty piece of work?" Viper said. Though her mouth was full of the Lorelei's flesh, the snake's voice synthesizer sounded with perfect clarity. "*I'm* worse than most? *Me?*"

The snake shook her head, ripping at the Lorelei's inner organs. Alyssa held on to the snake's tail, trying to pull Viper loose but unable to do so. Viper's tail-knife twisted wetly in Alyssa's hands as the snake thrashed wildly. Alyssa managed to keep hold, but couldn't stop the blade from writhing in her grip with a slashing splashing fury.

Then green goo erupted from Balla, in his place around Alyssa's forearm. The goo flowed smoothly to Alyssa's hand, and as fast as running water, it gushed onto Viper's metallic skin. It raced up her body in a gritty green wave; Alyssa thought of how algae had sometimes clotted on the outside of her scuba tanks if she got too close. When the green reached the point where Viper's teeth bit into the Lorelei, the flow split in two directions: half the algae flooded down Viper's throat, while the other half wormed into the Lorelei's torn flesh, soaking into her blood.

Suddenly, both robots fell still. Alyssa waited, until her heart had pounded out a dozen beats. She relaxed her grip and panted, treading water. She wiped her face hard; her nose stung from all the water that had splashed into her nostrils during the fight.

"Breathe slowly," her aut said. "Your heart is beating too fast."

It was Balla's voice, not the aliens. "Balla!"

"Now your heart is beating even faster," he said in disapproval. "Maybe you've had enough exercise for today."

"Balla," she said, "are you all right?"

"My diagnostics are far outside acceptable boundaries," he said. "But I feel fine. I'm afraid there's a gap in my memory—my data-storage circuits seem to have been offline."

"I'll explain later," Alyssa said. Still treading water, she looked at the Lorelei's giant silver sphere looming over her head. "Hello?" Alyssa said.

"Anybody home?"

"We are here," the aliens said, speaking from both the Lorelei and Viper. "It will take time to accustom ourselves to these new environments. However, they have many similarities to the aut, so we should acclimatize quickly."

"Ball and snake going to get sick?" Og asked.

"In time," the aliens said. "Not soon. We are learning how to cause less metabolic flux in terrestrial tissues."

"You shouldn't stay there indefinitely," Alyssa said. "They aren't nice machines, but it's bad to enslave anyone."

"We can find other hosts," Eve said.

"Absolutely," Spymaster said. "Some of the robots in this station are dumber than earthworms."

"But first we'll go back to the comm center," Alyssa said. "Call Earth. Tell them the plague isn't a problem anymore, and that we have visitors."

"Oh yeah," Spymaster said. "Nothing eases world tensions like telling folks that aliens have arrived."

"We have an excellent speech prepared," the aliens said. "It is most reassuring. It mentions peace."

"I'm sure it will be great," Alyssa said. "We'll just take things one step at a time. I'll call my parents . . . and the head of the Dolphin clan . . . and . . . I don't know."

"We note," said the aliens, "that this device called the Lorelei has an extensive list of contact persons on Earth. Many are tagged as having high political importance. The Lorelei also has a collection of files labeled BLACKMAIL INFORMATION. Is that of value?"

"Oh baby!" said Spymaster. "We got leverage!"

"Yes," Eve said. "Over the years, the Lorelei has listened to massive amounts of coded message traffic. It's not surprising she's collected blackmail material on people and governments."

"We also observe," said the aliens, "that the *largest* blackmail file consists of data about the General. The Lorelei has labeled it DYNAMITE."

Alyssa couldn't help smiling. She had no idea how one went about blackmailing a robot—or anyone else for that matter—but she assumed the Lorelei had figured that out. The blackmail files would surely contain detailed plans for squeezing "favors" out of many important people.

Alyssa said, "We'll talk this over on the way to the comm center." She swam back to the edge of the pool. Viper and the Lorelei followed her docilely.

As Og lifted her gently from the water, Balla suddenly let loose a squealing dolphin chitter. Alyssa looked at him in alarm . . . but the dolphin face on his screen was simply laughing with glee.

About The Author

James Alan Gardner got his Master's in Applied Math (studying black holes), then decided to write science fiction instead. He has written seven novels and numerous short stories. He lives an hour away from Toronto, where he practices kung fu and tries not to waste all his time on the Internet. Just for fun, he's started a B.Sc. in geology.

A Strand in the Web

Anne Bishop

Dedication

For all of us

Author's Note

Many years ago, three things happened around the same time. I read a quote by Chief Seattle about humankind being one strand in the web of life. I was playing a game called Sim Park and not having much luck keeping my ecosystems balanced. And I saw a bumper sticker that said, "One Earth, One Chance." I wondered what would happen if you could have a second chance. That wondering eventually became "A Strand in the Web."

Chapter 1

"Oh, yuckit," Zerx said as she looked at the cup in her hand and made squinchy faces. "I asked for it hot, and this is barely even warm!"

"That sounds like the date I had last night," Benj said, snickering as he walked over to his console to begin the morning's work.

No one responded to Benj's remark. That was how we handled these typical morning comments—with polite silence.

"I don't see why the maintenance engineers can't fix this thing," Thanie complained, taking her mug from the food slot. She sniffed it to make sure it held tea, then took a cautious sip.

"I heard Marv finally fixed the warning light problem," Whit said as the data for his part of the project filled the screen in front of his console.

"What warning light problem?" Stev asked.

Whit swiveled his chair to face the rest of us. "A warning light on one of the main panels has been flashing intermittently for the past several weeks, warning of a circuit failure in one of the minor systems."

"It's probably our food slot," Thanie grumbled.

"Of course, the engineers checked the system out every time and didn't find anything wrong," Whit continued. "When the warning light started flashing again yesterday, Marv gave the control panel a thump with his fist. The warning light went out and hasn't come back on since. Problem solved."

The computer chimed quietly, the signal that the morning class had begun.

As the rest of the team settled into their places, Zerx complained loudly, "Why do *I* have to do the insects?"

Before any of us could remind Zerx—again—that the computer had done a random draw to give us our parts of the assignment and that every part was equally important, Benj said, "Because you *look* like a bug."

Unfortunately, that was true. Zerx had gathered two segments of hair at the front of her head and used some kind of stiffener on them so that they stood straight up and looked quite a bit like insect antennae.

Benj turned away, satisfied with his retort. He didn't see the look on Zerx's face before she went to her own console. Zerx could be very unpleasant when she was in a snit, and that look on her face always meant payback.

Tuning out the usual morning grumbles, I carefully checked my own data, feeling the shiver of excitement go through me as it had for the past month when I sat at this console.

My teammates kept acting like this was another computer simulation that was part of our classwork. Oh, it was part of our classwork all right. In fact, this *was* our classwork now. Only this. But this wasn't a computer simulation where time was accelerated and a planet year was contained within a classroom day. This was *real*.

There were six teams at this stage of our education. We'd had to take an extra year of schoolwork while we waited for our city-ship to reach this world—and *another* extra year after that while we waited for the Restorers to prepare this world for the life we would give back to it.

You couldn't apply for a Restorer's team until you proved you could work in real time and maintain Balance in your part of the project. So, we had waited and studied and done the computer simulations and watched our simulated worlds crumble into ecological disaster—much like the worlds the Restorers committed themselves to rebuilding.

Now each team had part of a large island. Each part had a strong force field around it to prevent any accidents or disasters from going beyond the team's designated area. Now we were working in real time. We couldn't just delete plants and animals to make it more convenient when something got out of hand because we were given an allotment from the huge, honeycombed chambers holding the genetic material for billions of species from all over the galaxy. That allotment determined how many of each species we could deposit at our site. Now, every life counted—not just for our own final scores in the project, but for the well-being of the planet.

I was assigned the trees for this project, which pleased me very much because my name is Willow.

As I scanned my data, I took a deep breath and let out a sigh of satisfaction. The number of trees had increased since I last checked. I had planted some mature trees, but most of my allotment for this area had been used for saplings and seeds, and the seeds were beginning to grow.

I keyed in the coordinates and the command for a planet-side picture on half my screen. A moment later, I was staring at a tiny twig with two leaves—a baby oak tree. Someday its roots would spread deep into the land. Its thick trunk would support the strong branches that would provide nesting areas and shelter for birds. Its acorns would feed chipmunks and squirrels, and it would produce oxygen that the animals needed to breathe.

A tree was a wonderful piece of creation.

"You look pleased," Stev said as he approached my console.

"Tree," I said, grinning like a fool.

"That *is* your assignment, Willow," he replied, trying to maintain a somber expression. Then he glanced at the screen and his eyes narrowed. He looked at my twig of a tree and then at the numbers for each species. "How'd you get that many trees out of the generation tanks so fast?"

I stiffened a little. But there was nothing in his voice—like there would have been in Benj's or Zerx's—that implied I was getting preferential treatment because both of my parents were Restorers. "I requested 20 percent of the stock as mature trees old enough to begin self-reproduction, 30 percent as saplings, and the rest as seeds."

It could take days for the generation tanks to produce a mature specimen, depending on how fast the growing process was accelerated. But it didn't take the tanks more than a few hours to produce healthy, viable seeds.

Stev whistled softly. He didn't say anything for a minute. Then, with his eyes fixed on the little oak tree still on my screen, he said, "The Blessed All has given you a gift for this kind of work, Willow. You'll be on a Restorer's team the moment you're fully qualified."

With a smile that was a little sad, he went back to his own console. And I went back to staring at the little oak.

Restorers. That's what the eighty-seven people who are the heart of our city-ship are called. They give purpose to what would otherwise be an aimless wandering through the galaxy.

The Scholars say that a very long time ago we lived four score and seven years. Our people now live *forty* score and seventy years—870 years. They say that the Blessed All granted us the knowledge to extend our life spans so that we could make Atonement. That is why the city-ships that are now the home of our people were created—so that we could make Atonement by restoring worlds ravaged either by external disasters or by disasters caused by their inhabitants.

And it is part of our Atonement that we live in a world made of metal, that we never walk on a world we have restored, never feel the breeze that ruffles the leaves, smell the wildflowers ... or press our hands against the bark of a tree that we planted.

The Scholars never say why we have to make Atonement, but they know. You can see the sorrow that's always in their eyes after they complete their training and are told the Scholars' Secrets.

So, this restoration of damaged worlds is our way of making Atonement to the Blessed All for some failure long in our past. The Restorers and their teams are the ones who shoulder that responsibility.

I can't remember a time when I didn't want to be a Restorer—not because of the prestige that goes with the title, but because I love to watch things grow.

My console chirped a query, reminding me that I had work to do.

Blanking my screen, I called up the dot map that would show me the placement of the trees. I still had acorns, some sapling ash and birch, and one young willow left from my first allotment of trees, and I wanted to use them for the start of a new woodland.

As I brushed my finger over the direction pad on my console, intending to shift the dot map and look at the coastline, my hand jerked. I shook it, wondering why it had done that since the muscles didn't feel cramped.

The Scholars say that sometimes the Blessed All shows us our path in very small ways.

When I looked at the screen, my hand poised above the direction pad to shift position back to my team's designated area, I saw the other island. It was to the west of the students' island and about one-third the size—which didn't make it a small island by any means.

Curious about who the Restorer was, I keyed in the coordinates and asked the question. Every Restorer had a specific code so that other Restorers could quickly find out who was working on a particular section of the planet.

There was no Restorer code for that island.

Thinking I'd made a mistake when I keyed in the coordinates, I tried it again.

No Restorer code.

That wasn't right.

I requested soil analysis data. Maybe the Restorer teams had missed this island when they had carefully laid down the microbes and bacteria that were the first step in restoration. Maybe the land was still too toxic to support life, and that's why no one was working it.

No, the land was fertile and waiting.

I closed my eyes. It was rash. It was foolish. I would never be granted a land mass that size for a special project. And even if I was, I wouldn't be able to achieve Balance without a team to help me.

But I could feel an ache in my bones that I knew was the land's cry to be filled with living things again.

I wanted to answer that cry so much.

A soft warning beep reminded me that I had other land to tend.

I called up the screen that listed the trees and the numbers of each species.

My mouth fell open. For a moment, I couldn't breathe.

During the time when my thoughts had been elsewhere, 10 percent of my trees had been destroyed!

Yesterday, Dermi had placed three deer in the meadow that bordered the woodland—which was fine because the meadow was already well established and could feed them.

Now, *fifty* deer had been plunked in the middle of the woodland. There was nothing else for them to eat, so they were devouring my seedling trees.

My fingers raced across the keyboard as I wrote an Urgent request to Dermi for the immediate transfer of the deer to other viable positions within our designated area.

I could have just shouted across the room—and, sometimes, we did that—but every request had to be backed up with written data. The computer could override any request that *wasn't* formally made because, in part, that trail of requests and memos was what our Instructors used to judge our work. And that was sometimes very frustrating. We weren't graded just on our *individual* work, but on the *team's* ability to maintain Balance.

I sat back, trying not to bite my nails while I waited for Dermi's response. It wouldn't take long. Urgents always got top priority.

Minutes passed.

I swiveled my chair and looked at Dermi. She was sitting there, inputting data as calmly as you please.

I sent another Urgent request . . . and waited.

I attached a verification requirement to the third request to confirm that she *was* receiving the Urgents.

The verification came back. Dermi had gotten the requests and *still* wasn't doing anything.

Throughout the first part of that morning, I continued sending requests while I watched the number of my remaining trees fall . . . and fall . . . and fall.

When midmorning came, I sent an Urgent request to Fallah, who was handling large carnivores, and asked for a sufficient number of predators who ate deer to be brought to the woodland. At that point, I didn't really care what kind of carnivore she used as long as they would start eating the deer before the deer ate the entire woodland down to the ground.

By the time the computer chimed the signal for the midday break, there were 125 deer in a woodland that wasn't ready to support even one and still maintain Balance.

Instead of transferring deer *out*, Dermi had responded to each Urgent request by sending more deer *in*.

And Fallah hadn't sent one carnivore.

I blanked my screen before going to the food court where the older students gathered for the midday meal. When Stev asked me what was wrong, I brushed him off. I didn't mean to be rude; I just couldn't talk to anyone. Still, he brought his plate over and sat at the same table. Not next to me or anything, but he was there, along with Thanie and Whit.

I picked at my food, choking down only enough to give my body fuel for the rest of the day.

As we headed back to our classroom, Thanie tugged on my tunic sleeve to slow me down. Not that I was eager to go back in and find out how much damage had been done in the past hour.

"I overheard Dermi and Fallah talking," Thanie said in a low voice. "You're not going to get any carnivores."

"Why not?" I said loudly enough to have Thanie shushing me.

"Because Dermi's in a snit because Stev went to the concert with you last night, and Fallah is Dermi's best friend."

"Stev didn't go to the concert with *me*," I hissed back at her. "A group of us went together—including you."

"*I* know that. But Dermi wanted Stev to ask *her*. So *she's* not going to give you any help and neither is Fallah."

I'd spent a month creating that woodland. A month's worth of work, and all that *life* I had drawn from the genetic material so carefully stored. All of it wasted because Dermi was jealous.

As I walked to my console, I looked at Dermi. She and Fallah had their heads together, whispering. There was something smug and mean about the way they stared at me.

I called up the data on my screen, and for the rest of the afternoon,

I watched my woodland die.

I didn't give Dermi and Fallah the satisfaction of seeing me cry.

I also didn't plant any trees to replace the ones that had been devoured.

I just sat there . . . and watched.

Toward the end of the day, when we were supposed to write the day's activity report for our Instructors to review, Zerx sprang her nasty little surprise—her payback for Benj's bug remark.

I wasn't paying attention to much of anything until Whit yelled, "*ZERX!*" He sent a planet-side view to each of our consoles.

Swarm after swarm of locusts were descending like black clouds onto the meadowlands. Zerx must have used almost her entire allotment of insect life to create them.

And there was nothing any of us could do until class began again the next morning.

I think that's why I did it.

Instead of writing my activity report, I used my personal computer pad to write a request for a special project, a piece of land where I would have complete control, where I would be the only one responsible for achieving—and maintaining—Balance.

I asked for the other island.

I requested a Restorer screen around it, which meant that life-forms could be transferred through the force field around the island with my consent, but nothing could slip through on its own. I requested monitor blanking—a Restorer could override that request, but no one else would be able to see what I was doing unless he or she knew my password.

I sent in my request, blanked my console screen, and went to the living quarters I shared with my parents.

Mother always says that a person must have a life beyond the work. She belongs to a musical society. Father belongs to a theater group. They seldom talk shop at dinnertime unless something special happened. Or they talk about their work as a way to answer the questions that usually spill out of me while I tell them about my classwork.

I didn't talk about what happened in class that day. Since they both seemed concerned about something they were obviously reluctant to talk about while I was there, I also didn't tell them about requesting a special project. After all, I wasn't sure I would get it. Student special projects were usually limited to a few acres of land, not a whole island.

As soon as dinner was finished, I mumbled something about needing to prep for class tomorrow and went to my room. Normally, I would have spent at least an hour going over details and getting requests ready to submit to the techs who oversaw the generation tanks.

Instead I took the hologram from its special place on the shelf, set it on my workspace, and turned it on.

When I was a little girl, my mother asked me what I wanted for my birthday, which was still a couple of weeks away. I told her I wanted a tree.

The day of my birthday, just before the time when Mother usually programmed the food slot for the evening meal, Father muttered something about having a bit of business to take care of and left.

Before I could express my disappointment that he wasn't going to celebrate my birthday with us, Mother held out her hand and smiled. "We have a bit of business to take care of, too."

We went to the room where her team worked. It was the end of the day shift, and there were only a couple of her assistants in the room. When they saw us, they smiled and left. At the time, I was too young to realize that a Restorer's room was *never* left unattended and there was something unusual about them *all* leaving like that.

Mother led me to the large console where she worked. She sat me on her lap, and with her hand over mine, she opened a screen that showed a planet-side picture of a creek. Her hand guided mine as we set the coordinates and issued the command codes.

A few minutes later, a young willow tree stood near the bank of the creek.

"There's your tree, Willow," Mother said quietly.

I don't know how long we sat there, Mother with her arms around me and her cheek resting against my head, just watching the light breeze flutter the willow's leaves.

When she finally blanked the screen and we returned to our living quarters, Father was waiting for us, his smile a little hesitant.

And I knew then that, just as my mother had arranged for me to plant that tree, my father had personally overseen its growth in the generation tanks. But that wasn't his business that evening.

After dinner and the birthday sweet, I got my other present—a hologram of that young willow by the creek. While Mother and I had been planting the tree, Father had arranged to have the hologram made so that I would be able to keep that moment.

In all the years that have come and gone since then, that hologram has remained my most treasured gift.

I turned off the hologram and carefully put it back on the shelf.

There was nothing I wanted to do about the class project. There was nothing I *could* do about the special project. So I read for a while and then went to bed.

And spent a restless night full of terrible dreams about destruction.

Chapter 2

I checked my personal computer pad the moment I woke up. I checked it before I left for class. I checked it the moment I got to the classroom.

Nothing. No confirmation or denial for my special project.

The locusts had been busy since class ended yesterday, and everyone could see this was leading to disaster. Requests zipped back and forth, mostly requests to the Instructor who was our advisor to be allowed to terminate the locusts down to a workable population. The same message came back every single time: termination was unacceptable. Balance had to be restored by natural means—which meant transferring into that area or producing enough birds, reptiles, and mammals to consume the locusts.

Requests for predators poured to Stev's and Whit's consoles since they were the team members who were training to become a Right Hand—a Restorer's primary technical assistant—and had some pull with the generation tank techs. They forwarded the requests, which were acknowledged but put in the queue with the rest of the student requests. That meant all we had to work with was what we already had.

The lack of response caused a lot of muttering and grumbling.

The locusts weren't the only problem. The deer had eaten my young woodland right down to the ground. All I really had left to work with were the mature trees and the acorns and saplings I still hadn't planted. And I had no intention of sacrificing *them*.

Then Benj thought to check the team rating and discovered that it had dropped so low *none* of us would qualify for *any* kind of starting position on a Restorer's team.

That's when the yelling *really* started.

Of course, Zerx, Dermi, and Fallah were the ones who yelled the loudest.

The rest of the morning was filled with scrambled panic. Dermi started transferring the deer any old place within our designated area. Fallah finally released some of her carnivores and plunked them down in the middle of the deer. Benj dumped mice, squirrels, and rabbits into the meadowlands already covered with locust, not giving any thought to whether or not any of those animals would help with the locust problem. Thanie transferred her songbirds to that area, and Dayl poured in a load of reptiles.

It was a mess.

I did very little throughout the morning. I politely answered requests for more trees and made no promises. When the requests became more forceful, I said my order for saplings was already in the student queue and I would begin establishing the woodland as soon as trees were available.

It was almost time for the midday break when I keyed in the coordinates for the other island.

I stared at the screen for a long minute, my heart, and my hopes, sinking.

The island now had a Restorer code.

The midday meal was . . . unpleasant. Stev, Thanie, Whit, and I sat at a table by ourselves. None of us wanted to talk. Thanie was the only one who tried—once.

"It's early in the project," she said, looking hopefully at each of us. "We'll be able to restore Balance soon and get our rating back."

"The only good thing about all of this is that the force field won't allow our stupidity to spill into anyone else's area," Stev replied with enough bitterness that none of us dared say anything else.

Judging from the angry looks that were flashing between other tables around the food court, our team wasn't the only one having problems. Which didn't make me feel any better.

It was toward the end of the class day when I finally checked my personal computer pad again. My parents sometimes left messages to let me know if they would be working late or if there was a particular chore I should take care of.

There *was* a message for me. I read it three times before I finally understood what it said.

My request for the island had been granted. The code I had seen was the one that had been assigned to *me* for the duration of the project.

Feeling dizzy, I hugged the computer pad and tried to draw in enough air to breathe properly.

A warm hand settled on my shoulder.

"Willow?" Stev said, sounding concerned. "Are you all right?"

"I'm fine," I said, trying not to gasp out the words.

Stev studied me carefully. "You don't look fine."

"No, I'm fine. Really." But my hands shook as I tried to remember how to close up my console.

Stev brushed my hand aside and closed the console in the proper sequence.

"Come on," he said. "I'll walk you home."

"I'm fine," I said again. At that moment, I wasn't sure if I was going to dance down the corridors or burst into tears. I *did* know that I really needed to be alone for a while to think this through.

Stev walked me to my family's living quarters. He didn't ask any of the questions I could see in his eyes, and I was grateful.

I spent an hour in my room staring at that message.

The island was mine. *Mine.*

I couldn't possibly build a viable ecosystem for a land mass that size and maintain Balance all by myself. In fact, it would be totally foolish to even *try* to establish an ecosystem over the whole island all at once.

I wasn't sure how much time I would have. Sooner or later, someone would realize that a student had been given an island that should have been handled by a primary Restorer. But if I could establish a full ecosystem in a few thousand acres to *prove* I could do it, maybe I would be allowed to continue—or at least be part of the team that finished restoring the island.

I couldn't do it alone. Life-forms, from the smallest to the largest, had to be established. Each link in the chain of survival had to be formed carefully and in the right order. I needed someone who would act as an RRH—a Restorer's Right Hand. I needed someone who would support my work without trying to change it to suit his own vision, who could work independently, someone who could be counted on to value Balance.

I needed Stev.

Since I had an hour before my parents got home, I keyed in the island's coordinates and requested lists of all the species that were viable for this world and for that particular island.

The computer immediately requested the password.

Huh? I hadn't *set* a password yet.

I went back to the message that had given me the Restorer code. At the bottom of the message was the password: unicorn.

An odd word, I thought as I sounded it out. And it seemed equally odd that the password had been chosen for me. But this was no time to quibble. I made my request for species lists, added the password, and waited.

The lists were daunting. I'd had no idea that so many of the species that were stored in those vast honeycomb chambers were suitable for this world. No wonder the Restorers were looking a little dazed.

The computer chimed the warning that the hour was up. I saved the lists under my password, closed down the computer, and went to make dinner since it was my turn.

When I pressed the pad next to the food slot to indicate I was about to place my order, I was still muttering, "Earthworms, grubs, tadpoles, flies." Fortunately, the computer suggested that I place another order from the available menu. I could just imagine Father's reaction if I set a platter of tadpoles and bugs over earthworm pasta in front of him. No, this wouldn't be a good time for a lecture on keeping my mind focused on the task at hand. Not a good time at all.

I chose meatloaf, which would please Father, and a variety of vegetables to go with it, which would please Mother.

I had the table set when Father came home. Mother arrived a few minutes later, looking distracted.

She filled her plate without any comments, then sat there, pushing her peas around with her fork.

After a few minutes, Father said, "Has Britt made a decision?"

"She's stepping down as a primary Restorer," Mother replied.

"Britt?" I said, snapping to attention. "Why is Britt stepping down? Is she sick again?" Britt was the oldest Restorer on our ship. Forty score and seventy were the years allotted to us for Atonement. Britt had celebrated her 800th birthday several months ago, shortly before she became very ill. She had recovered and seemed fine whenever I saw her, although I remember Zashi, her RRH and life partner, had been very concerned for a while.

"Zashi is also stepping down," Mother said, still rearranging her peas. "He says he wants to concentrate on his tale telling."

Zashi was a wonderful tale teller. Whenever one of his story hours was listed in the activities, I was there. But if Britt and Zashi were no longer going to lead a team . . .

"What's going to happen to Britt's team?" I asked.

"Oh, they'll help out wherever they're needed for a while," Mother said, sounding vague—which wasn't like Mother at all.

"Then Britt didn't name a successor?" Father asked, frowning at his meatloaf.

"Not yet."

And even if she had, a new Restorer would form a new team, so there would be the inevitable shuffling as people settled into new assignments.

Father sighed. "Looks like some of us will have to shoulder the extra work in order to take care of the area that Britt had intended to restore."

"No," Mother said, a funny catch in her voice. "Someone has taken responsibility for restoring Balance to the island."

I choked.

Mother gave me a light thump on the back. "Better?"

I nodded, not trusting myself to speak.

I'd been given Britt's island. *Britt's*. Blessed All, she was the most talented Restorer to come along in several generations. Everyone said so.

"Are you all right, Willow?" Mother asked, brushing her hand over my forehead. "You look pale."

That got Father's full attention.

"I'm fine," I lied. "Really."

Mother smiled, but it wasn't her usual, easy smile. I could tell she was straining not to say a lot of things. Which made me wonder if she knew who had taken responsibility for restoring Balance to Britt's island.

I spent the evening in my room. Father had gone to a rehearsal for a play that his theater group was doing. Mother was listening to music.

My feelings kept going round and round. First feeling overwhelmed by the task I'd been given, then excited, then scared.

Finally I sat in meditation to become attuned to the Blessed All. In that silence, I found the quiet stillness within me. And then all I felt was joy.

I could do this. I *would* do this. I would bring life back to the island—not only for my sake and the land's sake, but now for Britt as well.

Chapter 3

The next morning, just before the computer chimed the start of class, I sidled over to Stev's console.

"Stev, I've received permission for a special project. Would you help me?"

His eyes lit up with pleasure. "Sure, Willow." Then he added reluctantly, "Will you credit me for my work?"

I hesitated a moment too long. And remembered a moment too late that other people had asked for Stev's help on a project and *hadn't* given him credit for his work. I'm sure the Instructors were aware of his part of it, and there was probably a private note in his file acknowledging the work, but it wasn't *formally* listed on his credits—and that could make a difference in earning the qualifications necessary to work on a Restorer's team.

His eyes dimmed. His face hardened. "Just tell me what you need," he said—and turned his back on me.

He didn't sit with Thanie, Whit, and me during the midday break. He didn't say a thing to me during the whole day.

When the computer chimed the end of the class day, I gathered my courage and approached him.

"Could you stay a few minutes?" I asked quietly, noticing the sullen looks Dermi was giving me and the way she was lingering so that she would leave at the same time Stev did.

She left in a huff when Stev finally noticed her and gave her a cold stare.

Dermi was one of the people who hadn't given him credit for his work on one of her projects. Why she kept expecting him to ask her for a date after pulling that stunt was something the rest of us couldn't figure out.

"What is it?" Stev asked, not sounding the least bit friendly.

I took a deep breath. "If this project succeeds, I'll be very happy to give you credit for your work. But if it doesn't—"

"Succeed or fail, I either get credit or I don't," he snapped.

"I think you should see the project before you say that."

Going to my console, I keyed in the coordinates and asked for a red line to show the boundaries of the project.

When the red line appeared, all I could do was stare. The message granting my request for the special project *had* contained the dimensions of the area that was now my responsibility, but I'd been so stunned and excited about getting the island, I hadn't paid attention to the numbers. It hadn't occurred to me that my designated area would be *larger* than I'd requested.

Not only was I responsible for the island, I was also responsible for a band of salt water that surrounded the island. Which meant I was responsible for a small part of another entirely different ecosystem.

Stev studied my screen for a minute. "You've got that little island off the main one a Restorer is working on?"

"Not exactly," I said weakly. Stev was looking at a tiny island off the east coast. It probably had been connected to my island at one time.

"So what *is* your project, Willow?" Stev said a bit impatiently.

"Well . . ." I gestured vaguely at the screen. "Everything inside the red line."

Stev's mouth fell open. "*Willow!*" He braced himself against the back of my chair. "Do you know how *big* that is?"

I certainly did.

Stev took a couple of deep breaths. "So who do you have for your team?"

"Well . . . Actually . . . You."

It was more luck than intention that he ended up sitting in my chair and not on the floor.

"Are you *crazy*?" he shouted.

I knelt in front of him, grabbed his hands, and held on tight. "We can do it, Stev. I know we can! And we don't have to do *all* of it all at once. Look." I jumped up, keyed in the boundary lines of the area I'd decided to work on first. "We can start here, with just this much. That's enough land to create Balance. We can work out from there."

I wasn't sure if Stev couldn't think of anything to say or didn't dare say what he was thinking.

"We can do it," I said again.

"That's a Restorer code," he said slowly as he studied the image on the screen.

"That's the code I was given for this project."

He took another deep breath. "With a Restorer code, we wouldn't be stuck in the student queue. We could use any generation tank that was available."

"We'll have to start from the ground up," I said as my brain began its stubborn chant of earthworms, grubs, tadpoles, flies.

"This really is crazy." Then he smiled. "Count me in. Have you made any lists for what's suitable for that land?"

"I'll transfer copies to your personal computer pad," I said happily.

Stev looked at the lists. Then he finally looked at me. "You're the Restorer on this project. Where do you want to start?"

I'd already thought of that. Balance. Always Balance. Every living thing needed a food source. "The simpler life-forms, especially the ones that aerate the soil. Seeds for grasses and wildflowers."

Stev nodded. "I'll do some checking. The generation tanks may already be producing some of these for other teams. With life-forms like this, the techs usually use enough genetic material to create in batches, then portion it out. That way no team is dependent on the genetic variables that might be in a single batch. We decide on a total number that we want in the designated area, then ask that a percentage of the total come from each batch until we reach our allotment. The grass seed won't be a problem. I'll go down to the tank rooms now and get that started. There should be some to distribute by tomorrow afternoon."

I smiled. He was talking to himself more than to me, which is what he usually did when he was focused and interested in the task.

He finally stopped, looked at me, let out a shout of laughter, gave me a fast hug, and headed for the door. When I didn't follow, he stopped. "Aren't you coming?"

Still smiling, I shook my head. "I have to close down. Then I'll work at home. You can reach me on my personal pad."

When he was gone, I keyed in the coordinates I had searched for last night. My screen filled with a planet-side picture of a stream dancing over rocks.

Each link in the chain of survival had to be formed carefully and at the right time. But the simpler life-forms and the grasses would not be the first bit of life I gave back to this land.

There, by the stream, I planted the young willow tree that I had saved from my student allotment.

Chapter 4

I got to class early the next morning. Stev was already there.

"The first batch of grass seed finished early this morning and is now in a holding tank," he said. "There's also a memo asking that the holding tanks be emptied as quickly as possible since there's a lot of material going down to the planet and full holding tanks will slow up the use of the generation tanks."

"Then let's get to work." I'd spent part of last evening working out where we should start. Accessing the data Stev had sent to my personal pad, we had enough seed to cover several hundred acres. I keyed in coordinates for half the acreage and sent the command to the holding tank for dispersal of half the seed. As the commands were relayed through the city-ship's various systems and dispersal began, a green tint began filling in the dot map that I had called up on my screen. When it was done, I sat back and grinned.

"You've still got the other half of the seeds to plant," Stev pointed out.

"No," I said, "*you've* got the other half to plant."

His eyes widened when I sent the password to his personal pad. His fingers danced through the command codes.

Grinning like fools, we watched the green tint fill in another part of the island.

We both jumped to change the image on our screens when the door slid open and Whit walked in.

"I don't know why the two of you are looking so pleased," he grumbled. "If we can't get this project under control, we'll have to ask for complete termination and start over. And *that* will definitely be on our formal records."

The rest of the team began to file in. Dermi and Fallah walked past me as if I didn't exist. Thanie slunk into the room, looking like she'd had a very bad night. Even Benj didn't make any of his usual comments. And none of the others had anything to say as they took their places and called up the data for their part of the project.

Whit was right. It was awful. So much of the plant life had been consumed, there wasn't enough for the animals to eat. And there was no chance that the remaining plants would reproduce and repopulate the area fast enough. If we dumped the next class allotment of plant life into the area without doing something to adjust the number of animals and insects, it would be consumed immediately.

What it came down to was this: if we were going to restore Balance, we would have to wait out the depletion of life. That, too, was part of Balance. Creatures consumed one kind of life and were, in turn, consumed.

For a while, the predators—both those that walked on the land and those that soared in the sky—would feast. They would mate and produce young who would also feast. But their prey, who ate the plants and seeds, would starve and produce no young. The predators, in their turn, would starve. And the land would start building the links in the chain of survival again—the grasses and flowers, the shrubs and trees, the insects that would pollinate them, and on and on until, once more, there was Balance.

But sometimes a world goes too far out of Balance. Sometimes too many links in the chain are broken too severely, and a world spirals into destruction.

Those are the worlds we restore to Balance as our Atonement to the Blessed All.

The computer chimed the start of class, and I got to work.

There were several requests from Dermi, of all people, for seedling trees. Checking the coordinates she had indicated, I realized she wanted me to put down seedlings in the middle of the deer herds to give them a food source. My next allotment of trees would only feed the deer for a few days at most, and that wasn't going to help the situation.

But I was still part of the team, and I had to do something to honor the request.

Remembering what Stev had said about the holding tanks, I released all the sapling birch and ash with a Priority attached to the planting command. I planted half the acorns I still had. I ordered the other half for aboveground dispersal. I winced about that, but they *would* provide some food for the nut eaters.

I didn't plant or disperse any of them where the deer concentrations were the highest. I felt bad for the deer, but sustaining them today only to have them starve tomorrow wasn't going to help the team restore Balance to our area.

I also put in a request to Whit's console for oak and beech trees that were mature enough to reproduce. I didn't think it wise to send *all* my requests through Stev, even though I preferred working with his specimens. Whit would use the full acceleration feature of the generation tanks; Stev never did without a very strong reason.

I breathed a sigh of relief when the computer chimed the midday break.

"Well, that was an interesting morn—" Stev started to say as the door slid open and we stepped into the corridor.

It was *cold.*

"Blessed All," Whit said. "Some of the heating system must have gone down." He shivered. "Come on. Let's get to the food court and get some hot food."

"If there *is* any hot food," Thanie grumbled, hurrying after him.

The rest of the team rushed past us. Stev didn't move.

"Stev?" I put my hand on his arm. His muscles were so tight, they didn't feel like flesh anymore. And he was very pale.

"This is how it started the last time," he whispered.

"No, Stev," I said, shaking my head. "*No.* Part of a system went down. The engineers are probably already working on it, and it'll be fixed in no time."

His eyes were haunted when he finally looked at me. "Of course it will," he said.

He didn't believe it. He had reason not to believe it.

But we couldn't afford to believe anything else. As part of our Atonement, we lived in a world made of metal. If something really *was* wrong with the ship, there was nowhere else for us to go. Nowhere.

Dermi returned from the midday break in a major snit. When she checked her data and realized what I'd done, the snit exploded into a prime tantrum.

"You . . ." she said, stomping across the room toward me. "You . . ." She called me a very rude thing. "You did this deliberately."

"I provided what I had available," I replied, trying to remain calm as I stood up to face her. "I've also requisitioned my next tree allotment."

"That's not going to help my deer *now*, is it?" Dermi shouted.

"Hey, Dermi," Zerx said, looking wary and guilty since it was *her* snit that had given us the locust problem. "Willow is just doing what—"

"Stay out of this, bug-brain," Dermi snarled. "She did it on purpose."

The way you poured deer into a woodland that couldn't support them? "I provided what I had available."

"You're doing this just to make me look bad," Dermi said, so angry she was turning pale. "The deer need food and *you* could have provided it."

I took a deep breath. "You could ask to transfer them. Maybe one of the other student teams need some deer. One of the Restorer teams might be planning to bring that species of deer into another area. You could—"

"You get *demerits* on your score when you ask to transfer," Dermi shouted. Then her voice dropped to a quiet that was far more menacing. "Of course, *you* never get demerits for *anything*."

Maybe I should have realized this wasn't really about the deer. Maybe I should have remembered that Dermi wanted the special student privileges I had without doing any of the work I'd done to earn them. She always wanted something from people without ever being willing to give anything in return. Maybe I should have realized how much she resented my friendship with Stev. Maybe I would have been prepared for what happened.

But I really didn't expect her to *hit* me because harming someone violated our strictest rules.

And I can't honestly say which of us was more stunned when her hand connected with my face.

I staggered back into the arm of my chair. As the chair swiveled, my body twisted with it. I reached out to grab the console, but I was too off-balance to catch myself. My right hand slid. My head hit the console with an awful *thud*.

I must have blacked out for a few seconds. When I could see again, Dermi was sitting in the middle of the room crying her eyes out, and Whit was doing his best to hold on to Stev, who had his teeth bared and his fists clenched.

I tried to push myself into a sitting position, but something was wrong with my right wrist. I yelped in pain and flopped back down on the floor.

At least that made Stev think of something besides punching Dermi, which would have gotten him into trouble.

The next thing I knew, I was cradled against Stev's chest and Thanie was kneeling in front of me, crying quietly, holding out a wadded up piece of linen that had a lot of colored threads dangling from it. After songbirds, Thanie loved embroidery, and she always carried a little sack of stuff with her.

She tried to press the linen against my face. It hurt, so I tried to push her hand away.

"You're *bleeding*," Thanie said.

Well, that explained why my face felt wet.

At least she had remembered to take the linen out of the embroidery frame. I just hoped she'd also remembered to take the needles out of the cloth.

"Can you walk?" Stev asked.

"Sure," I said, not sure of anything at all.

"Close down our consoles for us," Stev said to someone. It must have been Whit since he was the person who answered.

I wanted to go home. I got walked to sick bay. The medic frowned at the bruise on one side of my face, grumbled about the sprained wrist, and said some very rude things while he took care of the gash on my forehead.

By the time Stev walked me home, my head was pounding so bad it made me sick to my stomach. I barely made it into the bathroom before I threw up.

That didn't make my head feel better. But what made me feel worse was realizing Stev was hovering outside the bathroom door, probably wondering which would be more helpful—coming in or staying out.

If he *really* wanted to be helpful, he would have gone as far away from the bathroom as possible.

Sometimes boys have no understanding at all of how girls think.

Of course, that was what my emotions wanted and not what my body needed. Stev was right to stay close by and my emotions were wrong for wanting him to go away—which, by the time I left the bathroom, made me very cranky.

Stev told me in a quiet, soothing voice, "The medic said you're going to be fine. You just need to get some rest now." He took my shoes off and tucked me into bed.

Then Father burst into the room.

"The medic contacted your parents," Stev whispered before he stepped away from the bed.

Father had that look on his face—that pale, tight, angry look he got when I was really sick or hurt and there was nothing he could do about it.

He didn't say anything. Not one thing. Not a scold, not a soothe, nothing. He just walked over to the bed and very carefully placed his hand on my head.

"I'm fine," I lied, trying to smile.

Nothing. That was a *very* bad sign. When Father was this angry and wouldn't say *anything*, it meant that he was about to explode.

I wished Mother was there. I didn't think my head could stand Father exploding.

"The medic said someone should stay with her," Stev said quietly. Then he added, "I'll stay, sir."

Father straightened up, turned, and looked at Stev.

Stev straightened up and tensed.

The air between them seemed to crackle.

"I'll check in," Father said. Then he walked out of the room.

Stev let out a deep breath. His fingers lightly brushed my hand. "Get some rest, Willow."

I must have dozed off, because I sort of remember hearing Mother and Stev talking quietly. Then I fell asleep and didn't hear anything at all.

⚜️

I woke up sometime later.

Stev was sitting in front of my computer, quietly working.

All the muscles that had tensed as I fell were now aching along with my head and wrist. My mouth tasted like what I imagined the bottom of a swamp did, judging by pictures I'd seen of swamps. And I couldn't get my body to listen to my request to sit up.

Stev looked at me, saw me struggling, and hurried over to help me up.

"How are you feeling?" he asked.

How was I feeling? Very aware that I was sitting with a boy who I might like as more than a friend, looking like some swamp dweller and not being well enough to do anything about it. Which Stev wouldn't understand at all, so I said, "Thirsty." I looked at the computer. I just wanted to forget about this afternoon and fuss over my trees for a little while.

"You need to stay warm," Stev said as he went over to the storage cupboard that held my clothes. He came back with my robe—the worn-out robe that was my favorite piece of clothing and that I wouldn't ever let anyone but my parents see me wearing.

Before I could tell him to bring something else, I was bundled into the robe.

"Slippers," he muttered, looking around until he spotted them. Those made him pause.

Mother gave them to me last year as a funny present. I don't know where she got the idea for them or how she got them made, but I loved them.

They were fuzzy, blue bunny slippers. I wore them so much the "fur" was all matted. The ears, because I tended to play with them while I was thinking through a class assignment, weren't as stiff as they used to be and would wave at people when I walked.

Stev didn't say a thing as he stuffed my feet into the slippers. He helped me to the other chair at my workspace. "I'll get you some tea," he said, then hurried out of the room.

He brought back mugs of chamomile tea for both of us.

"Your mother has been checking in every hour," he said as he sat down. "Your father has been checking in every fifteen minutes." He sounded both annoyed and approving.

"He's worried about my head," I said.

"Your head isn't what he's worried about."

At least, that's what I *thought* Stev muttered. I let it go. I didn't feel well enough to try to figure out why Father and Stev were acting odd about each other.

"Where are we?" I asked as I tried to focus on the screen. That was a mistake. My head immediately started to pound.

Stev hesitated. "Based on where you had indicated woodlands and meadows, I've made a list of the species that will inhabit those areas."

That was good. At least one of us hadn't wasted the afternoon.

"We'll have to wait until we get back to class tomorrow to plant anything," I said. We could do all the planning on our computers or our personal pads, but we needed a console to send requests to the generation tanks or command codes for the distribution of species on the planet.

Stev put his mug down. He took mine and set it down before taking my hands in his.

"Willow . . ." He sighed. "You've been dismissed from the class project. The message came in a little while ago."

"Dismissed?" I stared at him in shock. "I've been *expelled* from the Restorer program?"

"No," he said firmly. "It didn't say you were expelled from the program. It said you were dismissed from the class project."

"But that's the same thing," I wailed. "At this stage of training, it's the same thing." Then I really *looked* at him. "They dismissed you, too, didn't they?"

"Yes." He looked down at our linked hands. "When the message came through your computer, I checked my messages and . . ."

"Was Dermi dismissed?"

"There's no way for me to know that, Willow."

Of course there was—Whit. The team would have to be told that Stev and I were dismissed so that our work could be distributed among the rest of the team. If Dermi had been dismissed as well, Whit would have known by the end of the class day—and he would have told Stev.

So Stev and I were out of the program, and Dermi . . .

"The island," I gasped. "What about the island?"

"Nothing was said about the island. Your code is still there, the password still works. You still have the island."

"*We* still have the island."

Stev smiled slowly. "We still have the island." He looked at my computer. "But we need to find a console to work from."

"We'll find one. And we'll do the work while we can."

He gave me an odd look. "Yes. We'll do the work while we can." Turning away, he started closing down the computer.

"We can still—"

"Do you want anyone else to know about the island yet?"

"No."

He continued closing down. He must have understood something about my father's check-ins that I didn't because Father arrived home a few minutes later—well before his usual time.

And there I was, sitting next to Stev with my face bruised and bandaged, wearing my grubby robe and my bunny slippers.

When I saw my father, I flung myself at him and burst into tears. "Daddy, I've been *expelled*."

I don't know which startled him more—me calling him Daddy, which I hadn't done since I was a little girl, or crying all over him. But he held me and rocked me and told me everything would be all right. And because for that little while he was once again Daddy, I believed him.

By the time I'd wound down to sniffles, Stev was gone and Mother was home.

They didn't fuss over me too much that evening. That was Mother's doing, I think. I stayed in the living area most of the evening, drifting on the music Mother had selected. I could hear them talking very quietly, but I couldn't focus enough to make out the words.

I drifted on the music and found my way to the deep stillness within me—that place where answers are sometimes found if you're willing to listen.

When I finally fell asleep, I knew exactly where to find a console Stev and I could use.

Chapter 5

It took three days before I felt well enough to work anywhere other than my room. Stev worked from his room, too. It would have been easier if we could have worked in the same place instead of always checking our personal pads for messages, but Stev pointed out that the only way he could have spent the day in my room without Father spending it with us would be to explain the special project.

I could see his point, sort of. Since we didn't have any class work, it would be difficult to explain why we needed to work together without explaining what we were working on.

So I made lists. I planned. When I had finished working my way through the links in the chain of survival for the land, I switched to the freshwater systems: plants, insects, reptiles, fish. By then I was too restless to do nothing more than make lists that I couldn't turn into reality, so I went hunting for a console.

Every Restorer team had a main room where they worked. Each team also had an auxiliary room with a handful of consoles.

I figured that, since Britt and Zashi had stepped down, Britt's team wouldn't be using their auxiliary room. Any assistance they were providing to other teams could be done from their main room.

So that morning, with my head still a little achy and my nerves stretched tight, I stood in front of Britt's auxiliary room and put my Restorer code into the keypad next to the door. When the door opened, I slipped inside the room.

I wasn't alone.

Britt turned away from one of the consoles. She studied me for a long moment while I tried to think of some way to explain what I was doing there.

"How are you feeling?" Britt asked quietly.

"I'm fine," I replied. Which had been a lot truer before I'd been caught sneaking into an auxiliary room.

Britt's eyes were far too knowing, but all she did was smile as she walked to the door. Then she hesitated.

"I was about the same age you were when I created my unicorn. My horned horse," she added when I stared at her. "Mine didn't have the elegant equine tail yours did, and it had a beard under its chin." She stroked under her own chin to illustrate. "I'd added that bit because my uncle had a beard like that, and I was fond of him." She smiled again.

When the door opened, she started to step through, then stopped. "We need to do more than what is correct for this world, Willow. We need to do what is *right*. This world . . . *This* world is our true Atonement."

When she was gone, I stumbled over to the nearest chair, sat down, and tried to sort out the messages beneath Britt's words.

The horned horse. The unicorn.

One of the projects necessary to qualify for a Restorer team was to create an "oddity"—to take some of the genetic material from the honeycombed chambers and create a new creature that could survive in a natural environment. I suppose the fact that most of the "oddities" couldn't survive outside the lab was supposed to instill in us a realization of the difference between being a Restorer and being the Blessed All who is the Creator. It also showed that there was no room for ego in the work we were choosing to do. When a creature had to be created in order to fill a niche in an ecosystem, it had to be done with care. A world could only tolerate so much ego indulgence before it rebelled.

I had created a horned horse. On the surface, there was nothing else that distinguished it from other equine species, but it *was* different.

I remember when Britt had been a guest Instructor for one of my classes. She had said that sometimes all the barriers between a person and the Blessed All were flung open. When that happened, it wasn't something that could be described, but it was something that you recognized. And when that happened, what flowed from you was more than what you could point to on the surface, was more than you could knowingly create.

I remember that feeling, that dreamlike quality. It had flowed through me the day I created the horned horse. And when the specimen had been grown and all its data inputted into computer simulations to observe how it reacted to its environment, I had no explanation for why things were the way they were.

In every simulation, wherever a unicorn lived, there was Balance. Somehow, its presence kept omnivores from overfeeding in an area so there was always food for every creature that lived within its territory. Predators wouldn't touch it while it lived. When it became old and was ready to return to the Blessed All, predators would follow it at a distance and wait. It would finally choose a spot and lie down. As it took its last breath, the horn would fall off. Then the predators would approach the offered flesh. But before any of them consumed so much as a bite, one of them would dig a hole nearby and bury the horn. It didn't matter what kind of predator it was, whether it traveled in packs or alone. It would bury the horn.

The Scholars and the head Instructors were more than a little startled when they reviewed my project—and some of them were openly upset. But nothing was said to me, and I was accelerated through a couple of levels of study because of that project.

Stev, on the other hand, had almost been thrown out of the program because of his bumbler bee.

It was a bee, a pollinator like other species of bees. Except that it was bigger and looked a little furry. Its wings weren't in proportion to its body size, but it was still able to fly. It "bumbled" from flower to flower, which is why he'd named it a bumbler bee.

The Scholars had grilled him mercilessly because of that bee. What research had he used, where had he gotten it, what sealed files had he accessed. When he insisted that he'd followed the project instructions and had come up with the bumbler bee on his own, they didn't believe him. They acted as though he had found a way to look at the files that contained the Scholars' Secrets—or had done something equally bad. Because of that project, Stev wasn't advanced with the rest of his group. And shortly after that, he switched from the Restorer program to the Restorer's Right Hand program.

No one at that time or since then has ever explained what it was about the bumbler bee that had gotten him into so much trouble.

But it left a scar on Stev's heart that still wasn't healed.

Now, thinking about what Britt had said, I wondered how much she'd had to do with my acceleration through the Restorer program—and how much she'd had to do with making sure Stev hadn't been dismissed from the program altogether.

I sent a message to Stev's personal pad, telling him I had a console and where to meet me.

When he arrived a few minutes later, he looked nervous. "Willow . . . if we get caught in an auxiliary room . . ."

"We won't get caught," I said, then added silently, *Britt will see to that.* I couldn't have explained why I was so certain of that, but while I'd been waiting for him, I'd reached two conclusions: Britt knew who had taken responsibility for restoring Balance to the island that had been hers before she had decided to step down as a primary Restorer. And Britt approved.

As soon as I accessed the console, there were three polite, but somewhat impatient, requests that I remove my material from the holding tanks.

"I don't *have* any material," I muttered as I double-checked to make sure the requests were meant for me.

"Willow." There was a funny catch in Stev's voice.

As we reviewed what was in the holding tanks against the lists we had made, we realized that what we had available was exactly what we needed. Oh, the quantities didn't *quite* match Stev's figures, but close enough. The grass, clover, wildflowers, and groundcover that were at the top of our lists were waiting for us. There was also an unsigned suggestion that we increase the percentage of mature trees.

"Let's think of this as a gift," I said. And, really, that's what it was. By using what was already there, the three days when we couldn't do anything for the land hadn't been lost.

Stev spent the morning working through our lists and sending requests down to the generation tanks for the rest of the "foundation" life-forms—that is, the insects—as well as a variety of shrubs and berry bushes. I spent that time dispersing the seed that was in the holding tanks.

By the time the midday meal came around, a light rain had begun over the island—just enough to give the seeds the water they needed and also settle them into the earth.

The food slot, which had been a bit whimsical all morning about what it chose to give us, decided to quit altogether when we tried to get a more substantial meal.

"Come on," Stev said, steering me toward the door. "We'll go to one of the food courts."

"But—" I didn't want to go to a food court, especially the one for the older students. It was going to take a while before I could bear to sit in the same room as Dermi.

"Your eyes—and the rest of your head—need a break from staring at that console screen all morning," Stev said firmly.

What was it about Stev that made me the most annoyed with him when he was right?

I began to wonder how much of a break my eyes *really* needed when we met up with Thanie and Whit outside the older students' food court.

"Why don't we go to another food court," Whit said as he glanced nervously at the other students who were going through the door. "There's another one a little ways down the corridor."

"We can't go there," Thanie said in a hushed voice. "*That* one is used by the Restorer teams."

"Well, we can't go into *this* one," Whit snapped.

So we went to the other food court, feeling very self-conscious when we walked through the door. There were a few glances, a few polite smiles. It wasn't that we weren't *allowed* in this food court. It was just that this was a gathering place for the adults.

We got our food and chose a table as far away from everyone else as we could get.

The first bite was enough to remind me that I really was hungry, so I applied myself to my meal. I was halfway through it when Thanie blurted out something that made me lose my appetite.

"As soon as she heard you were dismissed from the class project, Dermi asked to handle the trees," Thanie said.

"*Thanie,*" Whit said in a warning voice.

Thanie was too upset to heed the warning. "She used the whole allotment of genetic material to create seedlings."

My fork slipped out of my hand. My stomach began to hurt. "So the deer got their food after all," I said dully.

"She hasn't done a *thing* about bringing the deer population into Balance. By this morning, they'd eaten all the seedlings. Dermi requested another allotment of trees and was told her next allotment wouldn't be available for another thirty days, so now she's in a *major,* major snit." Thanie paused. "And she blames you."

Whit glared at Thanie while Stev said *very* rude things.

"Why does she blame *me?*"

Finally realizing how angry Stev and Whit were at that moment, Thanie hunched into herself.

"She blames you because she's more of a bug-brain than Zerx," Whit finally growled. "If Dermi had bothered to read the project parameters, she would have *known* that tree allotments are given out in thirty-day cycles. And what's worse is Fallah, who's supposed to be her best friend, keeps encouraging her rash decisions. The results will put our team score right into the waste recycler, but it will sure make Fallah's individual score look good compared to everyone else's."

"Excuse me," I said, pushing away from the table. "I—Excuse me."

When Stev started to rise, I put my hand on his shoulder to keep him in his chair.

As I headed for the door, I glanced to my left.

Zashi was watching me, a concerned look on his face.

I tried to smile in greeting. I couldn't quite manage it, so I hurried out of the room.

I sat in the auxiliary room, glad to be alone for a while. I told myself over and over that the student project was no longer my concern, that *those* trees were no longer *my* trees, that I had other work to do—other land to restore to Balance.

I understood that Balance was give and take, that life-forms lived . . . and life-forms died. I understood that some life-forms became extinct, not because of carelessness or indulgence, but because their time in the world had come to an end. When extinction was a natural part of the ebb and flow of the world, something else would come along to fill that space. It was when a life-form ceased to exist before its time was done that a hole was left in the world. That was when Balance itself could become extinct.

By the time Stev returned from the food court, I had pretty much convinced myself that one allotment of trees used foolishly wouldn't *really* make any difference to this world.

That night, one of the generation tanks failed completely, and there was nothing any of the techs could do to save the life-forms that had been growing inside it.

Chapter 6

Over the next few days, we worked. The grass seed we had initially dispersed had sprouted and was growing well. Some of the flowers had begun to sprout. Following my directives, Stev began accelerating some new plants to the point where they were in flower.

During that time, two more generation tanks developed problems. The techs, who were now extremely vigilant, immediately sounded the alarm. The engineers were able to stop the system failure on those tanks, but a memo came through from the techs strongly recommending that those two tanks shouldn't be used at more than 50 percent capacity.

A lot of ants could be created in a tank that could only function at half capacity, but that recommendation would have a serious effect when it came to larger life-forms.

During that same time, the problem with the heating system had spread from the corridors into the living quarters. My room would change within the space of an hour from freezing cold to being hot enough to make me sweat.

Stev didn't say a thing about the heating system or the problems with the generation tanks, but I knew what he was thinking.

Our city-ships are very, very old. Our people had been wandering through space for many, many of our generations. There were spaceports that belonged to other races where we could stop and make repairs once in a while. But we couldn't build new ships to take the place of the old ones because the generation tanks wouldn't work in any ship but the ones they had been built for, and we no longer had the skill to make new tanks.

It was as if, for one brief point in our people's history, we had been given the gift of knowledge to create the piece of technology that would give our people a chance to make Atonement. Once the ships, and the generation tanks, were built, that knowledge faded away, never to return.

Our engineers could maintain and repair the tanks, and they understood, *in theory*, how to build them. But they simply couldn't build one the size and complexity of the original tanks. The engineers have been trying for generations. Sometimes a very small tank was built and actually worked, but it could only produce one small specimen at a time. The results of trying to grow anything larger than a rabbit were ghastly. And trying to grow more than one specimen of *anything* in one of those tanks . . .

Sometimes one healthy specimen survived. Sometimes.

Everything has a life span. Even a ship.

Slowly, one by one, our city-ships have been dying.

We seldom meet another ship that belongs to our people. When we do, we travel together for a while. These rare meetings are the only way for us to bring new blood into our population. Sometimes people want to leave their own city-ship because of some unhappiness in their lives. Some people leave because they fall in love, and one partner is willing to give up family and friends to be with the other.

It takes courage and deep feelings to make such a choice because the chances are very slim that they'll ever meet up again with the city-ship that had once been home.

And then there are the survivors.

I was barely old enough at the time to remember when our ship picked up a weak distress call from a sister ship. It took weeks to reach it, despite the fact that we had headed for it with all possible speed.

When we got there, we noticed that the small shuttle ships were missing, and there was some speculation that a few people had tried to use them to escape. But shuttle ships, which were capable of transporting us between one ship and another, were not meant for long journeys. There had been no world within range that they could have reached.

The people of that ship had done what they could. What little power was left had been channeled to the honeycomb chambers that held the genetic material—and it had been channeled to the cryotubes. These tubes usually stored specimens that had been carefully grown so that fresh genetic material could be added to the honeycomb chambers to replace material that had become too old to be viable.

When the team from our ship had gone over to look for any sign of life, they had found the two hundred cryotubes filled with children. Only eight of those tubes were still functioning. Those eight children were brought to our ship.

One of them was Stev.

So I didn't offer him assurances neither of us could believe. We just did the work while we could.

—————————————⋙◇⋘—————————————

I discovered the problem in the honeycomb chambers when I put in my request for bees. A few minutes after I sent the request, the console chimed that I had an urgent message.

IF NOT USED IMMEDIATELY, THERE MAY NOT BE ENOUGH VIABLE MATERIAL AVAILABLE TO PRODUCE REQUESTED NUMBER OF SPECIMENS.

Muttering to myself, I spent close to an hour working my way through the command series that would allow me to view the honeycomb chambers that stored the genetic material.

Obviously, there had been a mistake. Somehow the computer had misread my request. Bees weren't some exotic species. They were *bees*. They went *buzz*, they helped pollinate plants as they gathered pollen for food, they made honey. And I had *checked* the amount of available genetic material just two days ago to make sure there would be enough, since I figured every Restorer team would want to disperse bees.

When I finally got to view the honeycomb chambers that held the genetic material for bees, I just stared at the screen. A shiver went through me—a shiver that grew and grew until I began to shake.

The honeycomb chambers had a color code. Green chambers held genetic material. White meant the chamber had been emptied; the material had been completely used. Pink meant the computer was picking up a problem within that cell that could damage the material. Red was a major alert that the genetic material was in danger. Black meant the material within that cell had died.

The area designated for bees was spotted with black and red cells. As I watched, two red cells turned black, and several pink cells changed to red.

With my heart pounding, I keyed in a Priority Urgent message warning every Restorer team that there was a problem with the honeycomb chambers. I also sent the message to the techs' consoles at the generation tanks. At that point, I didn't care who knew I had a Restorer code or that I was handling the island. The teams had to be warned.

As soon as I sent that message, I sent a Priority Urgent to Stev, who had gone down to the generation tanks to oversee the transfer of genetic material to start the field mice we would add to the meadows. I told him to put a hold on the mice and draw *all* the genetic material available for bees and get it into a generation tank.

A minute later, as I watched more green cells change to pink, I got back the query: *??*

DON'T ARGUE. JUST DO IT!!! I sent that message twice.

Stev didn't respond.

"Hurry, Stev," I whispered, clenching my hands so hard they began to cramp. "Please hurry."

More pink cells turned red. Some red cells turned black.

Then, finally, one by one, the red cells turned white. The pink cells turned white. Last, the green cells turned white.

I finally managed to take a deep breath—and realized I was crying.

There was a strong possibility that the material in the red cells wouldn't be able to create healthy bees anymore. Stev, being Stev, would have put that material in another tank so that it wouldn't contaminate the rest if it was no longer viable.

Whatever bees we managed to grow would have to be shared among the Restorer teams that needed them. There wouldn't be enough. We would need another pollinator.

I got a cup of tea from the food slot. Thought it over carefully—and followed my intuition.

When I did a little checking, I discovered that someone had taken Stev's little "oddity" and had been carefully growing more specimens from it. There were several dozen cells filled with its genetic material.

I waited until Stev sent a message that he was returning to the auxiliary room.

Then I sent another Priority message to the techs overseeing the generation tanks.

I was the Restorer for the island. I was the only one who chose what was given to that land, and I was the only one who would be held responsible for that choice.

Before Stev arrived, I got back confirmation from one of the techs.

When the next generation tank became available, it would be growing Stev's bumbler bees.

When I got home, Mother was crying her heart out and holding on to Father as if he were her entire world.

"There was nothing we could have done, Rista," Father said quietly as he rubbed her back, trying to soothe her. "Even if we had known about the problem before today, there was nothing we could have done. Those species aren't right for this world. They would have always been out of Balance."

"I know. I know. But . . . Jeromi . . . *Extinct*."

"We don't know that. There might be another ship—"

Father saw me at that moment and didn't continue. It had been a long time since we had heard from another city-ship. There was no certainty that there *were* any others out there anymore.

I don't know what he saw in my eyes, but I saw the conflict in his. He wanted to take care of the two people he loved, but he wasn't sure which one of us needed him the most at that moment.

I smiled at him and went to my room—not because I didn't need the comfort or the hug, but because Mother needed him more and deserved to have him all to herself for a little while.

Because Mother was from one of those other city-ships. She'd given up everything she had known out of love for another person.

I took my hologram down from its shelf and turned it on, watched it for a while.

An overloaded circuit was the reason that the warning about the cells never reached the techs' consoles. There had been a few erratic warnings a week ago, but the diagnostics showed no problem with the system, and the techs concluded that the warnings were a computer error.

Nobody understood why my accessing the information at that moment triggered the warning circuit, but my sounding the alarm produced an awful scramble in the tank rooms. In fact, my request for bumbler bees was the last confirmed request for the rest of the day.

While the techs were checking out the system, they discovered how much genetic material had already been destroyed. Fortunately, none of the now-extinct species were vital to this world, and some couldn't even have lived on the planet under any condition, but that didn't make the loss any better.

"Extinct" was the most terrible word we knew.

And if we *were* the last surviving city-ship, it was a word that would apply to us very soon.

Chapter 7

A couple of days later, while Stev and I were eating the midday meal in the Restorers' food court, Whit showed up. He got a plate of food and then just sat and stared at it for several minutes.

"Thanie resigned from the program," he said abruptly. "So did I."

"*What?*" I put my glass down before I dropped it.

"What happened?" Stev asked sharply.

"The . . . The songbirds were being destroyed from every direction. They were starving, and there were so many predators after them, the ones who weren't actually killed as prey were dying from fright and exhaustion. She just couldn't stand watching it anymore. So this morning, she sent in a request to have all the remaining songbirds transferred out of the area. The approval came in about an hour before the midday break. When the rest of the team realized what she'd done, you should have heard the way they shrieked about it. Dermi and Fallah were still yelling at her when she keyed in her resignation from the program, shut down her console, and left."

"What about you, Whit?" I asked.

His eyes were bright with tears. "What's the point of putting up with bug-brains like Zerx and Dermi and Fallah—or even Benj, for that matter? The ship is dying. Everyone knows it even if no one will admit it. There's no reason to do this since it's not going to make any difference."

His voice had risen to the point where several people around us had turned to look at us with not-too-pleased expressions on their faces.

"Not the Restorer teams," he said, his voice dropping back to normal. "I don't mean them. They're doing *real* work and they *are* making a difference to this world. But there's no reason for me to keep gritting my teeth and trying to work with the rest of those *people* in order to earn my qualification. There's no future in it." He tried to smile at a joke that was, in its honesty, obscene.

None of us finished our meals. Stev took Whit off to talk for a while. I went over to Thanie's and ended up saying useless things while she cried.

It was a couple of hours before I got back to the auxiliary room. Out of habit, I called up the screen that listed the species that were now in the area we were restoring. Several names popped up on the screen with the "new species" symbol next to them.

I stared at the screen. Birds? *Birds?* I hadn't *requested* birds yet. There weren't supposed to *be* any birds yet.

I keyed in the command for the computer to locate and provide a planet-side view of one of these birds.

There it was, a little sparrow that was barely able to hold on to the branch of a sapling oak tree.

"What's going on here? The Restorer screen is supposed to *prevent* things like this from happening," I muttered as I started to key in a demand to remove those birds. Granted, in a few more days, I intended to request birds from the generation tanks, but . . .

That's when it occurred to me to check my messages *before* I sent that demand to the tank techs.

There was a directive accepting a transfer of songbirds. The directive had a Restorer code that wasn't mine. It also had very specific instructions about the placement of the birds. They had been scattered over the several thousand acres of land that Stev and I were restoring. Despite being added prematurely, the birds really wouldn't be consuming more food than the land could provide.

Which wasn't the point, I assured myself as I muttered my way through the directive. Those birds shouldn't *be* there until *I* decided they should be there.

And then I got to the end of the directive. The Restorer code was repeated. Under it was simply—*Britt.*

I sat back, no longer sure what to think.

I checked my other messages—which I hadn't bothered to do since I hadn't expected any to come through on this console—and found the transfer request. It had been an open request. That meant it had been sent to every Restorer code the computer recognized, and anyone who wanted any of those birds could request them to be sent to the area that person was restoring.

Britt, for whatever reason, had initiated the transfer of the birds to the island.

No. Not "for whatever reason." They were living creatures. The person who had requested the transfer had done so in order to save them. In a few more days, I would have requested the same species. And I still would in order to bring the numbers up to a viable population.

But I think Britt, who sometimes understood too well, knew exactly what my decision would have been if I'd read the transfer request when it first came in.

Just as she understood exactly how Thanie would feel if she knew her beloved songbirds were safe with me.

Chapter 8

"Willow? Where are you going?"

Glancing over my shoulder, I saw Thanie hurrying to catch up with me.

"I have some . . . stuff . . . to do," I said lamely as I continued walking toward the auxiliary room.

"Can I help?" Thanie said. "It's just . . . Well, I thought since you didn't have class either . . ."

The entire walk was filled with her unfinished sentences, but I understood the gist of it. Thanie didn't want to sit home doing nothing while there was an entire world aching to be restored. She had no idea how I had been filling my days since I'd been dismissed from the class project and probably figured that two people doing nothing might create more of the illusion of doing *something*.

I was still trying to figure out what kind of excuse to give her when we reached the auxiliary room. As it turned out, I didn't need an excuse. As I approached the auxiliary room from one direction with Thanie, Stev approached it from the other direction with Whit, who had the same lost look that Thanie had.

I looked at Stev. Stev looked at me.

"Well," I said. "Four can do more than two." I put my code into the keypad. The door opened. "Let's get to work."

"Willow . . . ," Thanie said as she followed me into the room. "Students aren't supposed to be in auxiliary rooms."

"We're not students anymore, remember?" I replied as Stev and I started opening our consoles. "Thanie, why don't you take that console." I indicated the one immediately on my left. "Whit, you take the one next to Stev."

Whit looked around the small room. "You got permission to do a special project?" he asked, looking hopeful. "Could I—" He glanced at Thanie. "Could we help? Not for credit or anything."

That made me pause. I looked at Thanie.

This wasn't about getting credit. This wasn't about getting points on a score—or even getting formally qualified. They just wanted to do the work.

Stev was the one who broke the silence. "If you're going to be here," he said dryly, "we didn't expect you to just sit there and play with your fingers."

"So . . . what's the project?" Whit asked.

Stev and I braced ourselves to catch them as I called up the screen that showed the entire project. We didn't want to start the day with a trip to sick bay because someone hit the floor.

Whit and Thanie just stared at the screen, their mouths hanging open.

"Blessed All," Whit finally said. "You've done that much by yourselves?"

Pain and fury flashed in his eyes for a moment before he regained control. He was seeing the difference between what a *real* team, even if it consisted of only two people, could accomplish compared to what was done by one that was a team in name only.

"We've done that much," I said, feeling the pleasure of our accomplishment warm me. "And we've got a lot more to do. Thanie, you've got the birds."

"Willow . . ."

Since I was already at my console, transferring the data to *her* console, she took her seat. When she looked at the number of birds, tears filled her eyes. She knew where they had come from.

She sniffed a couple of times and then firmed up. "You don't have any hawks or falcons."

"They'll have to be added . . . along with the other bird species that are designated as being appropriate for this ecosystem."

I watched her take that in. She would be handling *all* the birds—and that included the birds that would eat the songbirds.

She closed her eyes for a moment, took a deep breath, and nodded.

In a land that had Balance, Thanie would be able to accept the give and take of life.

While Thanie and Whit spent the next couple of hours acquainting themselves with the project, Stev continued to work through the lists of species we would need, and I went through the messages that had been sent to this console.

Most of them were from the Restorers, basically offering understated praise for saving the bees. They also carefully indicated that they would like some of the bees if any were available.

Since I had initiated the order to grow the bees, I was entitled to keep as many as I wanted or needed. If I kept all of them, I would have a full population of bees for the island, but everyone else would have to scramble to find something else to take the bees' place in the ecosystems they were restoring. So we would share them.

Besides, I had the bumblers, which no one but the tank techs knew about yet.

The next message was from a tank tech informing me that all the genetic material for the bumblers had been placed in a generation tank and was being grown at the same slow acceleration rate that Stev had ordered for the other bees.

The message after that was from another tank tech informing me that the bees would be ready for dispersal in twenty hours. That message was copied to Stev.

The last message from was Zashi, who warmly praised my quick action concerning the bees and then gently offered his assistance. If I were willing to release the equivalent of two small hives—queens, drones, and workers—he would personally oversee using them as the genetic base to create more bees.

That was a tough decision to make. The generation tanks didn't require large amounts of material to start growing another specimen, but it seemed unfair to create something and then turn around and use it to create more of its kind without ever giving it a chance to live. But I was also aware that two queen bees would provide enough material to create close to fifty more queen bees. And fifty hives, that could then produce more bees on their own, would go a lot further toward giving every Restorer team starter hives.

I keyed in a message to Zashi taking him up on his offer. I copied the message to Stev, with an additional note that listed the Restorer teams who had requested bees. He would see that each team got an equal number of bees—or as close to it as possible.

By the time we were ready for a midday break, Thanie was bubbling over with enthusiasm. "Just wait until—"

"*No.*" I blocked the door. "This project is need-to-know *only*, Thanie. It doesn't get discussed with anyone who isn't working on it."

I knew she wanted to rub Dermi's and Fallah's nose in the fact that we were working on a major project, but there was still a chance that we could be shut down if this came to *too* many people's attention.

I saw her struggle with the disappointment. That was my real reservation about having Thanie work on this project. When pushed, she tended to blurt out confidential information in order to regain some emotional ground.

"What about my parents?" Thanie finally asked. "Can I tell—"

"They aren't need-to-know when it comes to this project," Stev said firmly.

Whit shifted uneasily. "You *do* have approval for this, don't you? I mean, you didn't . . . lift . . . the Restorer code or anything?"

"I have approval," I replied. "And there is a primary Restorer who is . . . aware . . . of the work."

That was enough for Whit and, apparently, Thanie.

Stev just gave me a searching look. After getting a message from Zashi, it wasn't hard for him to figure out who the Restorer was who was aware of our work. But I wasn't prepared to tell even Stev just *how* aware Britt was of our work.

And I wasn't going to start wondering *why* she was so interested in what I would do with the land.

Chapter 9

A couple of days later, while the four of us were eating what the food slots in the Restorers' food court had decided to offer for a midday meal, Zashi stopped by our table.

"The new bees are growing very nicely," he said, smiling at me. "They'll be distributed tomorrow." Then he gave me a speculative look. "I just came from the tank rooms. Since I was assisting you with the bees, one of the techs didn't see any harm in mentioning that your other specimens were nicely grown and ready for dispersal. I believe you'll find a message to that effect when you get back to work. I gather you want to give them a chance to prove themselves before offering them to anyone else?"

"Yes," I said, feeling my smile become brittle. "That's it exactly."

"I don't think you'll find that to be an issue—at least, not with any Restorer." He lifted his hand in farewell and went to join friends at another table.

"What other specimens?" Stev asked.

"I'll explain later," I muttered, not daring to look at him.

There had been a blend of amusement and sympathy in Zashi's eyes before he left us that clearly told me he knew as well as I did who was going to make an issue out of this.

When we got back to the auxiliary room, Stev read the message waiting for us and threw a fit.

"How could you?" he shouted. "How *could* you? I have spent *years* trying to put that behind me."

"They're pollinators. They're viable. They work in this ecosystem. We *need* them," I shouted back.

"They *aren't* viable. They *don't* fit! The Scholars and Instructors made that very clear when they reviewed the project."

"*I'm* the Restorer for this team, and *I* say they fit!" If there wasn't so much hurt under the anger, I could have punched him for being so stubborn. "They're *bees*, Stev, and *we need bees*."

He turned away from me.

Whit quietly cleared his throat. "Uh . . . Thanie and I have some . . . stuff . . . to do. We'll be back in a little while." Taking a firm grip on Thanie's arm, he dragged her out of the room.

I barely noticed them leave.

"They'll chew on you for this, Willow," Stev said bitterly.

"Let them try." I waited until he turned to face me. "I'll put our work up against *any* Restorer team. I don't know why the Scholars and Instructors made such a fuss over the bumblers. I don't care why they did. They were *wrong*, Stev." I was so angry at that point, I started to cry. "They were *wrong*."

"Willow . . ." Stev put his arms around me. "Don't cry, Willow. Please don't cry."

I did my best to stop, not because I was ready to, but mostly because seeing me cry made Stev feel helpless.

Stev sighed. "I guess no one will really notice a handful of bumblers."

Obviously, he had only gotten far enough into the message to read "bumbler bees" and hadn't actually taken in the *quantity* of specimens that were ready for dispersal. Once he had, hopefully he, too, would start wondering why someone had taken the time and trouble to produce that much genetic material for an oddity that had no value.

Now there was just the little problem of dispersing the bumblers. As much as I cared about Stev and would trust him without question at any other time, I couldn't be sure he wouldn't dump the bumblers under six inches of water somewhere if he was the one handling the dispersal. Since I'd ordered *all* the genetic material for the bumblers to be drawn from the honeycomb chambers, if Stev did something rash out of some misguided idea of saving the rest of the project, there wouldn't be any way of starting over and producing bumblers again.

Wiping my eyes with my sleeve, I checked my own console for messages while Stev slumped in his chair.

There was one message—from Zashi. All it said was, *Bumblers??*

Thank the Blessed All for Zashi. That message was an offer to handle the dispersal. Stev would have had another fit if I had asked Whit to take care of the bumblers, but there wasn't much he could say when a primary Restorer's Right Hand offered to handle it.

Yes, please, I answered.

A few minutes after Thanie and Whit returned, a message came in from Zashi, copied to Stev, thanking me for allowing him to participate a little and make use of his skills.

I busily avoided Stev's stare until he settled back to work.

And I smiled when, much later that evening after Stev had already gone home, I watched a bumbler land on a flower.

Chapter 10

We worked as long as we could and as hard as we could. It still wasn't enough.

Every day there was a circuit failure in yet another system. The engineers would just get one repaired and two more would go down. The tank techs were sending messages every morning, warning the Restorer teams about continued failures in the honeycomb chambers and which species were threatened. And every Restorer team was using the generation tanks at full acceleration now, even though there was more risk that a fully accelerated specimen might have less reproductive capability.

We just wanted to get as much life down on the planet as possible before a vital system in the ship failed—like life support or the ability to maintain orbit.

I was alone in the auxiliary room. I'd sent Whit and Thanie home because there was nothing else that could be done at the moment, and Stev had gone to check out something in the tank rooms before getting some sleep.

I was tired enough that I had slipped into that state of waking dreams. I stared at the screen in front of me, not really seeing it anymore.

Every link in the chain of survival had to be built in the right order and at the right time. That's what we'd been taught in every Restorer class. That idea was fine when there was more than enough time, but it wasn't going to work now. If I waited until I reached a particular link in the chain at this point, the genetic material might not still exist when I needed it. But if I *didn't* follow procedure, I risked the Balance the island now had.

As I stared at the screen, I felt a surge of energy flow through my body. I sat up. I really *looked* at the planet-side picture that was on the screen.

For several minutes, I watched a spider build a web and saw all my lists and plans in a new way.

Not a *chain* of survival—a *web* of *life*. A link was only connected to the links on either side of it. But a web . . . Each strand affected *every* strand in the overall scheme of the web, but in the end, there was Balance.

With the image of a web kept firmly in my mind, I looked over my lists again.

With the city-ship breaking down a little more every day, I might not be able to send enough of each animal and plant down to the planet in time to assure that each species would be able to sustain itself in the future. But now I knew how to fully restore a part of that island so that, for a shining moment, there would be Balance.

Chapter 11

The next morning, Whit and Thanie looked very confused as they reviewed the list of species I had requested from the generation tanks. Stev looked very concerned.

I knew what he was thinking: that I'd been working too hard and something inside me had snapped.

There was no way I could explain to him, but something inside me hadn't snapped, it was now wide open. Balance flowed through me in a way it never had before. I was no longer following the rules that had been laid down for us in class. I was the Restorer—and I finally understood what that really meant.

"Willow . . ." Stev said. Before he could go on, the door opened. Britt and Zashi stepped inside.

Britt's eyes met mine and held.

She had been waiting for this moment, had been wondering if it would come.

"Would you like some help?" she asked.

I just smiled.

Britt, Zashi, and I slipped into working together as if we'd always done so. After a couple of hours, Stev was almost in stride with us. Whit and Thanie were bewildered by the change in the project's direction and a little dazed at suddenly working in such close quarters with the most respected Restorer and Restorer's Right Hand on the ship.

At midday, Britt and Zashi excused themselves, saying they had other commitments during the afternoon. I thanked them both—and was greatly relieved when they assured me they would be back the next morning.

As they were about to leave, I overheard Zashi say to Stev, "Give yourself some time. You'll get used to working with someone like her."

Chapter 12

Later that evening, when I had finally gone home to get some sleep, I opened a file that had been sent to my personal computer pad. It was a picture of an old document followed by a plain copy of the text. I didn't need to be told that the document had come from the Scholars' secret files. I also didn't need to be told that the sender had taken great care to make sure access to that file couldn't be traced to me.

The document was a long list. A terrible list. At the top was the heading, *Lab Specimens Are The Only Specimens Now Available.*

Wolf, crow, hawk, falcon. Salmon, dolphin, fox, panda. Bison, zebra, elk, tiger. Nightingale, otter, cobra, seal. The list went on and on, naming plants and insects as well as animals. If I compared it to the list of species that were suitable for this world and were stored as genetic material in the honeycomb chambers, they would match. I was certain of it.

The next part of the list was much, much longer. Its heading simply said, *Extinct.*

Near the bottom of that list, I found the reason why the Scholars had been so upset with Stev—and why they had suspected him of accessing their secret files. The entry said *Bumblebee.*

Stev had re-created a creature that had become extinct before its time in the world was done. If the Scholars hadn't slapped him down to the point that he would never be willing to try again, who knows what other creatures he might have given back to the world?

The last part of the list said, *Myths.* The very last entry was the unicorn.

I looked at that entry for a long time. Then I deleted the file. I understood why Britt had sent it to me, and I understood that the list, and the underlying message, wasn't meant to be seen by anyone but me.

Chapter 13

We worked for another month while the ship failed around us. Whit had continued to disperse grass seed and wildflowers over the rest of the island whenever we could get them. Thanie dispersed seeds to build young woodlands while I planted the saplings that would give those woodlands an anchor. Britt added the deer. She had insisted on using the genetic material that was still available instead of transferring animals from another location. I was grateful to her for understanding that I could never have felt impartial about the deer if they had originally been Dermi's.

We had six breeds of horses. There were cows and sheep, hawks and falcons, foxes and hares, mice and owls. We had salmon and trout in the streams, and frogs lived among the cattails and water lilies in the ponds. We had woodlands and shrubs and meadows. We planted fields of oats and barley as well plots of every other vegetable the land would support. Parsley and thyme were among the herbs that had taken root. There was a small population of every kind of creature that belonged to this land. And we had the plant life to support it all.

In that one portion of the island, we had Balance.

We hugged each other. We cheered. We laughed until we cried.

We had Balance.

Over time, the plants and animals would spread out over the rest of the island and grow in number.

We wouldn't see it. But that didn't matter.

And then, the next evening, Stev told me something that changed everything.

Stev waited until the others had left for the day. Then he put his hands on my shoulders.

"Willow . . ." It took him a moment to try again. "Willow, I was talking to one of the tank techs today. In order to try to save the specimens that are needed to restore this world, they're going to start cutting the power to the rest of the honeycomb chambers. All the genetic material in those cells will die."

I felt a deep sorrow, but I understood the necessity. We wouldn't be traveling to any other worlds. We had to do what we could for this one.

"That includes the student projects," Stev said softly.

It took me a moment to understand.

"The unicorns," I whispered.

"I'm so sorry, Willow."

I closed my eyes and tried to wait out the pain.

"They can't die," I said. *Not again.*

I don't know why that thought filled my head, but once it was there, there was nothing else.

Turning away from Stev, I worked my way through the commands that would show me the honeycomb chamber that held the genetic material for my unicorns. When I found it, I couldn't say anything.

There was just enough material to create a small but viable population of unicorns. But if even one cell was lost . . .

Then I remembered something else. It took a few minutes more before I found the cells I needed.

Half of the cells containing the genetic material had turned black.

"If we made them all weaned foals, there would be just enough material for a small population. And *my* adult unicorns would look after them along with the other foals."

"We can't do it, Willow," he said, his voice thick with regret. "We can't put a species on this world that doesn't belong here."

I knew what he was thinking. I had saved his bumbler bees, and he had to be the one to tell me that I couldn't save something I had loved ever since I'd seen that one specimen that had been grown in the generation tanks.

He cared—and I loved him for it.

He was also wrong.

"They don't belong here, Willow."

I thought about the list of Myths I had seen. I thought about how, in the simulations, there was Balance where a unicorn lived. I smiled sadly. "Yes, they do. This is where they came from, Stev. This is their home."

His eyes widened. He stared at me as if he'd never seen me before. Then he looked at the screen and frowned. "Why did they put your genetic material into two different honeycomb chambers?"

"They didn't. Those are Britt's unicorns."

He seemed to have trouble breathing for a minute. "Blessed All," he whispered.

I waited.

He took a deep breath. Blew it out. "I'd better get down to the tanks and do this myself. You stay here and send me the cell numbers. That way I won't have to go through any of the tech consoles where this might get traced."

When he reached the door, he paused and looked back at me. "Zashi was right. It will take a bit of time to get used to working with you."

Chapter 14

Since they were the only ones available at the time, Stev used the two generation tanks that were working at half capacity. He set them at full growth acceleration so that they would be available again as fast as possible.

When a fully operational tank became available, he insisted on placing some of my unicorns in it.

I couldn't argue with him. The speed at which the cells were changing from green to pink to red to black was terrifying.

The techs weren't interested in what he was doing. They were scrambling to take care of what they could for the Restorer teams, and were happy that he was willing to do his own work.

Whenever he could, he jumped in and filled another generation tank before the techs could put other material into it. As soon as a tank finished the growth process, I issued the command code to send the unicorns down to the island.

I don't think either of us really slept for days.

Finally, the moment came when Stev placed the last surviving material into the generation tanks.

A couple of days after that, we sent the last of the unicorns down to the island.

The day after that, an angry group of Scholars and Instructors showed up at the auxiliary room door.

Chapter 15

Thanie was wracked with guilt and kept apologizing in between bouts of tears.

We'd warned her, again and again. But a couple of verbal jabs from Dermi and Fallah were all it had taken for her to lash out and tell them about the special project.

Of course, Dermi and Fallah immediately went to the Head Instructor and told *him* everything—including the fact that there were bumbler bees on the island. Which is what brought in the Scholars.

Stev and I were still groggy from lack of sleep. We were just sitting at our consoles, drinking tea and trying to wake up enough to function, when Whit and Thanie were herded into the room, followed by the primary Scholars and the Head Instructor. Behind *them* came Britt and Zashi.

Stev jumped to his feet. A younger person was supposed to rise whenever a Scholar or Instructor came into the room.

I remained seated. I sipped my tea and stared them down.

That made them furious. And, for some reason, nervous.

Accusations filled the room. I had deceived my Instructor by falsifying the information when I made the request for the special project. A *student* would never have been given a restoration project the size of the island. I had deceived the tank techs into believing I was a qualified Restorer and entitled to the special considerations I was given. I had *lied* to them in order to remove unsuitable genetic material.

During this harangue, Britt watched me.

I just sat there, drinking my tea.

When the yelling finally wound down, the Head Instructor said, "Well? What do you have to say to us?"

"Nothing," I replied calmly. "I have nothing to say to you. I do not answer to you."

"Oh?" said the Head Scholar. "If not to us, then who *do* you answer to?"

"The Blessed All."

They stared at me. Britt pressed a hand over her mouth.

I smiled at her. "I have something to show you."

I keyed in the coordinates and requested a planet-side picture.

A meadow, on the edge of a woodland. Butterflies flitted by. Birds flew from tree to tree. A bumbler went from one flower to another, doing its duty.

A minute passed. Two minutes.

Then, from among the trees came a white unicorn mare. Beside her were two fillies. One of the fillies had a beard under her chin.

Tears filled Britt's eyes. Then she started to laugh—a joyous, heart-deep laugh. "I knew you were the one. I knew."

"You took a risk," I said. "You could have gotten more of them out in time. We saved what we could."

Britt smiled at me. Zashi's eyes began to twinkle.

Somewhere—perhaps on the part of the student island that *hadn't* been designated for the students—there were more of Britt's unicorns. If I had failed this last test, there might not have been enough of them to survive. Britt had been willing to take that risk . . . because she needed the certainty of this last test.

"Willow is my successor," Britt said. She walked out of the room.

Zashi winked at me, smiled at Stev, and followed her.

The Scholars and the Head Instructor turned pale. Without another word, they left, taking Whit and Thanie with them.

It had come to me last night, just before I fell asleep for a few hours. All the other Restorers were referred to as *a* Restorer. Britt was referred to as *the* Restorer. She answered to no one but the Blessed All—because Britt was always in Balance.

And because Britt would not do just what was correct, she would do what was right.

Chapter 16

Tomorrow we are going to attempt to land our ship on the planet's surface.

The engineers have reluctantly admitted that it's *possible,* but they aren't sure we can do it. But if we *don't* try it, we won't survive another month out in space. If we succeed, we'll gain a few more years to continue our work before the ship dies completely.

The Scholars, of course, argued against it.

It was Britt who decided.

I've wondered if her decision would have been different if I hadn't saved the unicorns. If, without someone to take her place as *the* Restorer, she would have let her own people die rather than risk the world that is still slowly being restored to Balance.

I think I know the answer. That is why I will never ask her.

We have lived in a world made of metal, wandering the galaxy and restoring worlds to Balance because we have to make Atonement for something we had done long ago.

Now we have a chance to feel the earth beneath our feet, to feel the wind on our skin, to smell the wildflowers, to press our hands against the bark of a tree. We have a chance to live as one strand in the web. And we can never afford to forget that we *are* only one strand.

I don't think my people will ever again have the knowledge or the skill to go into space. This world is all we will have. If we fail it, we will be among the species that are listed as extinct.

Tomorrow we will land on the planet.

Britt was right.

This world *is* our true Atonement.

About The Author

Anne Bishop is the *New York Times* bestselling author of fifteen novels, including *Bridge of Dreams* and the award-winning Black Jewels Trilogy. She recently completed *Written in Red*, the first book in a new urban fantasy series. When she's not writing, Anne enjoys gardening, reading, and music. You can visit her at www.annebishop.com or keep up with news about her books at the official Facebook fan page, www.facebook.com/DarkRealms.

Stranded

Anthony Francis

Dedication

To Yseult, the First Centaur, who made all of this possible.

Author's Note

Almost a decade ago, I was working on a space opera starring a genetically engineered centauress from a supercivilization with all the toys. Wondering what her grandchildren would be like, I sketched a young centauress crossing a field of wheat towards impossible mountains, then drew her brother, a pudgier centaur with a straw hat reading a map of the universe … and carrying a staff that could take him anywhere.

Almost a decade later, my editor Debra asked me for a science fiction story about young adults finding their way. I gave that young girl her brother's staff and her grandmother's morals, imagined what would happen if she met a bunch of refugee children who were every bit as good as her in their hearts but who didn't quite have it all together, and made them all collide on that field of wheat before those impossible mountains. The result is "Stranded."

—*Dr. Anthony G. Francis, Jr.*

Stranded

Sirius flinched as sizzling grey bullets tumbled around him in zero-gee. The grey dented veligen pellets rattled through the cramped innards of *Independence's* life support plant, stinging his nose with the scent of bitter almonds. His hands strained at the yellow-striped master fuse. The girls shouted. They fired their guns again. More bullets twanged around him, ricocheting off the ancient, battered equipment, striking closer with every shot—but Sirius just gripped the hot, humming tube harder, braced both booted feet, and pulled.

Andromeda and Artemyst screamed for him to stop. Dijo, the engineer, screamed for their shooting to stop. Even the air screamed—out a bullet hole in a vacuum duct near his feet. But with every second, *Independence* shot a half million clicks farther into the deep, flying away from the Beacon that was their only hope of survival, so Sirius didn't stop: he just screamed too, pulling with both hands, shoving with both feet, jerking at the master fuse—until it popped out and he shot free into zero-gee, slamming into the hatch and bursting it open.

Sirius flew out of the life support service chamber into *Independence's* cavernous cargo hold. His head clanged off a handrail, knocking him into a dizzy spin in midair. He smacked into the tumbling brassfiber grille of the hatch he'd knocked free, halving his spin—and leaving him right in the crosshairs of Dijo, Artemyst and Andromeda, all clipped to orange handrails far out of his reach. All had their guns on him, red laser sights on, green safety lights off.

The girls of the ship called themselves "skybirds": most were budding teenagers now, bodies grown slender and toned in zero-gee, poured into soft pressure suits that came to their necks, patterned with shimmering scales and glittering feathers and rich animal prints.

Sirius tried to track them, but as he tumbled, the girls somersaulted around him, moving from anchor to anchor with deadly grace, keeping him off balance mentally as well as physically. It didn't matter—in the Engine Module, the skybirds had all the arms and the armor.

And they were proud to show it. They'd augmented their softsuits with scraps of ballistic weave printed like leathers and whipstitched with hullfiber, and decked out their communication cowls with feathers like tribal headdresses. The skybirds were savage, independent—free.

All very fetching, but the girls and their animal suits did nothing for Sirius, and that made him worse in their eyes than the "hullrats," the boys that Andromeda had exiled to the Command Module when she'd taken over the Engine Module—and with it, the ship.

Because if you weren't a skybird, and if you weren't a hullrat, you were a—

"Halfway Boy!" Andromeda cried, as the ship's lighting flickered and the whine of the air cycler slowly spun down. Her eyes were as wild as the spray of incongruous feathers sticking out of her snakeskin-patterned communications cowl. "What have you done?"

"Saved all our lives," Sirius said, still dizzy, still spinning. "You can thank me later."

"That's the master fuse for the lifeplant," Dijo said, staring at the yellow and black tube in Sirius's hands. Her eyes went wide, the patterned lenses that protected them from radiation making her look crazed. She dove inside the life support plant, cursing. "Oh, God damn it—"

"I told you, hullrats in the Engine Module cause nothing but trouble," Artemyst growled, squaring her shoulders and adjusting the sights on her gun. The veligen whined as its gyros compensated for movement, helping her keep dead aim on him. "Can I just kill him?"

There was a deadly pause. Sirius swallowed, squinting as red laser light sparkled off his forehead, but he was afraid to raise his hand. Not that she needed the gun to be a danger: Sirius could fight, but Artemyst had ten kilos on him and a mean streak. Then Andromeda spoke.

"And what then, Artemyst?" Andromeda said quietly. "Toss his body out the airlock? We can't afford the waste, and the boys have the recycler in the Command Module. Are you going to take the detail of chopping up his body and feeding it through the cycler in the shuttle?"

Sirius's eyes bugged, but Artemyst was equally appalled. Sort of.

"God, no," she said. "I'd make one of the fledglings do it—"

"Oh, shut it, Artemyst," Andromeda said. She kept her gun trained on Sirius, her voice rang out—but did it crack, just a little bit? "We can't cycle Sirius. He's our best pilot—"

"Carina can pilot," Artemyst said. "And we can throw *him* to the hullrats—"

"No. You know we can't do that. It was hard enough to get Leonid to take Toren, even with him getting as big as a bear," Andromeda said. "You have to think things through—like Sirius usually does. So, benefit of the doubt: why did you pull the fuse, Halfway Boy?"

"You know why. I told you," Sirius said, risking a dirty look at Andromeda despite her gun. God, why was everyone so stupid? Andromeda had been the one that split the girls from the boys, so she didn't even have the excuse of being a breeder! "The gliderdrive is about to fail—"

"Don't tell me my job," Andromeda said, glaring back at him. "Of course the gliderdrive is about to fail. *Independence* is seven hundred and fifty years old. Everything is falling apart! Why did you think deliberately taking out our life support would help?"

Dijo pulled out of the life support plant, tools rattling on her belt, feathered cowl in disarray. "The cycler is shutting down," she said, as breakers began tripping, one by one. "It'll need a full overhaul—and we're going to need oxygen. We need to dock. Anywhere. *Now.*"

Andromeda's eyes widened, and Sirius smirked.

"Now do you see why?" he said. "I told you, every second we flew further into the deep we flew closer to death, but you didn't believe me. I told you, we had to dock, to make repairs, but you didn't listen. So I made the point a little more clear—"

"Dammit!" Andromeda snarled.

"I know how hard this is," Sirius said.

"No, you don't," Andromeda said, face twisting up in unexpected rage.

"Yes, I do," Sirius said. "I was a kid on a five-person flyer, remember? It's been hard for all humans since the Dresanians kicked us off the Earth, and worse for *Independence*, with the adults gone, running from the next attack. But sooner or later, we have to stop and rest—"

"That's not it," Andromeda said. "Our reserves are more depleted than you know. I'm not sure we'd even make it back to the Beacon without supplementary life support—and the boys have what's left of the oxygen farm. That means . . . I'm going to have to talk to Leonid."

Sirius swallowed. The ex-captain she'd deposed. And her ex-boyfriend.

"Well," Dijo said, nervously looking back and forth between them. It was hard to read her expression beneath the smooth porcelain gloss of her engineer's facepaint, but Sirius guessed she saw that this had to be resolved, now. "If you don't want to . . . I could contact him."

Andromeda glared at her, then at Sirius.

Her hand tensed on her veligen; Sirius closed his eyes. Then she spoke.

"Contact the Command Module, Dijo. Tell Leonid . . . I agree to his demands."

Sirius squirmed, half from the narrow line of the zip tie cutting into his wrists and half from the unexpected weight of the cargo bay deck pressing into his rear. He'd expected to get a hero's welcome when the boys retook the ship—not a black eye while being taken prisoner.

In the zero-gee of the Engine Module, the girls had grown slender, and chose totems of flying birds and lithe snakes. But the Command Module spun to make gravity for the oxygen farm—and exiled to it, the boys had grown muscular—and for their totems, chose predators.

Where the girls had patchworks of prints, the boys had armor like leopards and tigers. Where the girls were acrobats, the boys were weightlifters. Biggest of all of them was Sirius's fellow Halfway Boy, the boy Andromeda had exiled when he hit his growth spurt—Toren.

Toren had become a bear of a man, with arms as thick as Sirius's thigh and a neck as wide as a support beam. His armor matched his image, a grizzly totem down to patchwork fur and a comm helm adorned with bear eyes, ears and teeth—over a human face as hard as flint.

Sirius had reached to hug Toren when he stormed through the airlock, but Toren had just punched him in the face. Now Sirius sat with the girls in the cargo bay, all huddled in a half-grav of rotation—with their hands bound behind them and armed boys ringed all around.

Leonid had set the ship to spinning in more ways than one. He hadn't just taken over from Andromeda: he'd disarmed the girls and bound them, then friction-coupled the Modules, setting the whole ship turning, making the girls groan in gravity they hadn't felt in years.

Then he set Toren to hunting down the stragglers.

"That's the last of them," Toren said, shoving Artemyst through the ring of boy guards. Her hands were bound behind her with a black zip tie, and when she tripped, she fell heavily onto Andromeda and Sirius. "Thought she could elude us by hiding in the sensor pod."

"Should have known not to use a tunnel to hide from a hullrat," Artemyst smirked.

Toren raised his hand to strike her, but Leonid clucked.

"Toren," he said curtly. "Thank you, but that's enough."

Sirius couldn't believe what had happened to Tori, the little Halfway Boy Sirius had befriended, then trained to defend himself against the other boys like Leonid. Tori had been his best friend—practically his boyfriend—but now acted like he never knew him.

Now Toren stood beside Leonid, his former persecutor. The blond boy with the lion's helm who had tormented the two of them when he'd ruled the ship was now back in charge—and Toren backed him up, folding his arms and glowering like a dark enforcer while Leonid spoke.

The world truly was upside down.

"Artemyst, you stupid girl," Leonid said, handsome as ever, frost-blue eyes gleaming beneath the lion's teeth of his helm. He didn't fold his arms like Toren: he simply spoke with authority. "We won't tolerate any more sieges, whether one of you or all together—"

"And just what," Andromeda said, "do you plan to do with all of us girls?"

Leonid glared. "Lock you all in cabins, individually. The boys will double bunk if that's what it takes," he said. A murmur began with the boys. They clearly didn't like it. But Leonid shouted them down. "Enough! We almost got killed by these irresponsible girls. So we do it."

Sirius's heart lifted when Leonid said irresponsible—maybe he got it. Maybe he saw how close the ship was to disaster; maybe he'd do something before the gliderdrive shut down and they were literally dead in space. Then Andromeda spoke, and Leonid proved Sirius wrong.

"You have us," Andromeda said with a smirk, "but how will you run the Engines?"

"Now that we have the Helm again, we don't need you right away," Leonid said, jutting his chin out at her, less like a lion than a defiant little boy. "When we do, we'll let you mutineers out, one at a time—but three to one. Two boy guards, one boy worker the girl will instruct—"

Now the girls were murmuring, and it was Andromeda who raised her voice.

"None of the girls," Andromeda said, voice quavering, "will tell you anything—"

"Enough!" Leonid shouted, firing his gun, and in the ricochets everyone went quiet. "*None* of the girls will touch *any* machine in the Engine Module *ever again*. No more than one girl is allowed in the Engine Module at one time, hands tied, instructing us. That's it."

"No!" Andromeda said, voice anguished, eyes wide. Sirius knew she'd made the Engines her life after she and Leonid had split—and that Leonid had to know that banishing her from the Engine Module would just kill her. "You . . . you can't mean that—"

"We still won't," Artemyst said defiantly, struggling to her feet. "We'll—"

Toren slapped her, and she went down again. "Enough," he repeated, and that casual slap quieted the room far faster than Leonid's gun. "You'll help us, or starve in your cells. You will instruct us. And when the boys know the machines—they'll have other uses for the girls."

The girls recoiled. Even the boys looked uncomfortable. Sirius scowled. This had been coming since the last adult of *Independence* died. Sooner or later, they'd all hit puberty. Sooner or later, they'd all be adults. And sooner or later . . . a new generation had to begin.

"You started this war of the sexes," Leonid said. "You had to know we'd win it."

Sirius eventually gave up hoping someone would show some sense and, as he always had to, took saving them upon himself. "Great plan—if you happen to be a boy, Captain," he said. "There's just one problem—it won't work. You don't have time for the girls to teach you."

"Shut up, Halfway Boy," Toren growled, and Sirius raised an eyebrow.

"Quiet, Toren," Leonid said. He smirked at Sirius, shaking his head—perhaps at the ridiculousness of Toren now pretending he'd never been a Halfway Boy himself. "Sirius, don't get ahead of yourself. Toren is right. Technically, you never finished your orientation—"

"Ha," Sirius laughed. "I flew years before you ever served a shift—"

"Not on this ship, on my ship," Leonid said—but before Sirius could object, he raised his hand, the smirk softening into a wry smile. "On a five-person flyer, not an NCE-class starship. You're a great pilot, but do you really think you've learned everything you need to know?"

Sirius glared, and Leonid just cocked his head, smiling at him. Weird.

"You're missing the point, pretty boy," Sirius said.

"No, you are, Halfway Boy," Leonid said, friendly smile fading into angry, defensive impatience. "You've not been initiated. Till then, you're not full crew, much less a full boy. You picked the right side, but you've got a long way to go to prove your loyalty—"

"I didn't do what I did for the boys, or to join them, or to prove my loyalty—though I did prove a point," Sirius said. "I did what I did for all of us on *Independence*."

"Do?" Toren said, and Sirius glared at his clearly former friend. "What did you do?"

"Did you really think Andromeda folded because Leonid withheld a few extra rations?" Sirius said. He smirked. "Do you think the girls gave up the Engine Module because they were scared of you, Tori? No. I did that. I made the girls fold. Me—"

Toren seized him by his softsuit and lifted him clear off the deck. "What did you do?"

"He . . . pulled the master fuse on the life support plant," Andromeda said.

"Oh, spraying sewage," Leonid said.

"We had to shut it down," Dijo said, flinching as Toren turned on her. Sirius stayed limp, dangling from Toren's fist: he'd seen the start of Toren's growth spurt but had no idea how strong little Tori would become. "It will take weeks to bring it back online—"

"God," Leonid said. "We'll run out of oxygen in days."

"Carbon dioxide could kill us in hours," Dijo said

"And you mention this now?" Toren said, and she again flinched back from him.

"This is what we tried to tell you when we surrendered," she said, not meeting his glare. "Even if the oxygen farm was up to the load, it just can't scrub the air fast enough. Most of us are going to have to suit up or retreat to shelters just to survive the day—"

"So you don't have time for the girls to teach you," Sirius said, not flinching at all as Toren lifted him off the deck again. Now both Andromeda and Leonid were looking at him. "You have to make port, now—and you're going to have to work together."

"Why, why did you do that?" Leonid said.

"The gliderdrive is about to fail," Sirius said firmly. "It was worse off than life support. And with the nearest habitable world light years off, failure of the glider means certain death. We were passing an interstellar Beacon. So I pulled the fuse. Now we have to make port."

"Not at that Beacon!" Leonid said. "It belongs to the Dresanians!"

"I don't care," said Sirius. "It's a registered Beacon tagged with a landing cradle—"

"Owned by the aliens," Leonid said, "who chased us off the Earth!"

"I. Don't. Care," Sirius repeated. "It's a dock and air and life—"

Leonid snarled, angular features mirroring his helm. "You son of a—"

"Like I told Andromeda," Sirius said, "you can thank me later."

Sirius smiled as Toren frog-marched Andromeda back into the long, narrow cargo control chamber. Not because Toren was strong-arming her—but because both of them glanced at Sirius, then looked away, embarrassed. So, even before Toren spoke, Sirius knew he'd been right.

"The gliderdrive *is* a day from cascading failure," Toren confirmed, giving Andromeda a halfhearted shove against an instrument panel. "We went over it together, end to end. The drive's totally overloaded. The next element that burns out starts a cascade, thanks to this witch—"

And he slapped her, knocking her headdress askew. Leonid's nostrils flared, but he kept staring into the flickering viewtank with Dijo and Sirius. "So, let's repair it," he said, moving the viewport. "What about that nearby station? Lore marks it inhabited, with a port—"

"That only looks close," Sirius said. He tapped the display; Andromeda had steered them deep into the Plume, a mammoth column of gas and stars that actually dented hyperspace. "We're way down the gravity well. We try to climb that gradient, the gliderdrive will fry."

Independence normally stuck to the edge of intergalactic space, where stars were scarce but their gliderdrive could live up to its name, sliding effortlessly over hyperspace as smooth as glass. But this deep in the stellar nursery that was the Plume, they had to maneuver carefully, charting a course gentle enough to not blow out their ancient, overworked hyperdrive.

"I can't believe you ran the glider this long without servicing it," Leonid said.

"After that last pirate scare," Andromeda said, "I hadn't found any place I felt safe."

"Fair enough," Leonid said. "Still, can't we shut the gliderdrive down, give it a rest?"

"Shutting the glider down won't help," Andromeda said, straightening. "Too many drive elements are burned out. All we'd be doing is sitting there, waiting to start it up again—and we'd risk a cascading failure from a cold start. We need to break her down, do a full refit."

"And you wanted to do that in the dead of space?" Toren growled, seizing her and lifting her off the deck. Seeing Toren do that to someone else drove home how big he was: had to be pushing two meters ten. "Also risking failure from a cold start, leaving us dead in space?"

"We . . . we had hoped to put in at drydock," Andromeda said, licking her lips, letting herself hang limply in his grip. Her blue facepaint and black eyeliner were smeared, and Sirius wondered if Toren had hit her in private. "At . . . at the Matriworld, if we could find it—"

"So you nearly killed us all," Toren said, "chasing a myth."

"Which if you'd succeeded at," Leonid said, "would have put all the boys in chains."

"You deserved it," Andromeda began—then squealed and flinched as Toren shook her.

"It doesn't matter," Sirius said. "We've got to completely rebuild the gliderdrive—"

"We can't do that. We'd have to take the whole Engine Module apart—and break containment in the cargo hold!" Toren said, releasing Andromeda and turning on Sirius. "For which we need the air cycler you denied us, Halfway Boy—"

"Halfway Boy?" Sirius said. "You're one to talk."

Toren clenched his fist, and the other boys murmured. "Those days are behind me."

"Sure they are," Sirius said. "But it doesn't matter. Outside the hull is dead space. Light years of it. Trillions of kilometers. Without the glider, on our best day, *Independence's* delta vee is a thousand kilometers a second. Even if we made straight for the Beacon—"

"It could take us centuries to get there—which means we've got to dock or land as soon as possible, before the gliderdrive fails completely," Leonid said. He scowled, then straightened. "Which means we make for the closest Beacon . . . which you found. Thank you again, Sirius."

"Thank you for listening," Sirius said.

"Don't thank me yet. The Beacon is in Dresanian territory—and the Dresanians are the ones who chased humanity off the Earth." Leonid turned to the others. "Andromeda, make sure our shields are at full strength. Toren, make sure all the boys are armed."

"That won't be enough," Toren said. "They're Dresanians—where are you going?"

"To the armory. These peashooters won't do us any good," Leonid said, tapping the veligen on his hip. "We've only got one working blaster left, but I'm going to break it out anyway. Though I doubt even it would do any good against a Dresanian force field—"

"Leonid!" Sirius said. "Do you think it's a good idea to go in packing?"

"You don't know what the Dresanians are like!" Leonid said. "They're tough as nails, practically immortal and they have all the toys! Even their philosophers are warriors, and their warriors are also philosophers! You have no idea what you've forced us into—"

"Given how ragged Andromeda ran us," Sirius said, "it's not like I had another choice."

Leonid grimaced, while Andromeda sagged like Sirius had punched her in the gut.

"Fair enough. None of us do," Leonid said grimly, turning to go. "Set course for the Beacon at Halfway Point, Sirius. As for you, Andromeda . . . just keep the glider running. Toren, keep it together until I get back. You'll all see what Dresanians are like soon enough."

Nine thousand light years away, wildsilk sheets slipped lazily around Serendipity's hooves as she stirred on her elegant burgundy-cushioned divan. Golden light poured between tasseled violet curtains she'd drawn back to wake her at dawn. The young centauress blinked, yawned—then smelled caffé and satsumas, and rolled until all four hooves hit the floor.

Serendipity Keltanya Kirkpatrick Saint George stared in mock horror at the breakfast tray on her desk. A handwritten note revealed her grandmother had once again beaten her—up before dawn, with time to make breakfast for Serendipity, before going on her own morning run.

"*Na'hai-ee*, Serendipity," said Tianyu, her minifox. The little robot had been curled up on the mahogany arm of the divan, watching her sleep as always, but now he stretched and fluffed his magnificent red and white tail. "Looks like your grandmother made you breakfast."

"*Dashpat*," Serendipity said, rubbing her forehead. "Oh—and *na'hai-ee*, Tianyu."

"Uh-oh. What's wrong?" Tianyu asked, jumping down. "You love breakfast."

"I do. But I drew the curtains to wake before her," Serendipity said, spreading her horsey legs, stretching her arms back over her horse barrel, left, then right, working out the kink she got at the join of her backs when she slept. "Hold a moment. I sleep locked. How did she get in?"

"Definitely is curious," Tianyu said, hopping up on the floating table and slinking past the hovering ball of caffé in its spiral holder. He sniffed the steaming eggs, the bowl of fruit, the triangles of toastwheat and glowcheese. "But she definitively laid out a spread."

Serendipity snorted. Of course. *She* was trying to keep Serendipity in shape for her stupid tournament. But she hadn't just saddled her with everything a young centauress athlete needed: she'd topped it off with bananaberry parfait with algurt and granula, Serendipity's favorite.

Serendipity sighed and stretched forth her hand. Her golden bracelet glittered, a satsuma levitated into her hand, and she began peeling it. One couldn't *be* a Saint George without learning to live in the shade of all those . . . those *impossibly* accomplished relatives.

Forget her father's side. Her mother? Renowned artist. Her uncle? Renowned reporter. Grandfather Kirkpatrick? Starship engineer. Great-grandmother? Intergalactic financier. At the trunk of the tree, her great-to-the-nth grandmother: the First Centaur, and genetic engineer.

All still alive, all still kicking, all still doing all those impossible things that made everyone want impossible things out of her. But the worst of all was her grandmother. Warrior. Author. Three-time winner of the Sagan Award for her work as a First Contact Engineer.

It would be hard for her grandmother to be more eminent: First Contact Engineering was difficult and dangerous work that had ultimately killed her. Now, back in a brand-new body, on well-deserved (and mandated) leave, she'd convinced herself she was Serendipity's best friend.

Serendipity nibbled a satsuma wedge, staring at a wood-framed holograph on her desk. Taken by Sistine, her mother, it looked like two young centauresses playing in Dover Woods: one a fiery redhead with quills and freckles—Serendipity—supporting, half atop her, a younger girl with metallic purple hair. But the "younger" girl was really her grandmother, and it was *her* leaning into the frame, almost pushing Serendipity out of it, that made the picture just perfect.

"Oh dear. I know that look," Tianyu said. He jumped as a dark shape passed the window. Moments later it dissolved into a moire of rainbow light and a delayed bass chiming—most likely, a bladeship popping into hyperspace. "Don't tell me you're still thinking of leaving."

"Not thinking," Serendipity said, stepping to the window, watching the sun glinting off starships swarming the skies of her homeworld, T'syar'lyeh. Every person on every one of those ships was going somewhere—except her. "I've set my mind to it. I have to get out of here."

"But T'syar'lyeh is our home," Tianyu said, curling up on the desk. "I like it here."

"I don't need to be coddled until I'm curdled," Serendipity said. "I need someplace exciting, where there's still room to do something new." She picked up her farstaff and twirled it, pointing it up through the roof at the invisible stars. "Someplace exotic: a far port, a distant colony, a long-haul spacecraft crewed by dashing space pirates. Anywhere—"

"Far from your grandmother?" Tianyu said.

"Anywhere," Serendipity said, lowering the staff, "out of the shade of the gods."

"You don't need to run away," Tianyu said, prowling back and forth on Serendipity's floating desk while she curled through a challenging tai chi routine her metaconscience thought she could finish before her grandmother got back. "Your grandmother loves you, you know."

"What are you, my metaconscience?" Serendipity said, hand arcing up. Then that same advisor program gave her a little poke, and she glanced over to see her minifox's ears drooping. "Sorry, Tianyu. It's just . . . since she got that new body, she's done nothing but hover."

Tianyu gave a little sniff. "Do you blame her? She just came back from the dead."

"I . . . no, I don't," Serendipity said. Then she sighed, finished, and straightened. She ruffled Tianyu's neck in apology. "I'm sorry, Tianyu. I do get an earful from my metaconscience program about it. I know it's been hard on her; it's just . . . I'm in need of a little space."

"I think you're being ridiculous," Tianyu said. "She'd be happy to help you—"

"Her 'helping' is half the problem," Serendipity said. "I've got to find my own way."

Serendipity wasn't sure when it had turned into a competition, but a competition it was. Anything she could do, her grandmother could do better. Serendipity loved to read; her grandmother was a writer. Serendipity was a foodie; her grandmother was a chef.

Science? *She* had a stack of degrees a mile high. Karate? *She* won her first tournament at the age Serendipity had started practicing. History? When Serendipity had started studying ancient Greek sculpture, *she* had traveled back in time to bring her a carving from Pompeii.

Even after Serendipity fell in love with travel, her grandmother still outclassed her. Serendipity had visited twenty-four worlds; her grandmother, thousands. For one brief moment, Serendipity had dreamed of becoming a professional traveler, at besting *her* at that one thing.

Then she found her grandmother had visited Andromeda before Serendipity was even born . . . and had sent digital copies of herself to two million worlds, using force-projectors attached to autonomous vehicles to collect data for her PhD thesis.

This was ridiculous. Serendipity had to find something to do that her grandmother hadn't done. And she couldn't do that on T'syar'lyeh: no matter what Serendipity chose, it was only a matter of time before her grandmother found out, decided to "help," and effortlessly outclassed her. Serendipity had to find a place that was her own, where she could make her own mark.

Even if it meant traveling halfway across the galaxy.

"Right enough," Tianyu said, curling up on the mahogany of her desk. "Show me."

Serendipity tossed the last of the satsuma peels into the mulchmoss of her brainsai and flicked her hand over the little tree to bring it to life. While tiny green teeth chewed up the peel, the branches of the tree glowed to life, projecting a map of the intergalactic Alliance.

"And here I thought all that time you spent researching colonies for your senior thesis was just an elaborate excuse for planning a vacation," Tianyu said, puffing a breath of air that ruffled the leaves of the brainsai and made the velvet expanse in the air shimmer.

"This whole summer was a vacation," Serendipity said. "Now it's time to go to work."

"You, thinking of work?" Tianyu said. Then he glanced at her and sat up. "Seriously, Serendipity? Your metaconscience must be broken. You shouldn't be thinking of work with only a primary degree. You've a scholarship waiting for you at the University of Geneva—"

"Go to U of G? Just like grandmother? Definitely not." Serendipity let out a snort. "And spend forever in school just for the privilege of following in *her* footsteps? Definitively not. I've no plans to spend my life retelling lives lived by others."

"Why specialize in history then?" Tianyu said. "The family tradition of masochism?"

"What? No! I wanted perspective," Serendipity said, peering into the starry map. The Dresan-Murran Alliance stretched ten million light years in every direction; how could anyone hope to make their mark in that? "I wanted to be able to see things others don't."

"There are cheaper ways to induce hallucinations," Tianyu sniffed. "What did you find?"

"The Alliance doesn't cover all the space it claims. It's just a collection of colonization bubbles around its homeworlds, like the one expanding from Dresan that had claimed Earth seven centuries ago, and like that new bubble, the Qorin bubble, just outside the galaxy."

Serendipity poked the map, and a star lit up brightly.

"And that knowledge helped me find," she said, "a waypoint smack-dab between them."

"Looks dreadful," Tianyu said, staring at the blinking star at the tip of a giant plume of gas six thousand light years long. He batted at it, zooming in so the edges of the colonization bubbles were barely visible. "Why did you pick that? It's past even the Frontier!"

"Halfway Point is a simply brilliant world," Serendipity said defensively. "An Earthlike moon around a gas giant with a yellow star? It has it all: living space, plenty of hydrogen fuel and a great big lump of mass that makes a perfect jumping-off point for a hyperdrive."

She flicked her hand at the display, making the world itself loom close. "There aren't ten thousand planets like it in the galaxy, and they always end up just spectacular. Dakaimetan, the capital of the sector; Pinyetaum, capital of culture; Murrarrenar, major trading point—"

"And yet no one has been to Halfway Point in ten thousand years," Tianyu said. He swiped at the star, making dataflakes puff out around it in a mind map like a textual snowflake. "According to this, they even tried to set up a port and failed. What does that tell you?"

"That war screws everything up," Serendipity said, flicking her hand to roll time back. The colonization bubbles shrank—then were split by an angry red neutral zone. "There, right after Halfway Point was colonized. That blockade lasted millennia. That killed it."

"So what makes you think you can bring it back from the dead?" Tianyu asked.

"Halfway Point went fallow because the war cut off this trade route, but it stayed fallow only because this region of space has been contested ever since the war," Serendipity said. "The rights only cleared up a few years ago, after, well . . ."

"Oh, don't leave me hanging. Wait—let me guess, if you've shut up then *she's* involved," Tianyu said. "So the rights cleared up . . . after your grandmother helped Earth join the Alliance, or after she negotiated that détente between the Alliance and the Frontier?"

Serendipity snorted. "It's called Halfway Point because they wanted to do what I want to do: set up a port between those two bubbles, which have grown so they almost touch. Shipping routes are still rerouted, but they won't stay that way. Halfway Point's even got a black hole—"

"Oh, wonderful," Tianyu said. "Sounds like a big KEEP OFF sign to me."

"Hush, love," Serendipity said. "The orbit's far enough that the inner planets are stable, but close enough to power heavy industry someday. In all the galaxy, Halfway Point is unique. I have no idea why it was overlooked, but I'm not about to let someone else step up and claim it."

They stared at the little blue-green moon, that forgotten jewel, curling around the rainbow pastels of its mammoth mother planet.

"I looked up *headstrong* in the dictionary," Tianyu said at last, curling up in a huff. "Your name was all over it: synonym, hyponym, see also, properly capitalized and everything."

"Be a good sport," Serendipity said, ruffling behind his ears. She cleared the breakfast tray, pulled out the satchels and saddlebags she'd packed last night, and laid them out on the desk so she could verify she had everything she needed. "Double-check my kit, would you?"

She was packing light: two boleros, four blouses, six tapestries of the style she loved to drape her horse barrel with—in combination, forty-eight outfits, not counting her overcloak, her spare slogs or accessories like her roseflower. She twirled the little computer in her hands, then decided to put it in her hair in place of the flutterby she wore now.

As the roseflower's filaments slid behind her horsey ear toward the port at the nape of her neck, Serendipity smiled: her hair had come in red today, nicely augmenting her freckles and flower. She always felt most like herself in red and freckles, and she winked and smiled.

"All very proper Simpson's Guide. Looks good to me," Tianyu said, patting the rainbow flutterby working its wings on her desk. He gently nosed it, pushing the smaller robot toward her satchel. "Your turn at the checklist. Unless you want to throw in another outfit."

Serendipity stuck out her tongue, then rummaged her bags, running her metaconscience's checklist, making sure she had two ways to do everything. Maybe this felt like a fun vacation, but it was still space travel, not a day trip to the islands, and she had to be properly prepared. She was a proper Dresanian, after all, never going into space without everything at least once redundant, yet leaving nothing wasted.

Serendipity preferred redundancy in overlapping threes. An omniknife, fabribox and nanoseed were her tools; a medical blade, survival pak and civilian Aegis were her shields. And to document her trip she carried a handlecam, memory slate and brittanica.

The most important of all of it was the nanoseed, of course, so she slipped the glassy ampoule from round her neck and flicked it with her finger, watching glowing diagnostics shimmer across the liquid metal shivering within its diamandoid vial.

The nanoseed distilled thousands of engineer-years' of effort down to a few grams of silvery nanoplasm, machine-phase matter capable of assembling anything atom by atom. With enough raw material it could make almost anything—but most importantly, more of itself.

Satisfied, she slipped the glittering vial back round her neck and flipped open the coppery disc of her civilian Aegis, running its diagnostic. Force field, life support, thrusters, scanners all checked out: the Aegis was practically a spacecraft in a belt buckle, a design pioneered by her grandfather. It couldn't get her to the next star, but it could keep her alive in a crash.

Then she checked the charge on her force rod, good for repelling animals and ruffians. Her grandmother preferred full arms and armor, but between her force bracelet and force rod Serendipity felt well armed, and between her Aegis and shield brooch she felt well armored.

Besides, her grandmother had trained her. Under the armor was no slouch.

Finally, she slid out her medical blade and ran a checkup—on herself. The long, slender blade looked like a machete made from circuit boards, but the complex fields it emitted could perform delicate surgery and the handle could extrude anything from a bandage to a cast. Soon the blade gave her a clean bill of health—and passed its own diagnostic, so she stowed it and began buckling up her saddlebags and satchel.

None of her gear was too big to hold in one hand, except for her macdonald and survival pak, similar coppery cases counterweighting each saddlebag. Altogether the whole kit weighed less than twenty kilos, but it would keep her alive for months even on a world with no air.

If all that failed, even Serendipity would be triply redundant. Naturally she'd bring her familiar, Tianyu: the ruddy little robot continually downloaded her memories so Serendipity could be reconstituted if killed—a beastly practice, but it had served her grandmother well.

But she'd also bring the fruit of her tree. She took her farstaff from the umbrella rack and stepped up to her table. She dinged the tuning fork atop the two-meter ironwood staff, the rings around the fork began spinning to life, and she extended her hand toward her brainsai.

The little tree quivered. The air around her rustled as the farstaff drew power. A glowing ball of light appeared in the brainsai's branches, accumulating leaves and moss. Serendipity's hair lifted and tousled as the humming farstaff built up an air pocket around her.

"Serendipity," Tianyu said softly, staring out the window. "Are you sure about this?"

"No," Serendipity said, as the hum rose. She hadn't the heart to tell her grandmother she was going, but she didn't want to be followed, so she'd filed a quasi-private travel plan: once they left, they'd be on their own till the end of summer. "You're right. This . . . will be a big move."

Light shifted outside, perhaps the sails of an airship, and briefly Serendipity reconsidered. She did love T'syar'lyeh and all its mazelike stairways, filled with hundreds of human and alien variants bustling on the endless steps winding beneath its mammoth angled trees.

But it had become a lonely place. Her siblings had fled the nest. She'd always been the youngest of her cohort, so her school friends were scattered across the ten galaxies. All she had left on T'syar'lyeh was her karate club—and they all saw her as sensei's granddaughter.

The light shifted again, and she stiffened at the sound of hooves striking the path beneath her window. Her grandmother was almost home, her parents were always away—and as for her so-called friends, all she really had were a pair of professional companions purchased for her.

"Even a move this big," she said, "can't possibly be far enough away!"

Serendipity snapped her fingers. The map of the Alliance collapsed into the tiny glowing sphere, which leapt from the tree and flew into her hand. Tianyu scampered up onto her shoulder and rubbed her cheek, and Serendipity rubbed him back as the farstaff chimed.

"Let's go on an adventure," Serendipity said—and in a twinkle of light, they disappeared.

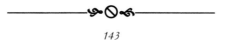

Serendipity skipped from world to world as if they were stepping-stones across a river, traveling the surface of the galaxy outward toward the six-thousand-light-year deep streamer of gas they called the Plume, at whose tip dangled the jewel that was Halfway Point.

Within an hour she'd traveled farther than she ever had in her life. Within the afternoon human space was far behind her. By evening, she was dining beneath mauve trees in a café by a glowing blue stream, talking via translation to creatures who'd never seen a human before.

Once they began climbing down the Plume, traveling became harder, worlds fewer. With a two-meter farstaff, she could travel at most seven millimeters of hyperspace—maybe a hundred light years each hop within the disc of the galaxy, but only forty when climbing out of it.

After three harrowing jumps, all airless, the last lacking even solid ground, Serendipity pulled out her mapping sphere. Hanging near a nub of a dry station, with five millimeters of air between her and space, she compared the map with the nebula towering before her.

Tianyu clambered up, rubbed her cheek. Serendipity rubbed back.

"It's not too late to turn around," Tianyu said, arching his furry eyebrows. The copper spine of a far trader slid by, seven kilometers of rarities from the Triangulum angling for its next jump. "We could hitch a lift, maybe for free if we trade the gravitics of our jump history."

"You're right. If we run home now, I've still time to train for the tournament."

She arched her eyebrows too; then he cracked up, and they both burst out laughing.

The gold disc of her Aegis glowed as Serendipity flitted to a trading pod where she bought an algasagna wrap, a tensor booster, and a small oxygen cylinder the alien trader called a "pony bottle," which made her suppress a smile and made Tianyu crack up.

Serendipity reserved twenty cubic meters a short distance from the pod. There, they had a little picnic in space, nibbling at the sandwich, hanging in space before the glowing lines of the map, planning their route with the galaxy sparkling beneath her black-booted hooves.

After they'd eaten their fill, Serendipity resealed the edible wrap around the grilled algae, tucked it into her satchel, and ran a thin life support line from her Aegis to the pony bottle. She grinned as cool oxygen began rippling around her, then, smile fading, clipped the tensor booster to her farstaff. The new route was better, five hops rather than twelve, but it needed not just the booster, but the bounce. She'd be traveling like a skipping stone.

"I'll stay in here, thanks," Tianyu said, hiding in her satchel.

"Right," Serendipity said. She took a deep breath of fresh air—and jumped.

Fifty-one light years. The stars flickered—jump. Sixty-five more light years. A stellar nursery sparkled below—jump. Fifty-seven more light years, the nebula loomed closer—jump! Thirty-five more light years, a new star shone bright—jump, another *seventy* light years—

And she was down on Halfway Point.

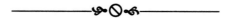

Explosions echoed through the whole Engine Module, staccato drumbeats as fuses blew in the gliderdrive. Sirius winced: he could barely think straight here, just beneath the drive, but since the girls had cut the trunk cables to the Command Module, the cargo control chamber was the only place with a functioning Helm—where he could directly fly the ship.

"Keep it running," he said, wrestling the twin grips of the glider's eighteen-axis steering bar. The computer was better than any human at flying in eleven-dimensional space—when it had a functional drive and a plotted course. Now, with the glider shorting out beneath them and space inexplicably torn up, it was taking all Sirius's experience and all the computer's finesse working together just keep the field alive. "Undervolt it if you have to!"

"The field will collapse," Andromeda said, whacking at a stuck breaker. "In minutes—"

"We only need one!" Sirius said, tapping a footpedal to zoom the holoprojection in close enough to show the approaching world. Space was somehow messed up here, but Sirius guessed they were still two hundred million kilometers out—far enough that they could still die before reaching port unless they were rescued. Sirius had no intention of dying just as they were within reach of safety. "One minute is the difference between a parking orbit and deep space—"

The gliderdrive groaned. Sirius shuddered. It felt like he was being twisted inside out. Sirius knew that feeling from a thousand jumps with his parents: this was the transition from dual to real coordinates. The gliderfield was collapsing.

"We're losing it," Andromeda said, throwing booster switches. "We're losing it!"

"Why are we losing the gliderfield?" Dijo said, the feathers on her helmet snapping back and forth as she glanced between a holographic projection of the space they were flying into and a flat monitor that showed the glider's vitals. The normally smooth, sloped waves of an approaching solar system were churned up into something Dijo called Christoffel surf. Flying into that mess, the glider was having so much trouble the row of sparklines on the monitor made it look like an old man going into cardiac arrest. "What's wrong with space here?"

"I'm not reading anything other than the Beacon!" Leonid yelled from the nav table.

"Screw it," Sirius said, kicking another footpedal to trigger an emergency launch into hyperspace. Capacitors discharged, the lights flickered, and fresh energy poured into the glider. They were already in hyperspace, so the launch failed, causing the rest of the gliderdrive's fuses to spark out all at once like a string of firecrackers. But it gave them a few more precious seconds of field—enough to close that final gap. "Everyone hang on!" Sirius yelled.

The whole ship shuddered now, steam roaring out of the gliderdrive as it tried to cycle. Everything doubled in Sirius's vision as field collapse played hell with the law of refraction. His teeth rattled, and the ship shook with a bang. Then everything went still.

The gliderdrive let off the last of its steam with a fading hiss . . . followed by an acrid smell of burned wires and blown fuses.

"Oh, God," Andromeda said. "Oh, God, it's overheating and we've boiled off all the rare earth water. It's going to burn up and we'll be stuck here—"

"And it's all your fault!" Toren said, shoving her aside from the glider service panel. "You and Leonid. This never would have happened if—dammit, you've changed everything since I last served a shift. Help me! We've got to flood the drive with potable water—"

"Potable won't take a tensor charge," Dijo said. "All that energy, lost—"

"But it will save the glider. Brilliant," Andromeda said, pushing Toren back aside, popping the service controls, exposing the patch panel, fingers leaping over the cables. "I'll reroute the water valves. Toren, stay on communications, get us landing clearance—"

"Agreed," Leonid said, moving to join Dijo at the glider control station, managing the console while she threw the safeties. "We'll try to bleed off the field—"

Sirius relaxed despite the many alarms. The ship had dropped early, the drive was frying, life support was still out, the beeping was getting worse—but his plan had worked. They were all working together, boys and girls together again—at last.

Sirius smiled with pride—then realized the beeping was a proximity alert.

"Hail, spacers," Sirius said. "Shouldn't the planet be farther off?"

They all turned to the forward viewer. The Beacon blinked before them, overlaid on a looming garden world—but it wasn't a freestanding planet, it was a moon around a mammoth gas giant. And it wasn't ten million clicks off like they'd planned. It was ten thousand.

"What the hell?" Leonid said, stepping back to the console he had just vacated, as the egg-shaped blue-green moon swam toward them, slowly eclipsing the banded pastels of the parent planet that wasn't listed in their Lore database. "I checked these readings—"

"Something took a bite out of space here," Dijo said, staring into the hologram that showed the shape of hyperspace. Even though the surf had faded, the map was hard to read . . . but still, this solar system almost looked . . . tilted. "Something really massive, bigger than that gas giant sitting atop our Beacon. That's why the drive overheated and the field collapsed early. On top of that, there's no trace of the Dresanian Relay, there's no other traffic—"

"And we're about to run straight into the Beacon," Sirius said, watching the world loom up upon them. He lifted the steering bar for the gliderdrive up and locked it, then pulled out the simpler paired joysticks for the maneuvering thrusters. "At nearly fifty kilometers a second."

"I'm . . . I'm not getting traffic directives," Toren said. "Maybe we should abort—"

"I've got the new mass distribution in," Leonid said. "Recomputing our options—"

A glowing cone showing their possible courses appeared on the holograph. The end of the ship's velocity obstacle was entirely contained within the surface of Halfway Point. Even if they could restart the glider now, it wouldn't fire until they were fifty kilometers underground.

"It's too late," Sirius said, as the ship struck atmosphere. "We're going down."

Serendipity gasped. She stood on rolling hills of wheat before a blue metal castle nestled in the shade of a floating lake. The shimmering green lake was a kilometer across, a fat, glistening oval twice as wide as it was tall. Beyond it, beyond the mountains, beyond even the clouds, the curved limb of a gas giant planet climbed the sky—Halfway Point's parent world.

Visible even in daylight, the roiling, turbulent clouds of the enormous sphere stamped a pastel rainbow watermark over half the heavens, but it was not alone. Beyond it, the Plume was also visible, a shimmering of stars and clouds, like frozen smoke from fireworks, given inconceivable depth and scale by hanging behind the planet before her.

"Wow," Serendipity said. "I mean . . . wow. This is why I voyage in space."

"Definitely not boring," Tianyu said, eyeing a butterfly-like creature suspiciously. It settled down on a waving frond, then trilled at him. Tianyu leapt back, hiding behind Serendipity's black foreboot. "And definitively not what was recorded on the map."

"Point taken, mister scaredy-but-not-cat," Serendipity said; her metaconscience had already called that to her attention. She reached into her satchel and released her mapping sphere, which flitted off to scout the area. Then she started forward across a field of waving alien wheat, toward a castle at the foothills of impossible mountains, where the floating lake hovered above the copper ribcage of the skeleton of a leviathan.

The low gravity was exhilarating, maybe seven-tenths Earth normal, less than half what she was used to on T'syar'lyeh. They hopped through the fields of wheat, covering vast ground, but even so, the castle was so far off she thought of flying on her farstaff. She'd picked a model more than long enough for her pony body, after all, and it could get her there faster than her four legs. But when she popped out the farstaff's kickstands and hopped on, sailing over a musty crevasse as though surfing a wave, she found she missed the feel of the wheat tickling her belly. So she hopped down at the other side and slung the staff, deciding to relish the journey.

As Tianyu bounced around her, Serendipity reassessed what she was seeing. The blue-white castle was a ruined spaceport; the floating lake was water collected in the focus of its landing cradle. The jutting ribs of the cradle, made of near-indestructible coppery *thact*, were weather-stained. Even the slender black spire of the Beacon, still flashing, looked ageworn.

The steep mountains beyond the port were barren, but all around her, especially in ruddy valleys between curious domed hills, were tattered remnants of a society. Lumps that could have been buildings. Stumps that might have been foundations. Giant coils of frayed wire.

Perhaps there was a Caretaker left here, a lone Andiathar, living in a cave, keeping things running. Or perhaps, the Beacon had simply survived that long: it was Dresanian equipment, after all. But the colony that had settled here ten thousand years ago had failed.

They paused in a clearing beside a stand of slowly swaying golden trees, giant cousins of the stalks of wheat. "I thought," Serendipity said, her voice unexpectedly weak even to her own ears, "I thought something would have survived. The Beacon's been running like clockwork."

"Me too. Definitely is a mystery. But . . . if you were looking for a place where your work was cut out for you," Tianyu said, hopping atop a jagged lump of glassy circuit slabs that might have been a household computer core, "you definitively found it."

"Headstrong, you said," Serendipity said, fists on her foreshoulders, farstaff slung over her foreback. She recalled the transaction she'd prepared in her neural weave and reviewed it carefully, making sure she'd gotten it right. "I prefer the term *determined.*"

The mortgage on the mammoth port before her, and the region of space it claimed with its Beacon, had been in default for almost ten thousand years—but after the war shifted the spacelanes, no one thought it worth claiming. She knew better, and hit *execute.*

When nothing happened, fear gripped her; she'd lost the Transference Relay, the data network that wove together the Dresan-Murran Alliance. Then she relaxed: the computer woven into her only had a one-centimeter transmitter, and here she was, atop a six-thousand-light-year-long column of gas. Direct connection to the Transference Relay was out of the question.

"Uh-oh," Tianyu said, canting his head. "I thought the signal loss was just me."

"You're not that much of an antique," Serendipity said. She frowned at the Beacon: nearly a kilometer tall, the black needle was still flashing as regular as a metronome. "That thing's got a connection. It let me file a travel plan, or at least appeared to. What's up?"

She pulled out her "archaeologist's spectacles"—round purple sunglasses with active ranging scanners integrated into each temple. Even from this distance, she could get a good read on the components of the Beacon, projected on the lenses in an augmented-reality view.

"*Dashpat.* The Beacon's half burnt out. The emission spire's still intact, the buffer pod is still receiving, but its local relay is totally shot." She squinted at the needle's base, then told the spectacles to run a diagnostic. "The relay almost looks . . . melted. We'll have to repair it."

"*We* have to repair *that?*" Tianyu said, craning his neck at the skyscraper-tall spire.

"Eventually, I mean," Serendipity said, giving him a little noogie. "If we want live access to the Transference Relay. Still . . ." She recalled her mapping sphere while she scanned the ruins, thinking. "Still, there's far more infrastructure to rebuild than I'd thought."

"Rebuild? I think you should declare a mulligan on Halfway Point and start over," Tianyu said, pawing at the cracked, dirt-stained slabs of computer core beneath his feet. On a second look, it seemed long buried, perhaps only recently exposed by erosion. "Fixing this place up could definitely take a lifetime." He canted his head again. "But isn't that what you want?"

"Maybe," she said, catching her mapping sphere. "Definitively, a big job."

The diagnostic of the Beacon completed and appeared on her spectacles: its structure was sound. She smiled. It had survived here, sending diagnostic packets every seventy-two years since before the dawn of recorded human history, and if it could, they could too.

"Well, what do we do?" Tianyu said. "If we can't even call for help—"

"Oh, come on, we teleported here. Surely we can improvise," she said. After a moment's thought, she unclipped the hypertensor booster from her farstaff and ran a filament from the nape of her neck into it. "See? This can be configured as a six-centimeter transmitter."

"Headstrong," Tianyu sniffed, "and completely hopeless."

Serendipity grinned at him. Then she looked back at the Beacon, the port, the ruins. It had all gone to rot when the war had cut off the shipping lanes, ten thousand years ago, but there was everything here needed to build a colony . . . and no one had yet stepped up to claim it.

Until today.

"Yes," she said, uploading the transaction she'd prepared into the booster's buffer. After a little thought, she added their recent memories and a few letters to friends and family, just to be sure. After all . . . she might be here for a while. "This *is* what I want."

She hit *send*. The booster surged, the message departed, and Serendipity felt a pang. Somewhere out there, ripples in hyperspace would become bits in cyberspace, then transactions in financial space, exchanging money for responsibility, and her inheritance . . . for this planet.

Serendipity was committed. It was her world now. She had to make it work.

"Have you seen my parents?" asked the small, scared voice of an Andiathar child.

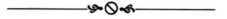

Serendipity flinched and nearly bolted, the voice was so close. She caught herself mid-wheel and stopped, staring at the scared little elf-monkey child with the shock of turquoise hair hiding in the stand of wheat-trees, wearing only a ragged cloak that looked like packing burlap.

"Oh my dear Lord," Serendipity said, her fingers pressed to her collarbone beneath the hem of her shrug. Andiathar were the dominant species of the Alliance, Dresanians-from-Dresan, elegant and refined after two hundred thousand years of continuous culture—but this boy looked like a refugee, with wan, splotchy skin, trembling tail and drooping ears.

"Definitely worse than we thought," Tianyu muttered silently over their comlink.

"They went hunting for food," the boy said in an older dialect of *derkesthai* just barely on the edge of triggering Serendipity's translator. Tail almost limp, he hugged himself, shivering, clutching a plain wooden staff. "There's not much edible here. But they never came back."

"How long ago was that?" Serendipity asked, peering at the boy with her archaeologist's spectacles. He couldn't have been older than eight, but his slender ears had the swiss-cheese look of the long malnourished—and his dialect was ancient, ten thousand years old at least.

Almost exactly the length of time the Beacon had been signaling like clockwork.

"I don't know," he said, hugging himself, his spray of hair falling in his eyes. Then Tianyu shifted in the grass, and the boy looked up, eyes hungry and desperate. Tianyu bolted behind Serendipity's hoof, and the boy fell back, scared. "Please . . . have you anything to eat?"

Serendipity swallowed, standing there frozen. She was acutely aware of her hearts beating against each other in her upper and lower chests. Her metaconscience remained silent—accusingly silent. Then she relaxed, reached into her satchel, and brought forth the wrap.

The boy eagerly reached to seize it, and Serendipity knelt before him, saying soothing words, inspecting the soundness of his skeleton and the balance of his blood with her glasses, desperately pinging her metaconscience for advice on how to treat Andiathar malnutrition.

Then a thunderclap struck them both like a hand of flame.

The screaming of the trees drowned out everything. Serendipity flinched back as the massive trunks quivered and shot back into the earth. Giant pores she'd mistaken for bunched roots clenched in their wake, leaving only the wheat, once golden, now burnt to a crisp.

Serendipity and the boy now stood howling on a burning, shuddering field as a spacecraft sheathed in red fire shot over their heads towards the landing cradle. Untouched by the flames, Serendipity seized the boy, brought him inside her shield, and watched the ship go down.

The grey and white ship was both ancient and elegant: its mammoth head was a slowly spinning cone and cylinder like something from the Apollo era, but the vast dark vanes erupting from the staggered cylinders of its cargo and engine pods gave it the appearance of a dragonfly.

The ship's repulsor field had ballooned to an immense size, driving before it a rumbling, crackling shockwave heated to a glowing red. From her primary school navigation labs Serendipity recognized the maneuver: emergency aerobraking, used to kill excess velocity without burning fuel.

But that was weird. This was a starship, not some in-system transport: blazing atop it was the katana blade of an emission spire in landing mode—a gliderdrive, Serendipity recognized, and with that she marked it: an NCE-class ship, one of humanity's last grand solo projects.

"This . . . this *can't be happening*," she whispered, shielding the boy in her arms.

Serendipity watched as that ship, that seven-hundred-and-fifty-year-old ship, that *priceless historical treasure*, barreled toward a landing cradle inappropriately filled with a floating lake. Too late it banked aside, the word *INDEPENDENCE* gleaming as it turned toward a mountain.

Earth plowed up around its field like muddy water splashing in slow motion. Seconds later an enormous *WHUDDDD* impacted her, followed by a heart-wrenching squeal as the repulsor field collapsed, the nose impacted the ground and the ship flipped upright.

The aft sensor pod sprang high in the air, its running lights flashing like a second Beacon, before twisting wildly as one of *Independence's* vanes struck a hillside and was near sheared off. The engine pod rotated a three-quarter turn while the nose kept grinding . . . then was still.

Serendipity stared at the downed ship in fear and horror. She was staggered by the loss of finding such a historical treasure just as it was destroyed. Then she was shamed by her care for the ship over its crew. And then she was terrified . . . for someone needed to go and help.

The child tore out of her grasp and began running toward the ship, running through the burning wheat as if the fires didn't bother him. Perhaps they didn't: Andiathar were tougher than humans, even if they didn't have human long-distance endurance.

"Where are you going?" Serendipity cried, quavering. "What are you doing?"

"Going to help," the boy said. "We have to help! My parents died like this!"

"Wait, what?" Tianyu said, tail standing up like a brush.

But the boy was off and running. Serendipity whirled, bolted, unlooping her farstaff and powering it up, hands trembling as she set the program. Fear gripped her, and she turned to her metaconscience for aid. Damningly, it gave her the worst kind of excuse it could: approval.

You should flee. Your rescue gear is inadequate. You can help most by going for help.

But she had rescue gear: A survival kit. A medical blade. Half a sandwich and a satsuma.

"Tianyu?" Serendipity asked, still holding the farstaff. "What—what should I do?"

"I'm just your familiar," Tianyu said softly, as he climbed up onto her shoulder. "I can't decide for you. I think your metaconscience is right: if you go for help, it's still help. Real help. You don't have to go to the wreck to help them. But . . . you don't have to run away either."

"Right," Serendipity said. Then she straightened her upper body. "Right."

Trembling, Serendipity slung her farstaff over her shoulder, swallowed and turned back to the shipwreck. The devastation was awesome. A burnt swath cut across quivering fields. Trees flattened and water sprayed from ponds where the ship banked. Then a rut of torn earth and the ship tilted against a mountain like God's own dreidel.

And a little refugee boy running straight toward it without fear.

Serendipity set her mind and darted after him. Quickly she paced the boy, extended her hand and lifted him, gasping, onto her back. He gripped her with the fierceness and claws of a cat, and she was stung by embers clinging to his cloak. But she kept running toward the wreck.

It took longer than she'd expected—the ship was larger, and had traveled farther, over rougher terrain, than she'd first imagined. But she kept running, thankful for all the endurance training her grandmother had put her through, while the child actually grew tired riding.

"How can you still be running?" the Andiathar boy said. "I'm so hungry."

The grey hillside whacked by the maneuvering vane was a landsliding ruin, so she cut to the left of the red rut. Shifting earth and sliding rubble worried at her, so she invoked her metaconscience's solver, letting it pick out a safer path that was far from obvious.

Slowly the distant dreidel that was the starship grew large, then loomed like a skyscraper over her. Here torn hull strips and smashed bits of equipment mixed through the sprayed earth, but overhead the ship's engine pod still blinked, whole.

The acrid tang of burnt plastics mixed with the rich scent of fresh soil. She jumped at a squeal far above—hot plasma venting from the engine. Her spectacles showed her the radiation was slight—and her metaconscience told her it was manual venting. She pressed on.

She crested a ridge overlooking the wreck—and froze, bewitched.

Climbing from the ship were the most beautiful people she'd ever seen.

They wore armored spacesuits, patched in a thousand places, and painted to look like animals. Helmets folded back revealed inner pressure suits decorated too: one girl in a leopard outersuit had a snakeskin helm, adorned with feathers, over skin painted a pale blue.

Serendipity gasped. These were adventurers. The gravity was clearly punishing their slender frames, but they kept going, crawling out of the smoking ship from every hatch, rappelling down on spacelines, tools jangling on their belts when their boots touched the broken earth.

Not one of them looked a day over sixteen.

That should have meant nothing—her grandmother didn't look a day over sixteen—but as fractured shale dislodged by her slogs crackled down the slope, they turned and stared at her with youthful shock. They had none of the smug poise of ancient souls newly young.

What Serendipity saw instead, and felt keenly herself, was fear.

Serendipity's gut churned as she saw the boys were armed—projectile automatics, maybe gyrostabilized, no immediate threat to one with a force field, but troubling all the same—but still she approached, watching their eyes widen at her four legs dancing over the rubble.

"*Hai-ee,*" she said, suddenly embarrassed she'd not said hello to the Andiathar boy now riding on her back. The spacer children gathered around them, the beautiful boys curious, the equally beautiful girls strangely subdued—except for the snake-helmed girl. She had ignored Serendipity, fallen to her knees, and was staring up at the ship . . . wailing.

Serendipity cleared her throat. "We saw your ship go down and came to—"

"Help!" cried a voice from the ship's upper reaches, where two boys, one older than the others, wrestled with a litter upon which a broken girl lay. Blood seeped out of her bandages—and the boys, struggling in the gravity, were about to drop her.

"Oh, dear Lord," Serendipity said, unslinging her farstaff. She could fly up with her farstaff, and . . . well, the gravity here was light enough that maybe between her farstaff and Aegis she could help them float the girl down. "Hang on," she said. "I'm . . . I'm coming!"

But before she'd rerigged her staff to take extra weight, the Andiathar boy moved.

With the grace possessed only by his species, the elf-monkey child leapt up through the wreckage, hopping from point to point, turquoise hair bouncing as he sprang up and up, his tail flickering out behind him as he landed atop the frame where they struggled with the litter—

The elder boy whirled, screamed—and fired a blaster into the refugee boy's chest.

Serendipity felt her nostrils flare, her eyes widen as the boy seemed to hang there, frozen in space with a golden flower erupting from his chest. Then he fell through the wreckage like a sack of potatoes, seemingly hitting every pole and protrusion on his way down.

Serendipity screamed and ran forward to the crumpled form, whose cloak was already stained yellow with blood. She started to scoop him up, but her metaconscience warned her off; so she pulled out her medical blade and swept it over him. There was no doubt: dead, dead, dead.

"This . . . this *can't have happened,*" Serendipity said, staring at the blade in her hand. Reflexively she holstered it, then scooped up the still form in her arms. Above her were screams and a crash, but she ignored them, cradling the alien child. "You brave boy."

The elder boy landed beside her in a crunch of boots and jangle of tools, and she looked up into wiry brown hair peeking out of a lion helmet, light brown skin flushed with exertion, and dark eyes swimming in white pools of fear—fear that rapidly turned to shame.

"He's dead. He's dead!" Serendipity said. "I didn't even know his name."

The elder boy fell to his knees, mouth falling open. Two others stepped up behind him—one an orange-haired slip of a boy that looked almost as elfin as the Andiathar refugee; the other, a big, brown-skinned bruiser who stepped forward with a look of grim satisfaction.

"Why did you do that?" Serendipity cried, cradling the refugee boy in her arms, feeling warm yellow blood seep through her fingers, wincing at the ugly singed scent of burnt flesh rising from his ruined chest. "We were trying to help!"

"I'm sorry," the boy said, blaster slipping from his shaking hand. "I'm so sorry—"

"And that," the big bruiser said, taking the blaster, "is the end of that experiment."

They took Serendipity's farstaff and Aegis. They emptied her saddlebags and took her force rod. They didn't get everything—they mistook her shield brooch and force bracelet for jewelry—but they might as well have: they'd bound her hands and left her no weapons.

Then they pressed her into service helping the victims out of the crash.

The first thing Serendipity noticed was how weak all the spacer children were. The boys were more muscled than the girls, but even they were mostly thin as sticks. Halfway Point's gravity, light by even Earth standards, was wearing on them. They probably spent most of their days in zero- or half-gee. Serendipity had triple their strength, not even counting her size.

Like her force bracelet . . . a hidden advantage.

So she grunted and strained at the litter they'd made her drag behind her, pretending it was hard to lift. The boys were remarkably contemptuous of the girls, and hadn't really noticed that her odd shape gave her far more muscle mass despite her height.

They could still swarm her. When it came time to escape, she would have to explode.

The boys were armed, but the girls had empty holsters. The boys and girls acted as if they hadn't seen each other in a while, but the girls were being treated like prisoners. It was serious: a pair of obvious siblings met with happy surprise—but the boy didn't free his sister.

The killer, Leonid, was in charge . . . but the baton was passing to the bruiser, Toren. He had all the muscle that most of his companions lacked, and a brutal personality to go with it. Night came too soon when the sun dove behind the gas giant, and while lion-helmed Leonid moped on a rock, the bear-totemed Toren organized a makeshift camp and campfire with a mixture of slaps and curses.

Admittedly, they were under the stress of a shipwreck disaster, and Serendipity had seen the spacers only for a minute before the shooting, but even so, it seemed like the real tension had begun when the Andiathar boy died. The girl they tried to save died, too, when Leonid went for his blaster and lost his grip on her litter. Now everyone walked around as if punched in the gut, and two bodies lay in shrouds not three meters from her.

A trilling sound called softly from the edge of the clearing. She looked: Tianyu.

"Definitely looks like you could use some help," Tianyu signaled silently.

Serendipity glanced around, then signaled back: *"Definitively, but be careful."*

The minifox darted from rubble to rock until he had snuck up behind her. Then Tianyu began gnawing at the zip ties that bound her hands. She heard one snap, then another, as the tough plastic fell to Tianyu's coppery *thact* teeth. Her wrists loosened a bit, and she tried to twist free, but one longer strap still held them. After trying to get at it, Tianyu switched his attention to the cord tying her wrists to the stake—then froze as a heavy tread approached them.

Broken rock crunched beneath Toren's boots as he squatted before Serendipity. She swallowed, stories of Frontier intolerance towards genetic constructs ringing in her pointed ears. It would have been hard to find two people at the crash site who were more different.

He was an unmodified human, walking on two legs; she was a centaur, walking on four. He was a Frontiersman, his battered spacesuit patched from years of use; she was a Dresanian, and her stylish finery had already autoshed the mud she'd picked up helping the survivors.

Almost alone among the spacer children in the camp, Toren still wore his armored outer suit. Its bubble dome folded back to a wedge, exposing an inner comm helmet made fierce with faux bear fur and teeth artfully sewn into it. His flinty brown eyes glinted at her beneath the fangs of the savage helm, and armored fingers brushed a dagger of hair on his chin.

"You, Dresanian," Toren said. Serendipity eyed him sidelong, silent. "What's your story?"

"I'm a human Variant," she said cautiously, wondering how he would take it. The Frontiersmen had fled Earth after the Genetics Wars, disgusted that the leaders of Earth had called in the alien Dresan-Murran Alliance to save Earth's biosphere. Her metaconscience gave a fifty-fifty chance of them treating her like a monster—either because she was a human Variant, or for her Dresanian heritage. "A genetic construct that—"

"I got that," he said, striking her upside the head. "I meant, how'd you end up out here?"

Serendipity winced: the blow had surprised her. Toren was a lot stronger than the others.

"I was exploring," she said. "It . . . it seemed like a nice world—"

"Then where's your ship?" Toren asked.

"You took it," Serendipity said, nodding her head at a pallet of equipment they'd made her carry—on which rested her saddlebags and farstaff. "That staff there."

Toren twisted round on the balls of his feet. "*That* thing?"

"Yes."

"Huh," he said, head tilting as he studied it. "How many can it carry?"

"Three of me, five of you," Serendipity said. Then she bit her lip. "Well . . . from here, me plus one. Halfway Point's far from any inhabited world, any charted one at any rate. I needed the booster just to get to a decent bounce point, and even then, you'd need your spacesuits."

"So where's your suit?" Toren asked.

"You took it," Serendipity said, jutting her chin at him. "That gold disc—"

Toren grabbed a fistful of her bolero and lifted her upper body off the ground.

"You think this is funny, you stupid girl?" Toren growled. Serendipity's eyes went wide as the cord tying her wrists to the stake broke. "You Dresanians chased us off our world, then chase us out here, dancing around us and laughing! I've had enough of you!"

Leonid sat heavily on a point of rock, eyes tracing upward through the evidence of his failures. Two bodies wrapped in shrouds. Their would-be rescuer, bound beside the campfire; the girls, bound in a huddle, while the boys sulked or avoided the increasingly erratic Toren.

And beyond them all, the spray of devastation around their downed starship.

Leonid felt physically sick. He'd been so paranoid about the Dresanians he'd shot one trying to help. He'd been so soft on Andromeda he'd let her run the ship into the ground. Well, maybe that part was her fault—but ultimately this disaster was his responsibility.

He had to accept that. He was the Captain. Time to start acting like one.

Some of the boys had pulled out tonesticks and were strumming; others were preparing meals; all looked confused about what to do about the girls. Sirius was shouting—knowing him, probably good sense badly delivered—and Toren was strong-arming their rescuer: typical.

Leonid stood. You couldn't lead by moping.

"Enough, Toren," he called. Toren looked over at him, and the Dresanian half-horse girl, the centauress, twisted free and stood on her four weird legs. Toren snarled and grabbed her elbow, but Leonid barked: "I said that's enough. Untie her. In fact, untie all the girls."

Everyone looked at him as he strode up to the campfire. No one moved.

"You heard me," Leonid said, scowling at the others. Of all the people in the camp, it was Sirius who had stopped what he was doing and looked at Leonid; the rest seemed to be trying to avoid his gaze. "We need to make camp and they need to help."

"After all they did," Toren said, the centauress still in his grip, "you're just going to—"

"The ship is down," Leonid said flatly, stepping up to Toren. The centauress, Serendipity she called herself, flinched away. Of course. He'd killed her friend. *Damnit.* One problem at a time, though: getting Toren under control. "We have to move on. That fight's over."

"You're dead wrong about that," Toren said—and punched him, hard.

Light flashed in Leonid's eyes, and he fell, jaw sore and throbbing.

"You want to lead?" Toren said, settling into a boxing pose. "Then take me down."

Leonid stared. He reached for his pistol, but Toren shook his head, touching the blaster. Then he raised his fists again. This was insane: Toren had the blaster, a gun and even a knife and yet wanted to duke it out. Leonid hadn't beaten him since he'd turned twelve. But he had to try.

The fight was over almost as soon as it began. No sooner than he'd gotten to his feet, a huge flying fist knocked him off them again. Leonid rolled up to a crouch and held his own for all of ten seconds before Toren dismantled his defenses and knocked him back to the dirt.

But then the centauress intervened, kicking at Toren with a black-booted foreleg.

"Hey!" she said. She wasn't as tall as Toren, and her lower body was no bigger than a very large dog or a very small pony. But when she rammed Toren with her shoulder, her mass nearly knocked him of his feet. "You can't solve this by dueling like a bunch of savages!"

Toren snarled and seized her by her elegant lace half-jacket, lifting her front legs off the ground. Leonid's eyes widened as muscles bulged in Toren's arm: he knew Toren worked out in the centrifuge but until that moment he hadn't realized how much of a monster he'd become. Leonid tried to scramble to his feet, but Toren, looking over the struggling centauress's shoulder, smiled viciously and shoved her down atop him. Her mass knocked Leonid's wind out.

"Who thought you up, you ridiculous thing?" Toren said to the girl, squatting to pick at her finery—her booted hooves, the tapestry wraps on her horse body, her fiery mane of hair. His hands touched some weird dark quills at her temples. "And what the hell are these?"

He ripped one off, and she squealed. Leonid, still gasping, clenched his fists.

"Attached!" she said, struggling to get off Leonid. "You ass!"

Toren snarled, his hand clenching, crushing the quill—then his eyes widened in fear at the spray of her red human blood on his armored glove. He jerked back, stood—and kicked her in the gut. Serendipity jerked, cheek scraping the shale as she curled into a ball, gasping.

"Leave her alone!" Leonid wheezed. "She's done nothing to you—"

"Shut up!" Toren shouted. "You're not in charge anymore!"

"I'm the Captain," Leonid shouted back, trying to get Serendipity off him.

"You were Captain until you *crashed our ship*," Toren said, and Leonid's gut churned. Toren walked closer to the fire, seized Andromeda, and hauled her to her feet, half knocking off her quezcoatl helm. "Which happened because you were soft on your girlfriend!"

Leonid was speechless. It tore him up to see Andromeda in pain—but even that feeling just confirmed what Toren was saying, what Leonid had already been thinking. Maybe Toren was right: maybe Leonid didn't deserve to be Captain.

Fortunately for Andromeda, though, she had another defender.

"Don't you touch her!" shouted Artemyst.

Toren laughed, but she uncoiled like a suddenly released spring and landed a blow on his chin, popping his head back. Unexpectedly, Serendipity laughed; clearly she didn't see how serious this was. Toren tilted his head, felt his jaw, and chuckled.

"I remember when you could throw a punch, Artemyst," he said, dropping Andromeda. Artemyst screamed and leapt on him, swinging, but he deflected the blows easily with one hand. "But you spent too long in zero-gee. Now . . . you just hit like a girl."

He backhanded her, knocking her to the ground, but Artemyst snarled, sprung back to her feet, and dove back on him. Leonid had always thought Artemyst and Andromeda had become an item after Andromeda split the ship; seeing how she fought for her, now he was sure.

"This is another shipwreck," the centauress said, trying to rise. "We've got to—"

"Don't interfere," Leonid said, putting a hand out to restrain her. God, she was muscled, but still, she froze beneath his hand; Serendipity really must hate him for killing the boy. Leonid understood; he did too, especially seeing one of the girls fight his battle for him. "This crash has been a long time in coming. We've got to let it play out. We've got to lance the poison."

Leonid watched Artemyst hit the dirt. Toren reached down, seizing Artemyst's head. Done, but not out, she screamed as he tore her bird-helm off and raised it in the air to the cheers of the boys. Then he threw her down by the two bodies that lay in shrouds, far from the fire.

"You cut us off! You called us hullrats! You called yourselves skybirds!" Toren said to the knot of girls. "But you are not skybirds. You are not Amazons. You're not even people! You're just the mutineers who wrecked our ship! We should have cycled the lot of you!"

The girls quailed, and Toren turned away, the hulking shape of their wrecked starship looming behind him. Leonid was shocked to see that he was fighting back tears. Toren's jaw clenched, he choked up—then he saw Leonid looking, cursed, and turned back.

"But we can't just toss you out an airlock, or into the recycler. It's done, along with our ship, our home," Toren said, pointing up at *Independence*. "We were supposed to travel forever, finding new worlds for Man and seeding them with colonies. Thanks to you, this is our last stop. We have to start over here—and you mutineers have all of our wombs."

"Oh, God," said Andromeda, eyes as wide as those on her feathered snake helm. Sirius, who had first gone to help Andromeda, and then Artemyst when Toren had thrown her down, stood up, glaring at Toren, clenching his fists.

"Once we treated men and women as equals," Toren said. "But you didn't want that. Then we tried letting the girls be in charge. We all know how that worked out. Now it's the boys' turn to rule—and the girls' turn to serve. And you will serve the boys."

The boys cheered and leered. The girls squirmed, but they were still bound. This was far worse than he thought. Now Leonid tried to get up to stop it, but Serendipity's weight pinned him down. She flinched when he moved. Rock shifted beneath her hooves, and Toren looked down at them.

"As for you," he began—but Sirius leapt upon him.

"The *Captain* said," Sirius yelled, cracking Toren's jaw, "leave her alone!"

This time, Toren was really staggered. Still he managed to knock Sirius away with a backhand—but he didn't knock Sirius off his feet. Instead, Sirius looked even more ready to fight—but before he regained his balance, Toren pulled the blaster from his holster.

Suddenly everyone got quiet.

"Tori," warned the smaller boy, raising his hands. "Don't—"

"Weaponsmaster!" Toren shouted, holding out the weapon, and Betelgeuse stepped forward, taking it and Toren's pistol. "Hold our steel. We have a challenge on our hands."

"Alright, Tori," Sirius said, cracking his neck. "If that's how you want it—"

And he leapt on Toren without a second thought.

Toren was bigger, but Sirius was better. After all, he'd trained Toren, trained most of the crew; his parents were bounty hunters. But Toren still had muscle on his side—that, and a row of cheering boys, who crowded around the sparring pair as the bound girls looked on in horror.

"How," Leonid said, "did we go so wrong?"

"Where were you going?" asked the centauress, rolling away from him.

Leonid sat up and reached out to keep her from bolting. He now questioned whether she should still be a prisoner, but she was still a prisoner. But when his hand fell on her horsey side, he unexpectedly felt her breathing. He hadn't realized she kept her lungs down there.

"Uh . . . good question," he said, realizing that it was something they should have asked themselves long ago. "A world. Any world. After the adults died, we got tired of running. We just wanted to find a place to settle. Preferably with a port but . . . we didn't agree on where."

He looked over at Serendipity, saw her hunching away from him, saw that curly red hair pouring over her face so all he could glimpse of her face was a violet rose and a marble-blue eye. "Please believe me," he said. "I am so sorry about your friend. I never meant—"

"He wasn't my friend!" Serendipity reared up, easily throwing off his hand as she rose with the strength in her four legs. But her hands were still bound behind her back, and Leonid rose with her and caught her elbow to keep her from running. Twisting, she tried to shake him off. "*Dashpat!* I just met him. Then you killed him!"

Serendipity glared at him, angry and hot. Leonid pulled her back harder than he meant to. She stumbled on a stone and bumped into him with a sharp yelp, and he found himself staring right into sparkling blue eyes over a spray of freckles, breathing her lavender perfume.

When he couldn't see her legs, she was human—and beautiful. Even the spots, the weird quills at her temples, even those elegant horsey ears didn't break the effect: they just made her more exotic. Leonid's breath caught. So did hers. Leonid's eyes widened. So did hers.

"Everyone, listen up," Toren said. He had a forearm around Sirius's neck, swinging him around; Sirius was squirming like a madman, but the fight was over. "Andromeda crashed the ship—because Leonid let her. So we're going to have some new rules around here—"

"I never meant for this to happen," Leonid said, squeezing her arm. "I'm sorry—"

"I'm sorry too," Serendipity said—and slipped her arms free.

Leonid jerked as he realized she'd gotten loose, and tried to seize her, but she ducked and reared, reaching out with one arm and collaring him with effortless grace. Leonid cried out, struggling—her grip was incredibly strong—and Toren turned towards them. Serendipity reached out—and a knife leapt out of Toren's belt and into her hand.

"Don't move," Serendipity said, holding the knife to Leonid's throat.

Leonid stood frozen, feeling the point over his jugular. "That's usually my line."

"Shut up. Everyone else, listen up," Serendipity said. "Stay back—or I'll kill him."

"No!" Andromeda cried, struggling to get to her feet. "Don't you do it—"

"Shut up!" Toren said. Then he turned to Leonid and smiled. "Go on, kill him then."

"Toren!" Leonid began—then shut up when she tightened her grip on his neck.

"You really want three people in shrouds?" Serendipity said.

"I—" Toren began, smile growing vicious—and fading when Serendipity dug in the knife, making Leonid yelp. "No, no, come on," Toren said, dropping Sirius in the dirt and extending his hands. "I didn't . . . we don't . . . no. We don't want you to kill him."

"I don't know what went on here," Serendipity said, jerking Leonid around. "And I don't really care. You're all acting like you're still in the deep of space, one bad decision away from death. Look around and relax for a moment. Your ship's down, but you survived—"

"Not all of us," Toren said, "and we're stranded on a hellhole—"

"An attractive enough hellhole to draw me nine thousand light years out here," Serendipity said. "Everything's a wreck right now, I don't know why, but this is a splendid world, not far off the shipping lanes. And I got here. And if I got here, I can go for help."

Toren stared at her. Slowly he relaxed. He kicked at Sirius, not hard, and Leonid felt Serendipity's arm tighten. But rather than spit more abuse, Toren simply said, "Siri, you've been right about every damn thing so far, so . . . what say you? Can we trust her?"

Sirius squinted at them. Leonid's mouth opened, but Serendipity gave him a squeeze—not a warning, but reassurance. But when Sirius cleared his throat, a distant rumble of thunder echoed, the quills at Serendipity's temples raised—and goose bumps rose on Leonid's arms.

The night sky lit up white—and every piece of machinery lit with blue fire.

Leonid screamed. Everyone screamed. Sparks flared up all around them. A new white star blazed in the sky, painfully bright, with a growing blue-white halo around it like feathers of blue flame—blue flame that matched the sparks streaming off anything with a tensor crystal.

"That's the black hole," Serendipity said, aghast. "And that's a tensor flare—"

She screamed, losing her grip on him, upper body flipping forward. Leonid leapt back from Serendipity as blue fire danced over her, too, rippling out from her spine over her arms and all her legs. Her hair began shifting through every shade of the rainbow, and she doubled up into an arch, wracked with pain. He reached to touch her, then jerked back, stung.

"We need to get back to *Independence!*" Andromeda yelled over a rising whine. Roiling flames rippled across the sky like a giant curtain, and in the distance a titanic bolt of lightning struck, followed by crackling thunder and a new tremor in the already shuddering earth. "The field's going to build up in the gliderdrive! We have to pull the coils—"

Leonid realized he'd been dumbstruck, that he should have done something, and failing him, Toren. He opened his mouth to bark an order he didn't know if anyone would follow, but it was already too late. *Independence's* gliderdrive had already started to glow, the same blue-white fire it glowed with when running, only brighter, and brighter, and brighter—until an explosion detonated in the Engine Module and the whole ship went dark.

Everyone was silent now. Even the curtains of light in the sky went quiet. In the stillness Leonid heard a hissing, sparking noise and glanced over to see the flickering light of the cargo pallet. Serendipity's farstaff was aflame, sparks spraying out of its top end at an angle.

Serendipity's seizure ended, and she slowly lifted herself off the dirt, struggling to sit upright, hair a frazzle of a dozen different colors. She saw the staff fizzle out, and her face drained to pale, making her look wan beneath her rainbow spray. "Oh, *God.*"

"You were saying," Toren said, cocking his head at it, "you could go for help?"

"Oh, God, no!" Serendipity wailed, and Leonid saw her reach not for the staff but for a little furry creature curled up on the wheatgrass. The tiny fox looked asleep, but its red fur was covered in soot, and it was dead in her hands. "Oh no! *Tianyu!*"

"Where did that come from?" Leonid said, swaying in a new earth tremor. Serendipity ignored him, cradling the dead creature to her breast. Then he saw a bit of zip tie in the creature's mouth, and realized that creature had freed her. "It must have eaten away at her bonds."

"Dammit. I didn't anticipate that. We'll have to watch the girls more closely," Toren said, hands on his hips, ignoring the increasingly unquiet earth. "Beetle, check their bonds."

Beetle laughed. "Sure, but I doubt any of the girls picked up a Dresanian familiar."

The earth shuddered again, and while Toren was off balance, Leonid quietly picked up the knife Serendipity had dropped. Toren had taken charge, for now, but he was too unstable to keep it. Leonid knew, if he kept his head, ultimately he'd win the crew back—

Low thunder echoed across the valley. The trembling ground shook, hard. Toren whirled. Leonid tensed. An immense tearing rent the air. Glowing cracks spread out over the smooth hillsides in the distance . . . and then the hillsides bulged and slowly lifted into the air.

"Oh my God," Leonid said. His voice quavered, drowned out by the thudding of falling boulders, the rumbling movement of displaced earth, the terrible cracking and tearing of some fabric below he couldn't yet see. "What . . . what is that?"

The hillsides were now vast rising balloons, the wheatgrass trees that covered them now waving like cilia. Huge tentacles uncoiled beneath them like mooring cables, sliding over the landscape—and vast eyes opened beneath them, blazing with blue-white fire.

"Of course," Serendipity said. "If there's a source of energy . . . life will exploit it."

"What do we do?" Toren said. "They're everywhere. What do we do?"

"Go deeper into the hills," Leonid said, pointing. "They're clear of the creatures—"

"I wasn't asking you!" Toren shouted. "We lost our ship following your advice! We don't know where they're going yet. We . . . we stay here, we sit tight, and we watch." He looked around, then motioned to Betelgeuse to return his gun. "We've got to make hard choices—"

Then Sirius sprang up, snatched Toren's pistol from Beetle and aimed straight at Toren.

"Go," he said, backing toward Serendipity and Leonid. To Toren he said, "Stay back."

"You little—" Toren snarled. He froze when Sirius raised the pistol.

"I'll shoot you in the face, Tori. Your suit will be no protection. You two, go!"

"What?" Leonid said, but Serendipity gripped his arm and began pulling him away. He realized Sirius meant to flee, that by going with them he'd be leaving *Independence* behind, leaving Toren in charge, and giving up any hope of remaining Captain.

"We can't just leave the ship—"

"We have to! Andromeda, come on," Sirius said, extending his hand. "Come on!" She stood up and started forward, but Toren punched her in the gut and she collapsed, wheezing. "Dammit, Tori!" Sirius screamed, stepping forward. "You're pushing it!"

"You gonna shoot me, Halfway Boy?" Toren smirked.

"Ironic coming from my other half," Sirius said, and Toren stiffened and snarled. Then he froze as Sirius stepped up, the gun just inches from Toren's face. "Tori! Have I ever had a problem with shooting people?" Sirius asked, and Toren squinted. "Try me."

Toren raised his hands, cocked his head. Quicker than anything, Sirius leapt back and turned the gun on Betelgeuse, who'd stayed frozen since Sirius snatched Toren's gun. But Beetle just raised his hands, making no move toward the veligen and the blaster on his own belt.

"Nobody's done anything worth shooting over," Beetle said. "You wanna go, you go."

Sirius backed up until he joined Leonid and Serendipity. "Let's go."

"What are you doing?" Leonid hissed, gripping his arm.

"If you've ever trusted me about anything . . . go," Sirius whispered. "Toren may not look it, but he's panicking. He's consolidating his power. And he's violent. Anybody he can blame for anything needs to be gone. I'd take Andromeda, Artemyst and Dijo if I could. Go."

Serendipity bolted forward and seized her satchel, slipping the poor broken fox robot into it. She started towards her staff and saddlebags, but jerked back when Toren raised his fist.

"Come on," Leonid said, pulling her away. "Sirius has a good head on him. If we'd started listening to Sirius earlier, we wouldn't be in this mess."

"On my back then," Serendipity said, now pulling at him.

"You are the fastest," Leonid said, lifting his leg and settling atop her. He found it very disturbing, putting his hands around her waist, more so when Sirius hopped on behind him and put his hands about his waist. "But can you carry both of us?"

"Like feathers," Serendipity said. "Sirius, keep them covered."

"Not a problem," he said—and then his voice faltered. "But where can we go?"

"I know a place," said Serendipity, "that's stayed safe for ten thousand years."

"Go on, run," Toren said, waving. He turned away. "Good luck on your own."

Even with two people on her back, the centauress could run faster than anyone Sirius had ever seen. At first she ran low, ducking and weaving through the hills until they were out of gunshot of the camp—but then she told them to hang on and bounded over the ground.

Behind them, what had been hillsides were transformed into a forest of looming balloons, moving over the landscape on slack, slow-moving tentacles. Toren was right about waiting and watching: the things hadn't started up into the mountains yet, but Sirius didn't want to brave those feelers combing the earth.

After a long leap, Serendipity yelped and stumbled. Leonid grabbed on for dear life, and Sirius did too—then he heard Serendipity yelp again, but more in startled surprise than pain. She moved Leonid's arm.

"Wandering!" she snapped, elbowing back at him.

"Sorry," Leonid said, though he didn't sound sorry at all.

Sirius hissed at the smug sound in Leonid's voice. This sucked. He knew Leonid had been with Andromeda, but Sirius had hoped that he'd wanted more than just another girl. Some part of him was even glad Toren had run them off—maybe now he could sound Leonid out.

The few times they'd met after the ship split, Sirius had thought he'd seen glimmers of interest—but here he was, practically wrapped round Leonid, and Leonid was so hopelessly girlsmacked he was already falling for—feeling up—another one, even one with four legs.

"Just another damn breeder," Sirius whispered, leaning his head against Leonid's back. This ride was as close as they would get.

"Is that it?" Leonid said. "Sirius, is that the Beacon that drew us out here?"

"Yes. It'd have to be. It's the only one," Serendipity said, winded. "I—I think we're safe now. Can we walk the rest?"

She skidded awkwardly to a stop, her legs splayed. Sirius hopped off; moments later, Leonid carefully set one leg down and lifted his other off her pony back. "Are you alright?" he asked, gently taking her hand and supporting her. Sirius clenched his fists.

"I'm right enough," she said, limping a little. "I came down hard over that ridge."

"Is it broken?" he said, kneeling, reaching out—but she pulled back.

"Mitts off," she said, slapping his hand away. "Probably just cut the frog."

"Sorry," Leonid said. "Didn't mean to feel you up back there."

Serendipity covered her breasts mock protectively. "Sure you didn't."

Sirius strode past them angrily, staring up at the glowing spire rising over the next ridge. This was the Beacon that had promised them safe passage, a place to land. Sirius suddenly remembered what he'd seen in that landing cradle and ran to the top of the ridge.

The landing cradle was huge: the floating lake hanging over its curved copper fingers had to be a full kilometer across. It gleamed underneath the white burning star, its rippling surface flashing every time the Beacon flared. Beyond, an imposing, castle-like structure loomed.

Serendipity and Leonid joined him, her limping, arm over his shoulder.

"Beacon's working," Leonid said. "I thought that tensor shock trashed everything."

"That's too big an antenna to fry," Sirius said. He'd seen launching rails smaller than that mammoth rapier pointed at the sky. "I bet most of the circuits are gone, though. Anything that wasn't physically disconnected from the circuit was probably destroyed by the surge."

"How does that work? What happened back there?" Leonid asked. "Up there?"

"I don't know," Sirius said, looking up at the glowing white star. It was no longer painfully bright, but it still had that weird halo of blue flame. After a moment, he shielded his eyes, then looked away. It gave him a headache, and his eyes had a spotty afterimage. "That's a black hole, right? A dead star, crushed so far not even light can escape—"

"The whirlpools of space," Leonid said, shading his eyes to look up at the white pinprick. After a moment, he too looked away, grimacing. "Normally, we just avoid them. How'd this one reach out and smack us?"

"Anything we make has a counterpart in Nature," Serendipity said. "That black hole's a natural phenomenon simulating a hyperdrive. It and this star dance around each other every seventy-two years, whirling around their common center, then flying out into the Plume—"

"And one's lit, but the other's not," Sirius said. "The black hole sucks gas in, but the star's hot. Its solar wind pushes away gas, but only so far—the heliopause, the boundary where we normally shut off the glider. When the black hole crosses that boundary—"

They all stared up at the Beacon as it flared atop the blue-white metal of the castle.

"It becomes half a hyperdrive," Serendipity said, "and burns up every matching circuit."

"Including all the ones in you," Leonid said. "Were you seriously hurt, Serendipity?"

"My weave was scrambled, but I'll be fine," Serendipity said, brushing her quills. "A century ago, even twenty-five years ago, it would have been totally ruined. But my grandmother got her implant burnt out by tensor shock, so my grandfather's team designed . . . upgrades."

She looked off, an odd mixture of bitterness and gratitude on her face.

"I'll be fine, Leonid," she said. "My equipment's repairing itself. Give it a few days."

"If you two are done flirting," Sirius said coldly—and both Leonid and Serendipity started—"I'm guessing this is the 'shelter that stood for ten thousand years' you mentioned. Yes? Can we get inside before the wind drifts one of those gasbag feeders over this way?"

They picked their way down the hill, encountering twisted, stunted trees with steeply angled trunks that Serendipity identified as Dresanian harvest trees, engineered to extract minerals and nutrients from the crust.

"We can't eat this—it's a molybdenum harvester," Serendipity said, inspecting a tree with stunted-looking metallic fruit. "These are used for nanotech. That's kind of odd for a colony this old—oh, hey." She bolted forward, seizing a fruit from another tree—then cursed.

Sirius stepped up. The fruit was half consumed by white fungi.

"A lot of the trees have the same fungus," Leonid said. "It looks . . . native."

"This explains why the refugee boy was starving," Serendipity said.

She dropped the fruit and they went on, but Sirius kept an eye out for more of the tree Serendipity had thought was edible. Most of the fruit were ruined by the same white fungi, but things started changing the further they went towards the Beacon.

"The trees are getting bigger," Sirius said, inspecting a dark blue-green leaf. At first the foliage had been spotted and crumbly, but now it was glossy, the angled trunks wrapped in dark peeling paper, their roots surrounded by bushy moss. "Everything's healthier, the closer we get."

"That's the crustal plug," Serendipity said. "A biosphere's more than surface ecology. The roots of life go down kilometers. Dresanians are experts at grafting biospheres together. Looks like this one went fallow before the harmonies developed."

They followed a path down to the spaceport's mammoth door, hanging half off its hinges, with a narrow triangular crack lit from within by a flickering blue light. The path ended by a pool at the base of the door, where the water seemed to stop midair.

Sirius leaned over the greenish pond—a lazy fat fish wriggled there, but Serendipity warned him off—a "thinkfish," inedible. Sirius peered at the weird cliff in the water at the base of the door: it was almost like there was an invisible force field holding the pond back.

"Well, here goes," Sirius said, trying to leap over the water through the crack in the doors. He ran smack into an invisible barrier, right over the water's edge. The barrier flashed and rang like the bass note of a strumstick, and Sirius rebounded, falling back into the water.

"Let me try," Serendipity laughed, as he spluttered back to the path. She edged up along the path, then began speaking in *derkesthai*. Sirius activated his translator, and caught the end: " . . . *by confirmation code Third Falling Lothi Leaf of the Second Red Branched Bough.*"

Serendipity hopped through, with a little yelp when she landed, and spun to face them. Sirius noticed that the blue light inside gave her mane of rainbow hair the appearance of irregular light and dark stripes. *"And these are my friends, my allies,"* she said. *"Let them through."*

Sirius gripped the tilted edge of the door and leaned through the gap. Nothing barred his way; moments later, Leonid followed. Sirius gaped: the force field literally did stop the pond midair, and he could clearly see the thinkfish wriggling in the greenish water.

Despite the force field, debris had gotten into the spaceport, choking its floor with mud, leaves and branches. They picked their way toward the Beacon rising before them through the cavernous roof. At its base, the skyscraper-sized spire narrowed to a slender tip.

Sirius swallowed. Just meters overhead, the kinetic energy of a collapsed star was pouring into that antenna. Flickering foxfire rippled over it, building up to a silent crescendo, then crackling over the giant spheres and cylinders of the receiver like slow-motion lightning.

"I thought the Beacon had been signaling all these years," Serendipity said. Much of the equipment was burned out, but emergency lights glowed a deep red. "It was just the emission spire, echoing the tensor shock, every time the black hole entered the system."

"At least we'll have power," Sirius said. "If anything's working, that is."

"A Beacon's robust," Leonid said, inspecting some loading equipment, which seemed partially active. "That much I know. But most of the other circuitry seems fried. I bet everyone who was stranded here got eaten by those monsters out there."

"Will the shield keep them out?" Sirius said.

"If the spaceport was still conscious, maybe," Serendipity said, touching a panel. It looked whole, but remained dark. "As it is, no central will, running on reflexes . . . no."

She glanced at Leonid, then quickly looked away; Leonid was still also stealing glances. Sirius fumed: they *were* flirting. But even he had to admit she looked even more beautiful with her hair frazzled in every color, the lighter threads highlighting the shape of her huge mane.

But she also looked hurt, tired, beaten down—and so painfully, painfully sad.

"Now we know why this system was left fallow," she said.

«My parents, have you seen them?» asked the voice of a child in Sirius's ear.

Leonid yelped, the voice was so close—and when Sirius did too, he realized the voice was translated. Leonid followed the arrows of his targeting indicator and found the voice came from a stand of wires. Hiding in them was a scared alien child with yellow skin and turquoise hair, pointed ears and long switching tail, wearing little more than a ripped tarpaulin.

The same boy that he'd shot back in the rigging of *Independence*.

«My parents, hunting they went, for food,» the translator in Leonid's comm cowl said, struggling to keep up with the boy's speech. The child hugged himself, shivering, leaning on a loose pole for support. «This place, there is little edible. My parents, they never came back.»

Leonid stepped forward, starting to speak—and the boy's eyes widened.

«You!» he said, flinching back. «You . . . you killed me!»

"It's right enough, it's right enough," Serendipity said, extending her hand to Leonid to stay back. She murmured something to the boy in *derkesthai*, the Dresanian language, and pulled something from her satchel. «Just woke up? Still hungry? Remember this? You can finish it.»

The boy stepped forward tentatively, then took the sandwich and ate eagerly. Serendipity adjusted the boy's tarp . . . and then looked over at Leonid, her face drained of color.

"Nanotech trees and inexplicable resurrections?" Serendipity said. "Now I really know why this place was left fallow."

Leonid opened his mouth, but Serendipity shook her head to discourage questions, and they watched the boy eat in silence. After a minute, Serendipity touched her forehead.

«A question, young one,» she said, still in *derkesthai*. «What are you called?»

Leonid clucked impatiently. "More importantly, what happened here?" he asked, with a sidelong glance at Serendipity. "Why was this place abandoned?"

"Let the boy talk," Sirius said. He paused as their helms finished babbling Leonid's translated questions. After they finished, he said: "Go on, kid. What's your story?"

«Norylan is my name,» the boy said. «My parents, they were settlers. When the dark sun rose, they went for help. Their ship crashed, then they died. After that, things were hard. My parents, they went for food, and never came back. Since then, it has just been me.»

"Wait . . . Norylan's parents died, *then* went for food?" Leonid said.

"After being resurrected," Sirius said, "just like him?"

"What did your parents come here for, Norylan?" Sirius asked.

The boy cringed and looked away. «The soulforge, I'm not supposed to talk about it.»

"To experiment with nanotechnological reincarnation," Serendipity filled in quietly. "Commonplace now, but highly illegal back when they came here. That's why they picked this remote world; that's why they never called for help. They didn't want to be killed."

"Your people would really kill this boy just because . . . because he . . ." Leonid said, realizing how bizarre it sounded, "because he came back from the dead?"

"Not now," Serendipity said. "But back then, we'd been through wars with group minds and nanomachines, and had all sorts of taboos. Today, people like Norylan's parents are regarded as heroes. Someone was probably covering for them when they stopped paying the mortgage."

"When was that?" Sirius said.

"Ten thousand years ago," Serendipity said.

"He's been here, alone, for ten thousand years?"

"And probably starving all that time," Serendipity said. "Norylan's brain is instrumented with nanomachines, stone knives and bearskins versions of the ones I have. Every time he gets killed, there's a capacitive flash that transmits his last memories back to a soulforge here."

«It's worse than she said,» Norylan said. «Sometimes I live for years. But I can't reset my pattern. Every time I screw up and die, all I am, all I've learned is stuffed back into this child. I stumble around traumatized for decades, dying every few weeks until I find my wits again.»

"If he comes back all the time . . . then what happened to his parents?" Sirius said. He looked as pale as if he'd run out of oxygen. "They came back at least once—"

"I don't know," Serendipity said, rising. "Let's go find out."

The soulforge was deep within the spaceport. The outside looked like a cargo bay to Sirius. Inside, however, was a decked-out lab, battered and dirty from long use. Banks of flickering lights and time-worn switches guarded a glowing shaft filled with blue fluid.

Sirius stared in admiration at the tall, humming cylinder. "It's still running."

"It's Dresanian equipment," Serendipity said, inspecting a glowing, floating orb she'd pulled from her satchel. Inside was a tiny tree with vibrant green leaves and sparkling blue moss at its base, but she called it a brainsai and treated it like a scanner. "And in good condition."

"Even after the tensor shock?" Sirius asked, inspecting grimy keyboards, their common keys worn shiny after centuries of use. In places *Independence* looked the same, but after a while the switches broke and had to be replaced. But here . . . "After hundreds of tensor shocks—"

«The soulforge is a failsafe against death,» the boy said. Suddenly he sounded far older, far more mature. «My parents, they designed weatherproofing against every calamity.»

"And trained you to maintain it," Serendipity said.

«Yes,» the boy said. «It was my first duty.»

"All alone for all these years," Sirius said, looking at Leonid.

"And always starving," Leonid said, looking back at Sirius. "God—"

«Most of the life-forms of this world are inedible,» the boy said. «The soulforge feeds off the crustal plug. It can rebuild me from atoms, but the food was all on their spacecraft—»

"We can fix that," Serendipity said, pulling a small orange orb out of her satchel. It had a pebbly surface and smelled delicious. "Care to resurrect enough satsumas for the four of us?"

The boy stared at it, then laughed, a strange kind of hooting laugh. He seized the fruit and ran off to a bank of equipment, which hummed and glowed to life.

"Ruggedized equipment survived here for ten thousand years," Serendipity said. "And so did this boy, with no more than eight or nine years of experience, and no food, being reanimated over and over again. God, I can't imagine that beastly treadmill . . . but he survived."

"Starving to death . . . forever," Sirius said. The thought made him sick. "Your point?"

"I," Serendipity said, plucking her brainsai from the air, "can make this world work."

"You?" Sirius said incredulously. "Is that your job, fixing planets?"

"My . . . job?" Serendipity said. "I'm a little young to have a job—"

"You have crew rotations where you come from, right?" Leonid said.

"Crew rotations?" Serendipity said. "Once on a summer cruise, once, yes—"

"A summer cruise?" Sirius said. "What's a—so you don't have a regular duty?"

"I'm only nineteen," she said. "I've a dozen years of schooling before I'm eligible—"

"You don't expect to do real work until you're thirty?" Leonid said.

"You're useless."

"I am not useless," Serendipity said with a snort. "I've studied history extensively—"

"So you've read a few books," Sirius said, "and expect to be able to rebuild a world."

"Yes," Serendipity said. She reached into her satchel. "I've been studying for months—"

"Oh, that's going to help us," Leonid said.

"Me studying something for months is like you studying something for years," she said. "Seriously. I'm half made of nanomachines with a computer woven through my nervous system, with access to an education system seven centuries ahead of yours." She held up a computer pad. "And I'm a historian. I've been planning to run away for months. I studied every new colony for four million light years . . . and fed them all into here."

"That's why you grabbed your satchel," Sirius said, staring enviously at the little pad. If he guessed right, it was a universal encyclopedia, another Dresanian treasure, containing as much Lore as a thousand ships. No wonder she'd gone back for it. "For your brittanica."

"Well, that and the sandwich," Serendipity said. Hearing that bit of forethought, Sirius found his estimation of her go up a notch. "The boy said there was little edible here, and if an Andiathar has trouble eating then humans won't fare too well either," she said—then scowled. "What we really need is my macdonald . . . but it's in my saddlebags."

"Which are in the camp," Leonid said. "That's why Toren wouldn't let you take them."

"So . . ." Sirius said. "You're gonna rebuild this world. And you've studied a gajillion colonies. Do they give you any bright ideas on how three and a half refugees can do that before being swarmed by Toren's goons when the gasbags chase them up here?"

Serendipity lowered the book. "Toren's a problem," she said. "I'm not worried about him coming here just yet—his best bet is to reboard *Independence* once the radiation dies down. I'm worried about what he's going to do to all the women on your ship. What the hell happened?"

"Leonid broke up with his girlfriend," Sirius said hotly. Leonid glared, but said nothing.

"Okay, good to know," Serendipity said, almost immediately blushing, and Sirius snorted. "But you have to give me more than that. An ancient ship, no adults, crashing—"

"*Independence* had a huge crew," Leonid said. "Three hundred forty-seven, three-fifty when we picked up Sirius and his parents adrift with a fried glider . . . what, five years ago?"

"Sounds right," Sirius said. "Those were the good times, when I first met Tori, and . . . anyway, the crew of *Independence* was wonderful to us. They kept looking for parts to fix my parents' flyer. And then, about four months later, we salvaged this old probe and . . ."

"And let loose a disease," Leonid said. "It killed almost everyone from thirteen to fifty."

"That's Halcyan's," Serendipity said, leaning back. "Near murdered my family—"

"We know what it was," Sirius said. "Almost killed my parents too, but they survived. They *survived*. We contained the disease to the cargo module, purged it, even set up a special pod for the survivors. But it left the ship so weak, so vulnerable, that when pirates attacked—"

Sirius swallowed, eyes welling up. He stood up and turned away.

Behind him, Leonid spoke quietly. "They killed the rest," he said. "They ambushed one of our survey recces and came back to claim the ship. His parents suffocated to death when the pirates pulled the plug on life support for the quarantine module."

"We got them, though," Sirius said, folding his arms. It hurt so much to think about his parents being gone, even after all this time—but at least he had the memories of making the pirates pay to console him. "We showed them—"

"My grandfather mobilized us kids," Leonid said. "We fought them off with his old collection of pistols and one remaining blaster. Surprised the heck out of them once, then again when he evacuated the cargo module with them in it. Since then, it was just us."

Serendipity swallowed. "Everything I've done seems so . . . small."

"And you think you can help us?" Sirius said, putting his hands on his hips.

"Yes," Serendipity said, cocking her head. "First by asking . . . what are we going to do?"

«Eat lunch!» the Andiathar boy said, bearing a whole basket of satsumas.

Sirius hadn't known how hungry he was until satsuma juice was dribbling down his chin.

They made a little picnic next to the soulforge, sitting cross-legged around Serendipity's glowing sphere, eating her strange orange fruit. Clearly not natural, it came apart into juicy and delicious slices, wrapped with a slightly bitter peel that Serendipity instructed them all to eat.

"Infused with elixirs," she said. "But we're going to need more sources of food."

"Clothing is covered," Leonid said. "At least for us—these softsuits are pretty tough."

Leonid was staring at Serendipity, more openly than usual, but then Sirius realized he was staring at her bolero and wraps. They'd laundered themselves back into a fresh-pressed state, so new it looked like it was the first time she'd worn them. Sirius looked at Leonid, who nodded.

"I'm guessing," Leonid said, "gear isn't a problem for you either, Serendipity."

"Toren has most of it, in my saddlebags," she said, scowling. "But I'll manage."

"We have shelter," Sirius said, wiping his mouth. "But we need to secure it."

"Why?" Serendipity asked.

"Because Toren is going to come and take it," Lenonid said. "Sooner than you think."

Serendipity glared, then tossed her satsuma back into the basket.

"*Dashpat*," she said. "What the hell is his damage?"

"He's bitter. He was training to be an engineer, until Andromeda took the Engine Module and kicked all the boys out." Leonid said. "This was about three years ago. I negotiated with her for the Halfway Boys, him and Sirius, to stay, but when his growth spurt hit—"

"She kicked him out," Sirius said hotly. "Now Toren hates all the girls—"

"Halfway Boy," Serendipity said slowly. "I don't like the flavor of that word—"

"Oh, it's got a nasty history," Sirius said, voice filled with venom. "Back in the dawn of the Frontier, when passengers were worth less than the crew who could keep the ships flying, a halfway person meant someone who got half rations of food . . . or air."

"That's ancient history," Leonid protested, avoiding Serendipity's eyes. "We never did that. I forbade partial rationing. Even after the mutiny, everyone always got their minimums. It's nothing to do with rations now. When the adult crew was on the ship, Halfway Boy just meant a boy of age who hadn't yet passed the crew test."

"But when Andromeda split the ship into boys and girls, it picked up a new meaning," Sirius said, glaring at Leonid, who looked away, ashamed. "It came to mean someone who didn't count as a 'real' boy—because they didn't like girls."

Serendipity's lip curled, eyes staring off in the distance with increasing anger.

"And there were just the two of us, me and Toren," Sirius said, staring into the basket. There were maybe a couple dozen satsumas in it. "Statistically only one out of twelve crewmen is homosexual. There were twenty-eight boys on *Independence*. Do the math."

Serendipity gaped at Leonid. "They were gay, so you sent them to the girls? What?"

"To protect them," Leonid said.

"Mostly from you," Sirius said hotly. "The boys picked on us, but Leonid was a beast—"

"I am so sorry," Leonid said. "I can only say that so many times—"

"You have no idea what it's like to be one of the only gay kids on a ship this size."

"Yes I do," Leonid said. "Yes, I do. It's a little higher than one in twelve, Sirius."

Sirius stared at him. So everything he thought he'd seen in Leonid . . . was real.

"But . . . wait," Sirius said, "you were . . . with Andromeda, with Serendipity—"

"Hey," Serendipity said. "We—"

"Sirius," Leonid said. "I'm bisexual. I could pass. It was easier that way."

Sirius closed his eyes. "Dammit," he said. "All that time you were picking on us—"

"Hiding in plain sight kept me out of trouble. Toren's doing the same dance now," Leonid said. "Butching up so the other boys will pretend to ignore what they know. Do you blame him? Once you get that . . . that pack going, you can't stop it—"

"Because you're doing everything wrong," Serendipity said. "Segregation is a recipe for prejudice. Your brains naturally build up snap judgments about other groups. You root them out by getting close, intimate, extended experience with people who are noticeably different—"

"I didn't split the ship," Leonid said. "It was Andromeda and Artemyst—"

"If you were Captain," Serendipity said, "it was your responsibility to rejoin it."

"Yes, it's all my fault, I know that," Leonid said. "We split, and we were both so angry, and she closed off the Module, but I thought I had to be the bigger, ah, man, and let things cool off. Truth is, I was just cutting her slack that I shouldn't have—"

"It was mutiny," Sirius said. "Toren wanted to storm the Module right away."

"And he was probably right," Serendipity said.

"And he knows it," Leonid said. "But now, three years later, with the ship wrecked, he's not going to be satisfied with I told you so. Believe me—he was my right hand man. At first I did it to protect him, but now . . . he's the biggest, and strongest, and has the blaster under his belt—"

"And thinks he should lead," Serendipity said.

"And he thinks he should punish the girls for their sins," Sirius said. "Andromeda split the boys and the girls. Leonid was planning to turn the tables and lock the girls out of the Engine Module. But Toren hates them. Who knows what he'll do to them—"

"We can't let this go on," Serendipity said quietly. "We can't survive here on satsumas. Your ship's done. Monsters rule the skies. We have to get the hell out of here. And not just us. All of us—we can't let Toren find some cave to live in and drag all the girls into a living hell."

"I don't see how the three of us can stop it," Leonid said. "We can't beat Toren—"

"What are you talking about?" Serendipity said. "Why do we need to 'beat' him?"

"We can't take on the whole crew, and we can't get them to follow us. Using weapons on each other is forbidden, so we have a sparring tradition—" and here Serendipity hissed "—and you saw what happened when Sirius tried. Me, I haven't beat him since he turned sixteen."

"Me neither," Sirius said, "and I was trained by bounty hunters. He's just too tough."

"What we've got to do is hide out, hole up, and wait for it to blow over," Leonid said, staring at a satsuma. "If we can find something Toren wants, like shelter or food supplies, maybe we can negotiate with him, get him to agree to ease up a bit on the girls—"

"What?" Serendipity said. "No! We can't let him set up a patriarchal system! Once they get started they last forever. The last time gender equality collapsed in human culture, it took eleven thousand years before women got decent rights again—"

"You're worried about the girls's rights?" Sirius said.

"I'm worried about the system Toren wants to set up," Serendipity said. "Egalitarianism is like diamond. It's the strongest natural structure—but it can burn away to vapor, or crumble to black dust, and when it's gone, it stays gone. Tolerance is only metastable."

"What?" Leonid asked.

"We all love living in a system that's tolerant, but it only has a perceived stability," Serendipity said. "You have to maintain tolerance, watch it, nurture it . . . or it crumbles."

"Egalitarianism? Nurturing tolerance? You're worried about social issues in another camp? You're crazy," Leonid said. "We can't worry about what Toren's doing out there. We have to worry about him coming here—"

"He's right," Sirius said, glancing between them, worried. Leonid got it. Serendipity clearly didn't. She could think, she could plan, she even clearly had some spacer training—but she didn't have any real experience. "Serendipity, we've got to focus on survival—"

Serendipity stood up.

"Twelve thousand, two hundred and forty-three," Serendipity said. "That's how many *human* colonies I surveyed before I came here. I know how they succeed—and how they fail. And they fail when someone puts survival above what's right—and it sticks. Forever."

"So tell us," Leonid said, glancing at Sirius, "what do you think is right?"

"Everyone is ultimately equal," she said. "If not in ability, in rights. Each creature has life. Each creature makes choices. And each creature should stand or fall on their choices, not on things they can't change. No creature should stand above another!"

Sirius clapped. "Very stirring," he said, feeling a wry smile creep onto his face: listening to this crazy pampered half-horse girl talk about ideals actually left him feeling a bit inspired. But just a bit—and they had serious work to do. "But we're talking about survival—"

"We are not on a lifeboat," Serendipity said. "We're standing at the foot of a Beacon of the Intergalactic Alliance, the largest civilization in the history of the universe. We're at the doorstep of its homeworld, Dresan, just fourteen thousand light years away—"

"Fourteen thousand light years—"

"Is a day trip," Serendipity said. "We are not isolated. We might be just off the spacelanes—but we are off the spacelanes. That has a consequence. Space is really big. No one will stumble onto us unintentionally. This place went ten thousand years between visits. For all practical purposes, whatever gets started here will keep happening forever."

"Forever," Leonid said, staring at Norylan. "You're really not exaggerating."

"No," Serendipity said. "But if we want to stop it, all we have to do is call for help."

"How?" Sirius said. "Wait for your circuits to heal, then you . . . just think 'SOS?'"

"No," Serendipity said. "We're atop the Plume, a huge column of gas. We need the eight-centimeter transmitter in my survival kit. It will reach hundreds of light years, enough to get some kind of aid, but it's got to be unpacked and the transmitter physically set up—"

"Let me guess," Sirius said. "You need it, so it's in your saddlebags—"

"In the camp," Leonid said. "We'd have to go through Toren."

"Exactly," Serendipity said. "That's our choice. Confront Toren, get to a transmitter, and call for rescue—or sit on our hands, and let Toren decide the future of every human on this world for the next ten thousand years. Sell the girls into slavery and scare the 'Halfways' into hiding."

"All the while pretending he's not a Halfway Boy himself," Sirius said.

"Oh, that's never happened in history," Serendipity said.

Sirius scowled. "Still, he's tough. Can we use the Beacon instead?"

"No," she said. "It's an older design—it could take months to discharge the power it accumulated in the surge, and what if there are aftershocks? It could kill me unless we dig up an induction fuse. No. I need my transmitter from my survival kit and its booster."

"Pity we can't use the link in *Independence*," Sirius said.

"The drive burned out," Leonid said. "How do we know the link wasn't fried too?"

"We shut it down before we dropped from hyperspace," Sirius said. "Standard procedure. Power will flow through a link if it's active, whether it's tensor shock or gliderfield collapse. Shut the link down, and it's just a hunk of matter that the shockwave passes by—what?"

"Treasures in the attic," Serendipity said, with a happy grin. "I've been on a ship like *Independence* before—*Deliverance*, when I was six. Some function my grandmother dragged me to. Even then, I dreamed of becoming a historian, and it's a famous colony ship. Naturally I wandered off to the historical exhibits . . . and touched all the display consoles."

"Naturally," Sirius said sarcastically. "How does that help us?"

"I'm laced through and through with nanomachines, and they're always learning," Serendipity said. "When I put my hand on those consoles . . . I downloaded the history of *Deliverance*, and all its original schematics. I think, with some work, I'm compatible."

"Even if a lot of the circuits are fried," Leonid said, "I bet the workshops are not."

"Of course we should use *Independence*," Sirius said, sitting straight up. "It's got an enormous emission blade. It decouples naturally from the glidercore when we pop to normal space. Attach a hyperlink, and we could call for help through nine meters of hyperspace—"

"Best idea yet," Leonid said. "Still . . . we'll have to get past Toren."

"Better than going head to head in camp," Serendipity said. "Still . . . I can take him."

"What?" Sirius said. "Are you serious?"

"I'm not saying we go in there swinging fists," Serendipity said. "But he thinks that might makes right, correct? If he catches us, I'll challenge him. The rest of the boys weren't comfortable following him. I could see that. If they know someone could defend them—"

Sirius stood up.

"And that someone is you?" Sirius said, gauging her. She seemed a bit rattled by the attention. "I trained Tori to fight, back when boys like Leonid were bullying him all round the innards of the ship once the adults died. No one's beaten him since he hit puberty—"

"I'm sure you trained him well," Serendipity said, "but it's nothing like what I've—"

"Oh, come on!" Sirius said. "You saw him! He's a monster! You watched three people take him on and fail. And you? You think you could fight him? You couldn't even beat me."

He punched her arm, hard.

"Stop it, this is pointless. I'm not fighting you," Serendipity said.

Sirius laughed and hit her again, harder this time.

Again she said, "Stop it!" Hurt and confusion spread over her face. She raised her hands feebly, fingers loose and forearms angled as if to defend herself, and Leonid got up and tried to intervene, pushing the two of them apart.

"You think Tori will stop just because you say 'stop it'?" Sirius said, ducking Leonid and punching her again, harder and harder, fists glancing off her protesting hands and striking her arms and shoulders. "You think he'll cut you a break just because you're a girl—"

He swung for her chin—and her hoof popped out and nailed his groin.

Lights flashed behind Sirius's eyes. He doubled over. He had a sudden vision of a huge knobbly knee coming straight for his face—and then everything went black, just for a moment. When he came to, his cheek was pressed to the deck by a booted hoof on his skull.

"I said, stop it," Serendipity said quietly. Sirius heard Leonid groan, and opened his eyes to see Leonid down on one knee, also doubled over, his arm twisted up crazy behind him by her deceptively gentle hand. "Both of you. And if Toren doesn't stop when I ask . . . he'll be sorry."

It took five minutes of talking for the two of them to calm Serendipity down enough for her to let them go. Sirius cradled his head gingerly as he stood up. Leonid had briefly struggled, and Sirius had felt a pop: he was sure Serendipity's boot had broken the bones of his skull.

"Don't worry," Serendipity said, peering at Sirius with a pair of round spectacles. Behind their dark purple mirrored lenses, light flickered, casting patterns on her face. "It's just a linear fracture. It should heal nicely on its own."

"I was just trying to stop it," Leonid said, feeling his arm. "You didn't have to—"

"Those who in quarrels interpose," she said, "must often wipe a bloody nose."

"So you can fight," Sirius said, feeling the side of his head. "You're an expert."

"No, no," Serendipity said. "I just know the basics. I hate fighting."

"Like, what basics?" Sirius said. "What are you good at?"

"Well, midrange for selfdef, of course," Serendipity said, as if her words were the most obvious things in the world, "plus traditional grappling and striking. Beyond hand to hand, I've only got proficiency in knife and staff. Never took zeegee and my sniping is terrible—"

"You learned all that?" Sirius said. "Before or after going into the space marines?"

"My grandmother invented her own martial art," she said. "A lot was expected of me."

"This is what I was trying to tell you before we ever hit this dogforsaken rock," Leonid said, glaring at Sirius. "You really don't know how tough the Dresanians are. They have every advantage. They're all immortal. They have centuries to get like this."

"It shouldn't take centuries, but it is why we can spend up to thirty years in school: to learn how to recreate our culture," Serendipity said. "Dresanian citizens are *civilization seeds*. I know how to throw a punch or set a bone, cook a meal or land a spacecraft—"

"And you're just nineteen," Sirius said. "What will you be like at a hundred?"

"Oh, Lord," Serendipity said. "That's what I'm going to have to do, isn't it?"

"What?" Sirius said.

"I ran away to free myself from my grandmother," Serendipity said, looking at her fists. "But if we want to survive . . . I'm going to have to *become* her."

Serendipity decided they should leave at parentnoon, when the sun was down but the gas giant still loomed full and bright. Technically, parentnoon was just solar midnight, but at its peak, the broad disk of the giant was almost as bright as Halfway's more distant star. The giant would wane as Halfway Point spun round it, giving them a chance to reach *Independence* in near darkness now, rather than waiting thirty-six hours for the next solar eclipse.

Even in the shimmering auroral gloom, the shift in topography was stark: behind them, bare jagged mountains scraped the gas giant's clouds; around them scrub Dresanian bushes grew on sloping hillsides . . . and beyond, a forest of glowing balloons loomed over a vast plain.

As they grew closer, Dresanian brush ended and rough earth began. Creatures like bees buzzed around the slope. A raucous flock of chirping things like birds wheeled about, landed as a flock—then turned themselves inside out, revealing flowers which the buzzers pollinated.

"If you've got a force field, activate it," Sirius said, unlatching his helmet wedge and flipping it up and over to seal his head. He lifted the edge of a flower: the creature had planted itself, roots digging into the earth. "You don't want spores like that rooting in your lungs."

"Agreed," Serendipity said, tapping her shield brooch—and pulling out a scarf and wrapping it about her mouth, just in case. Leonid, Sirius, and Norylan stared at her, and she shrugged. "Shield filters work best against microscopic objects."

Soon *Independence* loomed over them, a hulking shadow in the mists lit faintly by its running lights. A ghosting of bioluminescence lit the mounds of earth thrown up around it, like frozen waves, making Serendipity feel like they were rats swimming towards a giant buoy.

"Didn't the running lights die when the glider blew?" Sirius asked.

"Radiation has died down," Serendipity said. "They might have reboarded the ship, started to effect repairs—"

"Or at least posted guards," Sirius said.

"Well, that's just great," Leonid said. "Any thoughts on how to get past Toren?"

Serendipity called up the schematic of *Independence* in her metaspace viewer and studied it. "It looks like our best bet," she said, "is to make for the opposite slope, climb the torn radiator panel to the Engine Module proper, and board through one of the service airlocks."

"I was about to suggest the same thing," Sirius said. "That will get us to cargo control."

"You have the schematic of *Independence* wired into your head too?" Leonid said.

"No," Serendipity said, finding the emission blade, a katana sixty meters long, set in an induction housing atop the Engine Module. "But I've got a program called a solver that's great with mappings. It's projecting *Independence's* refits onto *Deliverance's* schematics."

"Fantastic," Sirius said. "Maybe that will help us with repairs. Let's go."

They skulked around the ship, carefully crossing the shifting earth of the impact rut while avoiding direct line-of-sight with the camp. A couple of bored boys threw rocks at the base of the ship: perhaps Toren had posted them there as guards once the radiation had died down.

From the opposite slope, *Independence* hulked in the mist like a castle. Its bent radiator panel stretched toward them like a crazy-tilt drawbridge, made of black metal shingles a meter long. They climbed onto the panel quietly, trying not to attract the attention of the guards.

Halfway up, Serendipity's hooves slipped. Leonid and Sirius caught her centimeters from the edge. They froze there, in silence, struggling with her weight, the guards far below. Then tiny little Norylan scampered down, planted his hand-like feet in the shingles, and pulled her back up.

«Thanks, young one,» Serendipity whispered. «Don't wear yourself out.»

"How can he possibly be that strong?" Leonid muttered.

"Andiathar have strength," Serendipity murmured. "Humans have endurance."

At the bend of the panel, the four of them hopped over cracked shingles. Then the radiator angled up steeper, and they climbed up slowly on hands and knees. Finally they reached the twisted knot of metal where the radiator panel had been half torn out of its housing.

There was no room for all of them to stand, so Sirius climbed up on the narrow ridge of the housing, tapping at the airlock controls while the rest of them waited on a mammoth metal drum. Serendipity cocked her head: the drum was a giant motor, something her solver identified as the radiator panel's "rotator servo." It was hard to believe the giant slanted bridge they'd just climbed could actually move. Finally, on his third try, Sirius got the airlock open.

The grey metal of the outer hull was behind them, and they were now in machine-lined corridors, once white, covered in centuries of graffiti. Only the equipment and rigging retained their colors: climbing handles in orange, circuit conduits in blue, warning stripes in red.

After a long slog up a nearly vertical service corridor, during which Serendipity blessed each push-up and chin-up her grandmother had ever forced on her, they climbed into the main cargo control chamber. It stretched at least ten meters up away from them.

"This place is a wreck," Serendipity said. It smelled of burnt wires, stained with soot, and littered with broken pieces from the glider. She inspected a piece of dangling wire . . . and found it sound. "But it's actually less damaged than I expected. I think we can do this."

"The auxiliary helm is up there," Sirius said, scowling up into the now nearly vertical shaft of cargo control. In normal gravity, the helm was clearly reachable; in zero-gee, it wouldn't be a problem either. But like this, it was inaccessible. "Maybe on Leonid's shoulders—"

"Even on her shoulders, with her on hind legs," Leonid said, "you'd barely reach."

«I could get up there,» Norylan said. «But I don't know what to do.»

"Maybe we don't need to reach it," Serendipity said, lifting on her hind legs to inspect an instrumented groove in the ceiling, which rose above them like a tilted wall. "This runs the length of the induction housing. My wireless is burnt, but I should be able to plug in—"

But when Serendipity pulled a tensor filament from the back of her neck, she couldn't make it reach—and couldn't quite guide it either. She hopped down, Sirius clambered up onto her shoulders, and they tried again. When she slipped, Leonid grabbed her about her barrel.

"Wandering!" Serendipity said, bopping him on the head with a hoof.

"Hey, I'm trying to help here—" Leonid protested, shifting his grip.

"Would you two stop flirting," Sirius said, trying to thread the wire, "and stand still—"

"Just finish the hookup," Serendipity said. A light went off behind her eyes as her filament found the port on the induction housing and began negotiating a connection. "Thank you. I'm going to set down slowly—keep play on the filament."

When she carefully touched down, Sirius handed her a loop of the filament and climbed off her shoulders. Serendipity started rattling off components, and quickly Leonid and Sirius found the equipment she needed to wire together the rest of the circuit.

"They'll notice when I send a signal, won't they?" Serendipity asked.

"Sending a message using the emission blade?" Sirius said. "In atmosphere, under that black sun, with this metric gradient? It will light like a torch, and we should expect company. Maybe we should send the signal and run. How long will it take for help to arrive?"

"Depends on if *she's* in the shower," Serendipity said, wrapping the filament with an induction fuse. Then she looked up to see Sirius staring at her bug-eyed. "Maybe thirty to forty minutes . . . or maybe three to four days. Depends on who's on call, what's up."

"Then we'll have to wait, not run," Leonid said, casually resting his hand on his gun butt. "We need to be close to the source if the signal succeeds, and we need to stay here to try again if it fails. If Toren shows up . . . he has three choices. Help us call for help, mount a challenge . . . or risk a firefight."

Serendipity stared at him. "Okay," she said, playing out the filament. "I'm ready."

Sirius wired up the hyperlink and Serendipity prepared the message; Leonid stood by a porthole, watching the camp while he kept the cargo control door covered. By the time Leonid called out that he saw movement from the camp, they were ready—and sent the signal.

Independence's batteries discharged. The filament glowed. Serendipity felt a shiver of current, only the tiniest fraction of the energy coursing through the circuit, damped by the fuse. Leonid leaned away from the black circle quickly as a bright flash lit up the porthole.

Within minutes cargo control began filling up—two boys and a slip of a girl who'd been working in the cargo section, a larger troupe of boys from the camp, Andromeda—and then Toren, who swaggered into the room with a bruised and battered Artemyst on his arm.

"What the hell have you done now?" Toren said with disgust, seeing the four of them. He squinted when he saw Norylan, but quickly he recovered his swagger. "I thought I told you to run for the hills and never come back."

"Actually, you wished us luck," Serendipity said, backing up. She even played up her limp a little bit, though the frog of her hoof was nearly healed. Toren soon had her cornered in what had been the forward wall of the cargo control chamber. "But I'm done running."

"Oh are you now?" Toren said, pulling his arm out of Artemyst's shell-shocked grip and pushing her away. He glanced at Sirius and Leonid, who stepped up to either side of Serendipity, grim, arms folded. "Well, if you want to stay, we're going to live by my rules—"

"No, we're not," Serendipity said. "This isn't the Frontier. This is an Allied world—"

"The hell it is," Toren said. "You chased us off our homeworld, but not this one—"

"I didn't chase you anywhere," Serendipity said, hands raised. "We both ran together. Your ancestors didn't flee the Dresanians. They fled Halcyan's Syndrome, the disease that ravaged Earth and nearly killed my great-to-the-nth grandmother, the First Centaur—"

"So?" Toren said. "What does that have to do with anything?"

"She didn't start out as the First Centaur. Her disease made her experiment with genetics. She wouldn't have remade herself without it—and I wouldn't be who I am," she said. "We're children of the same war. Without it, you wouldn't be here, and I wouldn't have these legs."

"We're not the same at all," he growled, stomping towards her. "Your ancestors stayed and let the Dresanians turn you into things. Our ancestors made the human choice: we didn't let the place change us; we left and explored until we found someplace better—"

"You're a spacer, master of the skies, and I respect that," Serendipity said, leaning away deferentially, so her upper torso angled back over her horsey body. "But I was raised in a gravity well, with all four feet planted on the ground. So there's one thing I don't do."

"What's that?" Toren said, looming over her.

"Hit like a girl," Serendipity said, unfolding an explosive right hook on his chin.

Toren toppled backwards, arms splayed out. Two boys leapt upon

Serendipity, but she knocked them down with two quick punches, then spun round, barrel knocking aside two more that tried to leap on her from behind. When she turned, Toren was rising. She drew her knife.

"Weaponsmaster!" she said. "Hold our steel. We have a challenge on our hands."

Toren stared at her from his sprawl—then snorted, drew his gun, and tossed it to Beetle. Serendipity tossed the knife. Toren levered to his feet, shifting, tensing, as a knot of boys closed around them, shouting; Serendipity relaxed, eyes on him, taking a deep calming breath.

Toren screamed and leapt upon her.

This wasn't like aikido practice, or a karate match, or even a cage match, all of which had rules, a certain polite rhythm to them. Toren had no rules, he just roared and came windmilling at her, a tornado of fists and kicks, always on her, shrugging her blows off, never giving up.

With someone this tough, Serendipity had no choice but to take him apart.

For all his strength, Serendipity could punch harder, so she pushed him back, out of grappling distance to the midrange, where she could land really solid jabs and kicks. He led left, so she started nailing his left thigh with fore roundkicks, each time feinting for his ribs, then punishing the muscle. Soon he started to limp, to favor the leg—then drop his hands.

Serendipity kicked his extended hand, hard. Toren howled and twisted back, hobbling. Serendipity followed, rearing, kicking his hands down with her forelegs as she sprang forward with her hind legs. While he staggered, she seized his head—and kneed his face.

Toren stumbled backwards, dazed but not out, and in that brief pause Serendipity felt the opening for her cage training. She stayed reared up, nimbly pushing his hands aside with her forelegs. That surprised him, and when he put all of his attention on fending her legs off, she snapped one hand out, cupping it behind his head, controlling his movement.

Then she really started punching.

"This whatcha want?" she snarled between punches, between breaths. She felt adrenaline surging within her, ancient fight-or-flight reflexes struggling to take over, but she fought it, trying as much to control herself as to control Toren. "Wanna get beat t'death by a girl?"

"I'll kick your," Toren roared, trying to throw her off, "kick your ass—"

"Spent six years training," she spat, "under the greatest martial artist in history—"

Toren popped her in the chin unexpectedly, struggling to get free. "I'll eat your face—"

"Settle down," Serendipity said, jabbing in his face again, jerking him around until he was completely off balance, "or I'll throw you to the ground and *step on your head.*"

That got through to him. Toren's eyes went wide as he realized she could do it—and what it would do to him. "You wouldn't. Don't—don't you do it—"

"*Kill you?*" Serendipity asked. He jerked away, head tugging against her hand, and with the sudden jerk she felt her nostrils flare. "I can do it," she snapped, punching him, even as she was struggling to get control. Blood flew as she smacked him again. "I *will* do it—"

Then Leonid's arm was grabbing hers. "Don't," he said. "He's not worth it—"

With that touch on her arm Serendipity realized just how angry she was. She'd seen this: even with trained fighters who were good friends, sparring could turn real ugly, real animal—and this was far more than sparring. Serendipity let out a breath, trying to calm herself.

But the intervention made Toren struggle more—and then Artemyst grabbed his arm. "Stop, Toren, stop," she said. "I think she means it—"

"Aren't you going to do something?" Toren screamed at his weaponbearer.

"You said stay out of challenges," Beetle said. "That you'd deal with them yourself—"

"And I have a force field," Serendipity said, arm slipping Leonid's grip and springing at Toren. "By the time Betelgeuse cracks it, I'll be scraping your brains off my hooves—"

"Dammit," Toren said. "Dammit—"

"Is this how you want it, Toren? Might makes right?" Serendipity said. "To get beaten to death by a girl and have her take over just because she's the biggest and strongest?"

Toren's bloodied eyes stared into hers. He caught her arm, trying to fend her off. They struggled, swaying there, Toren desperately giving it his all and Serendipity quietly holding back, drawing calming breaths while she matched him strength for strength.

Finally, Toren said, almost whispered, "No. That's not what I want."

"Me neither," Serendipity said, fist still poised over him. Not true:

right now, she wanted to bash Toren's head in. But no matter how much adrenaline rattled through her, she had to be better than that. The fight she'd set out to win was moral. The street brawl she'd let it turn into was anything but. "So . . . can we stop fighting?"

Toren's eyes tightened. "What do you want?"

"Respect," she said. "Not just for me. No more me versus you, boys versus girls, Allies versus Frontiersmen. No more halfway people either—everyone treated the same. All of us equals, all working together to survive."

"Of all the crazy," Toren said, flinching back from her fist. "You're crazy!"

Serendipity raised a hoof over his head. "Consider the alternative."

Toren's eyes narrowed. His muscles tightened. Slowly, he began to relax.

Then the room exploded in a flash of blue fire and a thunderclap of ice.

As the cold blue flames dissipated, Serendipity didn't even need to look to see what had happened—and *who* had arrived. The tensor fire was the remnant of a long-range teleport; the displacement thunderclap left veins of frost ice over every surface it touched.

At the center of the veins of ice, a centauress rose, layered in armor like an armadillo made of razors, bearing a double-ended scythe with black blades. "I am First Captain Porsche Lynne Kirkpatrick Saint George," her grandmother said. "Here, I am the Dresan-Murran—"

Shocked, the weaponsmaster fired his blaster. *Her* razor armor deflected the gold energy, spraying it over the room. Now burn marks were woven through the frost on the walls, everyone was screaming, and her grandmother raised her scythe, twin mirrored blades gleaming as—

"Stand down," Serendipity said. "I didn't call you here to slaughter children."

"Stand down? Really?" her grandmother said. Porsche Kirkpatrick Saint George raised one mailed hand and lifted her visor, and Serendipity saw a distorted echo of her own face with purple curls tumbling down over an arched eyebrow. "Looks like you need some help."

"No," Serendipity said, realizing how silly that sounded with the four of them struggling there. She turned her glare to Toren. His eyes flickered between Serendipity's grandmother, Serendipity—and Serendipity's fist. "I think we have it just about sorted."

They eased down gently, Serendipity slowly releasing her grip on Toren's head, her fist still poised. Then they were both standing, almost eye to eye, Toren still towering over her, but hunched, Artemyst supporting him as Leonid backed Serendipity up.

Sirius stepped between them and pushed them all just a bit farther apart.

"Who's that?" Leonid murmured. "Your younger sister?"

"No," Serendipity said. "My grandmother."

"So," Toren said, glancing between Serendipity and her grandmother, "so she—"

"She's not going to interfere," Serendipity said. Keeping her eyes locked on Toren, Serendipity raised her hand towards her grandmother. "Stay back. This is between us."

"As you wish," Porsche said.

"Alright," Toren said, locking his gaze back on her. "What do you want?"

"First I want all my stuff back," Serendipity said.

Toren blinked, shrugged. "Alright."

"Then I want you to stop treating the girls like slaves," Serendipity said. "We're—"

"You think this a war between the sexes? You think the boys are the bad guys?" Toren said. "The girls are the ones who turned on us. They tried to make us into farmers. All it would have taken is one girl to break ranks, but no. They stuck together and cost us our ship!"

"One girl?" Serendipity said. She reached out and seized the hand of a little slip of a girl, hiding behind one of the bigger ones with a raptor headdress. "Like this one? What is she, eight? How old was she when it happened, five? You're blaming her for not taking on an Amazon with a machine gun and coming over to your side?"

Toren stared, blinked. "No."

"And why'd you lump me with the girls when you met me?" Serendipity said.

"I didn't treat you like a girl," Toren said. "I treated you like what you are. An enemy—"

"An enemy? Offering aid and medicine?" Serendipity said. "Armed with little more than a self-defense stick, when all of you were packing? No. Besides—I overheard you. The other boys asked you 'what to do with the new girl'—and that's when you took me prisoner."

Serendipity flicked an ear at him, and Toren looked away.

"I know your history, Toren. The girls treated you like half a person. Thrown to the boys, you blended in to survive. You had to keep up your performance, had to make the point that no girl remained free. But that played well with the boys, so you put yourself on top—"

"It was never about me," Toren said. "It's about the survival of our species!"

"Mankind is alive and well, flourishing elsewhere, everywhere," Serendipity said.

"With four legs, quills, and rainbow hair?" Toren said. "You're not human anymore."

Serendipity glared, but Porsche laughed and turned away, inspecting a plaque on the wall of *Independence's* cargo control chamber. Serendipity's cheeks flushed. This boy had called her a monster, and her grandmother was actually mocking her.

"I'm human enough to want you all to survive," Serendipity said.

"You mean you're human enough to want to take charge," Toren said. "Okay, I treated you like dirt, but we'd just crash-landed because of those stupid—no, those mutinous girls. Someone had to get everyone moving and that someone was me—"

"It was me," Leonid said, "before you took over by force."

"It was that or let you keep shooting first and thinking later," Toren said.

"*I'm* the eldest," Leonid said. "I should have been in charge—"

"*I'm* the daughter of the Captain," Andromeda said. "I should have been in charge—"

"You are all idiots. I'm the only one who saw what needed to be done," Sirius said. Serendipity saw Toren look at him sharply, calculatingly. Sirius didn't flinch. "You all would have been dead if it weren't for me. *I* should have been in charge—"

«This is my home,» the elf boy said petulantly. «*I* should be in charge—»

Everything dissolved into talking over each other. Then Serendipity raised her voice.

"It's *my* world." Her voice boomed. "All of you are just standing on it."

Norylan looked at her in shock. «But I . . . my parents . . .»

«Your parents never finished paying the loan on that landing cradle,» Serendipity snapped, immediately regretting it when she saw the haunted look on his face. «The debt's been outstanding for ten thousand years. I bought the debt. I'm sorry, Norylan.»

"You bought it?" her grandmother said.

"You bought this world?" Toren said.

"I bought it," Serendipity said. "I spent my inheritance on it. It's my world—"

"Seren," Porsche began.

"It's my world," Serendipity repeated, "and you, Toren, docked without permission."

Toren's jaw clenched.

"Following the Protocols, now? Is that what you want?" he said, seizing Andromeda and shoving her towards Serendipity. "Then execute her. She took over our ship and forced us to crash it. She committed mutiny in violation of the Protocols. The sentence is death—"

"Is that what your Mission Commander decided?" Serendipity said, looking at Leonid. "I studied your Protocols—the Frontier is the space next door. Isn't the Frontiersman rule that the Captain doesn't have power of life or death? Only the Commander?"

Toren shifted. "Yes . . . but . . . we don't have a Commander."

"Then pick one—but until then, an execution *isn't going to happen*," Serendipity said, pulling Andromeda back and angling her body to shield her. "I'm granting Andromeda asylum—and as for the rest of you, you're under my rule as refugees without transport."

"So it's a monarchy now?" Toren said, lip curling.

"No, but this place became my responsibility when I bought that mortgage," she said. "You're holding unauthorized prisoners in Dresanian territory, and until we have a government here, *I* am the Dresan-Murran Alliance. I order you: release the girls from captivity!"

Toren straightened. "No. If you want to claim authority, then you owe us. We were a ship in distress. You had a Beacon. You owe ships access to a working landing cradle. We followed your Beacon, found no place to land—and now our ship is wrecked!"

Now Serendipity's jaw clenched. He was right. He was right . . . and it was possible.

"Right enough," she said. "But I've surveyed this ship. It will fly again. I promise you."

Toren laughed.

"Don't mock me," she said. "It may take years, but we can do it."

"With what equipment?" Toren said. "You don't have a spacedock—"

"I will," Serendipity said. "I didn't come here on a lark. I came here to start a port. We'll have to shutter it when the black sun rises, but this will be a great port. The first thing we do is flush the landing cradle. Then I charge every ship that comes here a tax—"

Toren laughed again, shaking his head.

"What?" Serendipity said. "It's my world, and I'm in charge—"

"Tell that to the indigenous population," her grandmother said.

"What indigenous population?" Serendipity said.

"The spores," Porsche said. "Surely you saw the biosphere wake after the tensor shock?"

Serendipity felt her face flush with heat. "Oh . . . shit."

"The spores," Sirius said. "Not the gasbags themselves, but their spores? What?"

"That's why this world was left fallow," Porsche said. "Right now you're seeing the first flowers of the summer of the black sun, but once the thundermounts are fully grown, this world will be swarming with intelligent spores, all competing with each other—"

"It wasn't in any of the assessments," Serendipity said. "There's no indication—"

"A couple of days of research should have picked up that—oh, *dashpat*. Because of the war a lot of that was classified," her grandmother said. "Still, you should have sent a probe or a survey team. What, did you rely on the prospectus of the investors that sold you the debt?"

Serendipity's face flushed. "But . . . it was from Gretgramama Clarice—"

"My mother?" Porsche said, with a bitter laugh. "And you believed her?"

"I did do my own research," Serendipity said, voice sounding unpleasantly petulant in her own ears. "And anything else, it-it was her duty to disclose!"

"A disclosure play?" Porsche said. "Oh, good luck collecting on that with my mother—"

"So," Sirius said, "I take it you're from what they call a dysfunctional family?"

"Oh, shattap!" Serendipity said, her voice cracking, embarrassingly, into the clan's English Enclave accent.

"Never mind," Leonid said. "What about your deal? Did you squander your inheritance?"

"No," Serendipity said firmly. "Even a patch of a world can hold a port. Right enough, Gramama, you've informed me of a possible indigenous claim, thanks, I'll have to do a Contact assessment before we do extensive development. You can be my First Contact Engineer—"

"I can't do it," her grandmother said. "And we can't stay either—we've got to evacuate *now*. Tensor pressure is worsening the deeper the black hole plunges into the system. We have to teleport back within the hour, or we'll be completely cut off for months—"

"The hell with that," Toren said decisively. "We spent centuries fleeing the Alliance and we're not going crawling back to them now with no ship, no money, no status—"

"What?" Serendipity said. "You—you can't just stay—"

"Spacers, scatter," Toren ordered, and half the children bolted, just like that. "Back to camp. Tell them to break it down and prepare to move to the new site—"

"Wait," Serendipity said, seizing his arm. "You can't just go—"

Toren glared at her. "I thought you wanted to treat us like equals," he said, nodding at her hand on his arm. She let go, and he shifted. "We're your new indigenous population now. We'll make our way here. We may not have a ship, but no spores or centaur will stop us—"

"This ship will fly again," Serendipity said. "I swear it."

Toren stared at her like she was crazy, then laughed and walked out of the control room.

———————————⟆◊⟅———————————

There were eight of them now: Serendipity, Leonid and Sirius; Andromeda and Dijo, Beetle and the elf-monkey Norylan—and the elephant in the room, Serendipity's scythe-wielding, heavily armored grandmother, staring at her grumpily with folded arms.

"That . . . went well," Serendipity said.

"You humiliated him, Seren," her grandmother said. "What did you expect—"

"*Dashpat*, can't you let me have this?" Serendipity said. "We need to go get him—"

"No," Porsche said, oddly hurried and agitated, counting the crew. "Six, seven. Wait, where's Tianyu—oh, Seren, I'm so sorry. At least we have his memories on file. Right enough; seven. I think I can manage seven on the return jump, though it will be difficult—"

"Seven?" Serendipity said. "There are . . . how many crew on Independence?"

"Fifty-four," Leonid said. Then his face fell. "Fifty-three."

"We have to leave them," her grandmother said. "I can't track them all down—"

"What?" Serendipity said. "Of course you can! I know what you're capable of! And we can't just leave them. You saw Toren! He's more baggage than you travel with, and he's going to build his own little dictatorship here, with boy warriors and an army of girls as slaves—"

"We can worry about that later, Seren," Porsche said. "The tensor pressure is increasing. That black hole's like a giant thumb pressed down on spacetime. In a matter of hours, any jump will be impossible, for at least fifteen to sixteen months. We have to go, right now—"

"Can't you send a ship?" Serendipity said. "A rescue pod—"

"Seren, I'm here now to rescue you," Porsche said. "And it can't wait—"

"Why?" Serendipity said. "I almost had him. Why can't you come back when—"

"I'm pregnant," her grandmother said, extending her hand back to her barrel—and Serendipity's jaw dropped. Now she could see extra armor, on top of the usual, and a bulge. "This is my last long jump for a while. I shouldn't even have come—"

"Why . . ." Serendipity began. "Why didn't you tell me?"

"Your grandfather and I are planning to raise David on Harmony," Porsche said. "It's better to raise a child in one gravity well. The whole Project is moving. Site Omega's being shut down. I've been so busy, and we've been having so much fun, I just didn't have the heart—"

But at "fun," Serendipity flinched—and her grandmother caught it.

"Or at least, I thought we were having fun," Porsche said. She stared up into the vault of cargo control. "I thought I was worried about you being left alone, but really I was worried about me, leaving. *Dashpat*, I've gone and done it again, made everything about me—"

"You think?" Serendipity said, unable to hide the bitterness.

Porsche winced. "Sistine and Amin have to be gone so much, I thought I'd fill in—"

"You're not my parents," Serendipity said. "They're supposed to be there for me—"

"What if they were dead? Should I abandon you because 'they' were supposed to deal with you?" her grandmother said. "No. Don't waste a second of your life hurting yourself just because someone else 'should' do something. Accept the situation and make the best of it—"

"So I've a summer to myself before college, and you try to smother me?"

"Smother you?" Porsche said, shocked. "I just wanted you to

succeed—"

"By besting me at everything I ever tried to do?" Serendipity said, hating the petulance in her voice. "You have no idea how impossibly good you are at *everything*. Or, maybe, you do, at least physically. I've heard you: 'ninety-ninth percentile on all axes,' isn't that the phrase? I—"

But her grandmother raised her hand.

"I'm sorry, Seren. I have been smothering you. I just hated to leave you alone."

Serendipity felt a sudden pang. What if her grandmother had just left her alone?

"You didn't have to make it either-or," she said. "I—I could have gone with you—"

"But when you just heard I was going, you secretly felt relieved, didn't you?" Porsche said. "You ran halfway across the galaxy, Seren. You don't want to follow me to Harmony."

"No . . . no I don't," Serendipity said. "I'm . . . I'm sorry, Gramama."

"It's right enough," her grandmother said, biting her lip the moment she said it. "You're not the first daughter I've had who needed space to grow up."

Serendipity twitched. Then she stepped toward her grandmother, arms out, but paused at the razor edges of her bladed armor. Porsche tilted her head, and the armadillo blades flattened, leaving the surface of her armor a battered mirror when Serendipity stepped into her hug.

"I'm sorry," she repeated lamely. "Forget what he said, Gramama. We're not a dysfunctional family. We're just . . . different."

"It's just me and my mom and my dad that had the falling out," Porsche said. "All my brothers, sisters, children, *grandchildren* . . . I couldn't be more proud of you."

Then she shifted. "Still . . . it's time for us to go."

———————————&Ø&———————————

Serendipity stared at her. "You don't understand," she said. "I can't just leave them—"

"And we won't go," Leonid said. "We can't abandon *Independence*!"

"It doesn't seem to be much of a ship anymore," Porsche said.

"We . . . we can rebuild it," Leonid said, looking to Serendipity for reassurance. "She even said we could. And—and even if we can't, I won't abandon our crew."

"We can't take them all," Porsche said. "In fifteen months, we can send a ship—"

"And leave Toren in charge?" Serendipity said. "You didn't hear him earlier. The way he was talking . . . we'd be sentencing the girls to fifteen months of gang rape."

"She's right," Leonid said. "I won't go. I won't leave the girls back at camp to Toren."

"Thank you," Andromeda said, and Leonid squeezed her hand.

"You shouldn't leave the boys to Toren either," Serendipity said, looking away from that touch. "They're right at the age that they're most vulnerable to indoctrination into soldiering. He'll lure them on with the promise of power and booty, and they won't want to turn back."

"I won't let that happen," Leonid said.

"It may not be that easy," Serendipity said. "Militia structures can develop quickly—"

"You really think only you can save us?" Sirius said, stepping to stand with Leonid and Andromeda. He folded his arms. "You have a home to go to, and a way to get there. Take it while you can. We've got a lot of challenges, but we can take care of ourselves."

Serendipity stared at them for one frozen moment. Then she turned to Porsche.

"Fifteen months," Serendipity said.

"Now wait a minute," Leonid said. "Sirius is right. There's no need—"

"Fifteen months," Serendipity repeated. "You come back. Right here—"

"Seren, you'll be stranded," Porsche warned. "Between the pressure and the risk of aftershocks, no ship with a conventional drive will risk coming here. Until that hole is leaving the system, *you will be on your own.* Besides, Sirius is right. This is not your fight—"

"I'm making it my fight," Serendipity said. "I'm staying so that these children don't die."

"We're not children," Leonid growled.

"Staying, Leonid, so that Toren won't build a world where four thousand generations of women grow up under a man's thumb," she said. "Tell me Toren won't do that. Tell me you can stop him. Tell me that leaving doesn't mean that I'm leaving this world to be designed by a bunch of babies who don't know anything!"

Leonid didn't meet her glare. After a moment, Porsche spoke.

"Honorable intentions, but your diplomacy could be refined."

"You didn't raise a diplomat," Serendipity said. "I'm a warrior."

Porsche stared at her, a smile growing on her face. Then she shot out her hand.

"Your memories," she said. Serendipity pulled her hand back, but her grandmother pressed forward, glowering. "If you die here I have to be able to rebuild you, or your mother will kill me. Give me your recent memories or I'm taking you home. End of discussion."

Serendipity stared at Porsche's hand, then took it. She held it briefly, feeling the tingle as electrotensor fields interpenetrated and data flowed; then, when her metaconscience let her, she drew her hand back, feeling oddly like she'd gotten more from the exchange than Porsche had.

"Don't you go make some ghastly copy of me," she said. "I'm not going to die here."

"That's my girl," Porsche said. "Right enough, step back. It's time."

Serendipity watched her grandmother unsling her saddlebags and withdraw a tough metal prong, a military farstaff. Wordlessly, she roped out a resonator coil upon the deck, set the prong in the center of it, and released a ball of light, which quickly expanded to encompass her.

"Well," Serendipity said. "Good-bye, Gramama."

"Till we meet again," Porsche said, voice echoing inside the shimmering bubble. Then the armored demigod that Serendipity had run nine thousand light years from smiled at her. "I'd say make me proud, but you already have. Always have. Good luck, Seren—and God bless."

With a flash of light, Porsche was gone.

The seven of them stood there, staring, at the pattern of frost upon the deck.

"You could have gone with her," Andromeda said. "Really, why didn't you, Seren?"

Serendipity took a deep breath. She thought she'd been committed before. Now she felt like she should be committed. But she had what she wanted: a world to build, people to help, work to do, her own mark to make—without her grandmother looking over her shoulder.

She saw a bruise on Andromeda's cheek. "Let's have a look at that," she said, stepping over to the saddlebags Porsche had left for them and motioning for Andromeda to join her. Surely her grandmother had packed a medical blade. "And it's Serendipity."

"I don't know," Leonid said, stepping up beside her. "Seren. I like that."

"What did she leave us?" Sirius said, joining them in rooting through the supplies.

"Our own world," Serendipity said, raising a medical blade. "Let's make the best of it."

About The Author

By day, Anthony Francis programs search engines and emotional robots; by night, he writes science fiction and draws comic books. He received his PhD in artificial intelligence from Georgia Tech and currently works in research at the 'Search Engine That Starts With A G'. He's the author of the award-winning urban fantasy novel FROST MOON starring magical tattoo artist Dakota Frost, as well as its sequels BLOOD ROCK and the forthcoming LIQUID FIRE. He lives in San Jose with his wife and cats but his heart will always belong in Atlanta.

You can follow Dakota Frost online:
http://www.dakotafrost.com/
http://www.facebook.com/dakotafrost.

You can follow Serendipity online:
http://www.facebook.com/serendipitythecentaur
Or on Anthony's blog at
http://www.dresan.com/

CPSIA information can be obtained at www.ICGtesting.com
Printed in the USA
BVOW030141191012

303437BV00002B/2/P